P

MW00623337

"Wowie Wow Wow! I have been waiting with bated breath to get ahold of Iris, the newest installment in the Minnesota Marshalls series—Book 4! And it does NOT disappoint!! Action, Suspense, Intrigue, Romance, Family, all rolled up into one book."

STEPHANIE, GOODREADS

"Another fast-paced ride with another sibling of the Marshall family. Wow! Each book has so much drama, suspense, action, and bits of romance and you find yourself having to remember to breathe, or you faint because of holding your breath. This one is NO different. "

MARYLIN, GOODREADS

"A strong, capable woman + an Aussie Alpha male + death threat = Thrilling tale of football and adventures across Europe and Minnesota. I loved this book. I read it in less than a day! Fast paced action and a sweet love story kept me turning the pages."

HOLLY, SMWF STORE

"I couldn't put this down from the moment I picked it up. [Iris and Hud's] story was my favourite by far. My mind is still lingering on so many faith nuggets from the book"

M.P., SMWF STORE

IRIS

THE MINNESOTA MARSHALLS
BOOK FOUR

SUSAN MAY WARREN

IRIS

THE MINNESOTA MARSHALLS

ONE

S he simply couldn't ignore the bullets.
       Or the bombing.

Or even the last twenty-four hours hiding in a damp and dark cave under some cliffside in the Aegean Sea.

Regardless of how much Iris wanted to live in denial.

"You okay, ma'am?"

She looked up from where she sat, shivering on the bench of the fishing trawler, the sun from the cloudless Greek sky warming the towel she draped around her shoulders.

"Yes. Just...tired."

The man, mid-sixties, cast his shadow over her, cutting off the glare of the sun. His skin was the shade and texture of deep leather, with white whiskers, perhaps a couple days old, on his face. He wore a fisherman's hat that shaded his blue eyes, and a navy-and-white striped tank top, a pair of rubber pants, and connected boots held up with suspenders.

But it was his kind eyes that drew her, and now he gave her a small compassionate frown. "How long were you at sea?" His English was choppy, thick with accent.

She glanced at fellow castaway, Hudson Bly, who was now climbing aboard the trawler, being hauled up by a couple younger fishermen, perhaps the sons of the elder. He was pretty scraped up, given his heroics in the cave, his shoulders and back bearing the claw marks of the rocks. But under the sun, with his blond hair, that hard-athlete body, square jaw, dark-blue eyes, he still looked every inch a sort of Australian Adonis.

Who'd nearly lost his life because of her.

"Overnight," she whispered.

The fisherman handed Hudson a towel now also, and he slipped over to sit beside her on the bench, his body warm against hers.

Nope, she wouldn't think about the cave.

Or how they'd nearly died...again.

"Our boat blew up," Hudson said, wiping his face, then shaking his head like he might when he emerged from a shower after one of his Vienna Vikings football games.

"Engine trouble?" This from one of the younger fishermen, same blue eyes, dark-brown hair. He wore a T-shirt, the arms ripped off, and identical rubber coveralls.

"Something like that," Hudson said, and glanced at her.

Oh, she could barely look at him, because the man was so lying, and the truth of it just burned through her.

No, she wanted to say. Not engine trouble. Because someone bombed our boat.

Hudson might have read her mind, because he frowned, then gave the slightest shake of his head.

"Lucky to be alive," said the older man. "We will get you back to port." He nodded toward his son, the one at the helm, and the boat engaged. "We already have our catch."

He gestured to a pile of sopping nets in the front of the boat, writhing with small red lobster-type critters, hundreds of pale silver- or red-patched fish, and a few massive striped blackfish. The net seemed alive, the fish thrashing for air as the younger fisherman threw water from the sea onto the mess.

"We will take them to port and separate them," said the man. "Name is Xaris. That is Theo, my nephew, and my son Nico in front." He hung on to the canopy over the bridge as the boat churned up the water. "Nearly didn't see you. Could have run right over you." He raised an eyebrow.

Yes, it might not have been the best idea for them to swim out of the cave, shouting and yelling for rescue—and not only because the blue-and-orange trawler happened to be motoring by, picking up nets, possibly hooks hanging out. But because of other reasons.

People-hired-to-kill-her reasons.

The boat bounced over the waves as they headed out to the open sea between the island they'd hidden on and bigger Santorini. She'd stared at the lights for the better part of the night, tempted—well, at least until the tide had come in.

But now, as the boat skimmed across the water, cutting through the waves, frothy-tipped out here in the open, Hud had been right.

Better to hide, to take their chances in the dark maw of the cave than at sea.

But it hadn't been without cost.

"Funny that no one picked up your boat fire," said Xaris. "Or found you two floating in the wreckage."

Hudson nodded, his mouth a tight line.

She looked away but felt his hand move to hers, squeeze it.

So, clearly he didn't want her to tell anyone about their desperate underwater swim as bullets pelleted the water, the way they'd surfaced near shore, behind a bevy of rocks, watching as their boat burned black, then sank into the sea as another circled it before setting off down the shore, searching for them.

"Where'd you spend the night?"

Hudson looked at the man and drew in a breath. And just like that, she heard the voice, slightly accented, of a woman named Ziggy, occupation sketchy, who'd just happened to show up a step before trouble found them. *I found out who put the hit on Iris.*

A hit. As in someone wanting her *dead*.

Why, they still hadn't figured out. In fact, Hudson hadn't wanted to stick around to sort out the answers either.

Poor guy. He actually thought he'd been the one to get her into trouble. She could still hear his desperation in the hotel room in Athens nearly five days ago. *Listen. I'm sorry I got you into this. I'm not James Bond. I'm not even Tom Cruise. I'm just a lousy wide receiver with a leaky brain and need to get off this roller coaster ride. And I think you should come with me.*

"We spent the night in a cave," Hudson said.

Xaris's eyes widened. "Not Cave Aspro?"

Hudson lifted a shoulder.

"It's an all-white cave. They say it is covered in the tears of nuns," said Nico, climbing along the deck of the boat and jumping down beside them. "A pirate ship caught them and left them to die there. It's filled with stalactites and dead, jagged coral. At night, the tide completely fills it."

"We know," Hudson said.

Nico raised a dark eyebrow, his gaze going to Hudson's shoulders, the loosened blood that stained the towel.

"Are you on your honeymoon?" This from Xaris. Behind him, the shore grew, along with the port of Santorini with its fishing boats and houses built on the craggy hillside. Along the top of the ridge, like so many hats, sat the whitewashed buildings, one on top of another, many with domed roofs, all nestled together.

Magical. And the perfect place for a honeymoon.

Iris looked at Hudson. She'd used the lie only a few days ago when he'd been hospitalized, but—

"Yes." Hudson lifted their clasped hands. "We're staying in Santorini—just took a rental out for the day. I don't think we're getting our deposit back." He grinned, and wow, she'd seen his charm up close and personal, but now it had the power to loosen the aura of suspicion she hadn't noticed until that moment.

Then, he leaned over and kissed her on the cheek. "I'll bet you can't wait for a warm shower and a gourmet dinner, right, honey?"

She'd be happy for dry clothes and a vending machine sandwich, but she nodded.

"You look familiar," Nico said, frowning. "I don't know where."

Hudson lifted a shoulder. "I get that a lot. I sort of look like an actor."

"Hmm," said Nico, but the boat was turning into the harbor, and he left to pick up a line.

Iris glanced at him. Raised an eyebrow. "An actor?"

"Yeah. Didn't you see the new *Reacher* on Netflix? It's a series—Coach says I look like that actor."

She hadn't seen it, and frankly, Nico probably hadn't either, but, "Right." Because if the man was a fan of American football in Europe, then they both knew exactly why Nico recognized the six-foot-four, blindingly handsome, fit and sturdy wide receiver from the Vienna Vikings.

"Let's hope he's not interested in a selfie," she said.

They pulled up alongside other fishing boats coming into dock. The place smelled of fresh catch, salt, and oil, and dockhands tied up boats as fishermen sat on deck, sorting their fish from the nets. A road switchbacked up from the harbor to the pristine town. Horses snorted nearby, tied up, waiting to pull carts filled with today's catch to market.

Or at least, that's what Iris supposed. She also wanted to suppose that the nightmare was over—that whoever had shot at them yesterday, blown up their boat, and sent them to spend the most terrifying night of her life in a cave made of jagged shells might have decided to give up, and was most definitely not waiting for her in some nearby bistro, drinking coffee and eating baklava.

Her stomach growled as she got up.

"You can't walk around town like that, ma'am," Nico said.

She still clung to her towel, but under that she wore only her swimsuit.

Thank the Lord it wasn't a bikini. But still.

"Here," said Nico and reached for a grimy denim button-up shirt wadded into a cubby near the helm.

"Thanks." She managed a smile, then dropped the towel and pulled on the shirt. It hung about three sizes too big, the cuffs wagging, the tail of the shirt to her knees. "Who owned this? Andre the Giant?"

"My brother, Atlas," Nico said, laughing.

She glanced at Hudson, who appraised her, nodding.

"Thank you." First stop was a store.

Well, no. They might need money, given that her cash was currently swimming with the fish in the depths of the Aegean.

Hudson climbed out first, then held out his hand. "Thanks again for saving us."

Xaris shook his hand. "You know where you're going?"

Not a clue, but Hudson grinned, nodded. "We're staying at a resort nearby."

They were?

Hudson took her hand, and she climbed off the boat and onto the dock. Managed not to drop to her knees and kiss the cement jetty.

Nico stood in the boat, hands on his hips. "Really familiar. You sure we haven't met?"

"Really? You run into a lot of shipwrecked Americans?" Hudson reached down to shake his hand.

Nico laughed. "That's it. *In the Heart of the Sea.*"

Iris just stared at him.

"You're Chris Hemsworth."

A beat, and then Hudson laughed. Something loud and full, and even Iris had to smile.

"I wish, mate," Hud said, sounding decidedly Australian. "But I'll take it."

Iris rolled her eyes.

Hud took her hand. "C'mon, darlin'. Before more of my fans find me."

"Please." But she held on, because she was hungry and tired, and maybe he did, just a little, resemble a superhero.

Stop. She wasn't looking for a man in her life.

They were barely friends.

In fact, as soon as she could, she needed to ditch him.

Because, despite his words, this was all her fault, and she knew it.

But his hand warmed hers as he led her across the long boardwalk, away from the harbor and toward a row of cafés.

"I could really use a T-shirt or a dress or—anything."

He glanced down at her. "Not a fan of denim?"

"It smells like fish."

"The dogs like it." He gestured to a stray hunting her down behind them. "Shoo," he said, and the dog loped off.

The air swept off the sea, carrying with it the briny smell, and the sun shone down upon massive trees of bougainvillea that spilled over rooftops and walls, brightening the cliffside with vibrant pink flowers.

So maybe it wasn't a terrible place to be shipwrecked.

"Just take the shirt off."

"Not a chance."

"You don't like walking around town in your swimsuit?"

"Oh sure. It's my favorite. I'd wear one to work, but it could get breezy."

"Not to mention no one would ever catch a pass again." He grinned at her, then pulled her into a nearby shop.

A fishing shop, filled with net supplies and lures and buoys and all manner of seafaring goods. But he spotted something and pulled her over to a display of rain jackets. Picked one up. "This should fit."

"And what are you going to buy it with, Hemsworth?"

"I'm going to barter, like the Greeks do."

He walked up to the counter. A teenager—maybe sixteen, a

hundred pounds soaking wet, dark hair, and big brown eyes—looked at him.

"Would you trade for the jacket?"

The boy looked at him, then at her. "Trade what?"

And then Iris had nothing as Hud pulled off a ring he wore on his right hand. Gold, with a stone set in the middle. "What are you doing?"

He ignored her.

The boy picked it up. Looked it over. Shrugged.

Hud took the jacket and slipped it off the hanger. Then he handed it to her.

She stared at him. "What was that ring?"

"Just something I picked up in Vienna. Not important. Trade you."

"You wear the jacket."

"For one, it's too small. For two, I saw the way you were eying Nico and all his fisherman manliness—"

"Oh, for the love." She pulled off the shirt and handed it over. He gave her the jacket. She put it on, zipped it up. Lightweight, it still fell down to her thighs.

He, in the meantime, completely filled out the shirt.

"How about these shoes too?" He addressed the kid at the counter, holding up two pairs of short rubber boots—one pair for him, the other for her.

The kid nodded, and she slipped on the rubber booties. "I look ridiculous."

"I look like Chris Hemsworth." He too wore the boots.

"Don't let that go to your head."

"Way too late for that."

She followed him out into the sunshine. "Now what, Skipper?"

"We go to the resort."

"What resort?"

He turned to her. "The one we were supposed to stay at five days ago. It's actually not far from here." He pointed up the hill, the one with the switchbacks that led to the sprawling white village on the hill. "Except for the little hike there."

"Now I understand the need for my special shoes."

He smiled at her. "Hope you don't mind the honeymoon suite."

"You did not."

"At the time, you were my girlfriend. Thought it was time to take the next step." He started up the sidewalk.

Hudson. "Okay, stop."

He turned, squinting at her in the sunlight.

"This is...I don't know what's happening here, but this isn't a game, Hud. We...we nearly died. I thought—I've never been so scared in my life. And that was after the bullets and the fire. And you—you're hurt. You might even need medical attention. But more—people are trying to kill us!"

He held up his hand, glancing around. "Ixnay on the illkay."

She put her hands over her face. "Please, listen to me—"

"No, you listen to me." And then he was right there, invading her space, so close to her that when she opened her eyes, she had to put a hand to his chest—his very Chris Hemsworth chest—to steady herself.

"I know this is not a game, Iris. But I was there last night too, and I remember how unraveled you were—"

"I wasn't—"

"For Pete's sake, Iris!"

"Just—whatever, okay? I don't want to think about it!"

"Me either. In fact, right now, I just want a bed, and breakfast, and maybe not in that order, but the more I think about the last twenty-four hours, and even the last week, the more I'm back in that cave trying not to drown, so yeah, if I have to make jokes and pretend that we're on a honeymoon, and laugh at your attire and the way you flirted with Nico—"

"I didn't—"

"Kidding. See? You mad at me is better than you scared, right?"

She blew out a breath. "Yeah, I guess so."

"Okay then. Let's get to the hotel, and then if you want to fall apart, that's fine. I'll be on the phone to Ziggy trying to figure out our next step. Okay?"

"I'm not going to fall apart."

He met her eyes, held her gaze. "Right. Okay. Good." He stepped back. Took her hand. "Let's try to not die between here and the hotel, okay?"

She smiled. "You do look a little like Chris Hemsworth."

"I know." He smiled. "Let's hope the front desk clerk thinks so too." Then he winked.

And she followed him. Because maybe denial was exactly where she wanted to be.

Hud and his bright ideas had nearly gotten them killed.

Rent a sailboat. Sail the Aegean.

Get blown up.

Hide in a cave.

Spend the night fighting to stay afloat.

Wave down a fishing trawler.

Rent a resort room with his time-share points.

And now he hadn't a clue what to do.

"Hud, I'm going to order room service, okay?" The voice came through the wooden door to the bathroom where he was currently bracing himself against the tile of the shower, letting the rainfall head splash down over him, cleaning out the cuts from the cave walls.

Some of them seemed pretty deep, but the last thing he needed was a trip to the hospital.

Again.

Which might only lead to more medical follow-up and the

unearthing of his test results in Athens. He could only thank, well, God, maybe, that he hadn't suffered a seizure last night. His head had certainly felt like it might explode.

"Hud?"

"Yes. Get anything. I don't care." He closed his eyes, and for some reason her voice swept through him. *We're going to die, Hud!*

Nope. Not on his watch. He'd made promises—maybe foolish promises, but promises nonetheless—to her brothers.

He very much planned on getting Iris home, safe.

He just didn't know how to get from here to...wherever safe was.

Rinsing off, he scrubbed his hands over his face, wishing he'd asked the front desk for a razor. But maybe the shadow would help conceal his identity.

Chris Hemsworth. As if. Hud was at least an inch taller, had about thirty pounds on the guy. And could definitely beat him in the forty.

But okay.

He stepped out of the shower and grabbed a towel, turning to take a look at the damage. Some pretty good scrapes down his shoulder blades and a gash in the meat of his shoulder—he remembered that one. A brutal wave. He'd gotten his arm around Iris and pulled her against himself, his other hand gripping the coral wall.

Yeah, that crash had nearly blown her out of his grip. His hands were pretty torn up too, but he had tough hands. Strong, wide-receiver hands.

Good for gripping jagged rock all night long, holding himself and Iris afloat.

He brushed his teeth, ran his hands through his short hair, then grabbed the clothes he'd purchased on credit in the gift shop—linen pants, a matching pink shirt, and flipflops. He'd also purchased underwear and some swim trunks and another shirt, along with shorts.

Iris had picked up a dress—interesting—along with her own unmentionables and a pair of shorts, a linen shirt, a hat, as well as some toiletries.

Honeymooners, lost at sea. At least, that's what he'd told the desk clerk, who'd rebooked him the room he'd cancelled three days ago when he'd landed on the ever-so-bright idea to rent a sailboat.

Brilliant there, mate.

Although, maybe it would have been if—

If he hadn't been caught up in the what-ifs and been paying attention. Man, they should have been hiding, not joyriding around the Aegean.

He could still hear her scream right before he'd pulled her under the water, their sailboat in flames, the bullets zinging through the waves.

They should, by rights, be dead. And that left him weak, his adrenaline dropping as he stepped out into the main room.

Good thing he'd rented the honeymoon suite, because it came with a living room with a long sectional. The whole place opened to a deck with a private infinity pool that overlooked the sea. Teak lounge chairs sat under umbrellas, and someone had already delivered fruity drinks, now sweating on a table between the chairs.

"You okay, Hud?"

He looked over at Iris, who'd cleaned up before he had, leaning against the desk, holding the receiver and a menu card.

Oh, he should have asked for separate rooms, because wow, the woman was pretty, especially when she wasn't wearing the zebra suit of an ELF referee. Blonde hair down to her shoulders, she wore a peach linen dress, bare feet and legs, and no makeup, which only accentuated her blue eyes.

Yep, the sofa for him. Maybe the lounge chair on the deck.

"Yep," he managed.

"Very good," she said into the phone and hung up. "Okay,

they're sending us saganaki, a Greek salad, moussaka, and spanakopita."

"No burgers on the menu?"

"You're such an American. We're in Greece!"

He shrugged and walked out onto the deck. The sea stretched before him, the hour past noon, the sun still high. "It's so amazing that everything is white."

"Some say it helps keep the houses cool. But the official reason is that the military made them paint everything blue and white back in 1967 when they took over the island."

He glanced over at her. She braced her shoulder against the open door to the suite. "I read it on a brochure when you were charming the front desk clerk." She smiled, then came out to sit on a lounge chair.

He sat in the other. Closed his eyes. Took a breath. The air smelled of flowers, and he attributed it to the massive pink bushes that fell over the edges of the whitewashed walls.

Paradise.

Danger in paradise.

"I tried calling Ziggy while you were in the shower."

"With what?"

"I logged onto my online voice mail and retrieved her number. I back up all my voice mail online—I don't want to miss anything."

"What, like a call from your agent telling you the Minnesota Vikings want you?"

He blinked at her. "Um."

"Oh, Hud. I was kidding. I—sheesh, I'm sorry. Of course they want—"

"Stop, Iris." He closed his eyes again. "We all know that if I was going to play for the NFL, they would have already called."

A beat.

"Besides, the last thing—the very last thing—on my mind is whether some NFL team is considering me for a replacement wideout." He looked at her. "I'm so sorry, Iris."

She blinked at him. "What?"

"This is my fault."

"How—what are you talking about? I do believe that Ziggy said the hit was taken out on *me*."

"If I hadn't said yes to Ziggy when she asked me to hand off that drive to your cousin Tate—if I hadn't been so desperate to be, I don't know, *more*—then I wouldn't have been on that bridge in Prague. And you wouldn't have followed me to my hotel room, seen your cousin stabbed and bleeding, and been caught up in his mission to deliver the info—"

"To my brother, hello. Information that hopefully is helping him find his fiancée. So, um—"

"Yeah, but the last thing your brothers—*plural*—wanted was for you to get involved. And they asked *me* to get you home safely."

"Seriously. I'm a grown woman. I can take care of myself. Which I told you when you broke into my apartment in Lake Como." She shook her head. "I should have never gotten on a plane with you to Athens."

He let that lie there, because maybe not.

"Then again, if I hadn't, you'd have ended up face-first in your eggs, having a seizure in front of the whole world."

He sighed. "Yeah. Well, if the ELF finds out that you're now my girlfriend..."

"Fiancée."

He offered a small smile. "Just for tonight. Tomorrow you're getting on a plane—"

"To where, pray tell? Because Ziggy told us to lay low. And methinks that the last twenty-four hours says that maybe she was right."

He sighed. "I hope she's tracked down that guy—what was his name?"

"Alfonzo? Aka Alan someone? Ex-CIA spy turned rogue agent? And now I sound like a movie trailer. Good grief." She leaned back in her chair. "If you should be blaming anyone, it should be me. I was the one who agreed to spy on you at the bridge, thinking you were a traitor."

"You were duped. Don't be so hard on yourself."

"I'm trained to see things. To not miss anything—"

"I don't think that applies to rooting out spies." He looked at her. "Unless said spy is also a cornerback from the Prague Lions with his hands in my face, about to trip me."

She met his gaze. "You're such a drama queen. Besides, we both know that wasn't a penalty."

He narrowed his eyes at her.

"You going to tell Coach Max about the seizure?"

"If I do, then...probably that's the end. The Vienna Vikings will release me, and then I have nowhere else to go."

She was still looking at him, and he hated the compassion on her face. "I'm sorry."

"Let's just focus on not getting shot. Or bombed."

"Or poisoned."

He looked at her. "That's an option?"

"I dunno. I was just adding to your list of potential ways to die."

"Like setting fire to your hair? Or getting toast out with your fork?"

She blinked. "Dumb Ways to Die."

"My brother Harry loved that song. It was a PSA from the Metro Trains in Melbourne, Australia. My mum is from Melbourne, so they knew all the words, sang it all the time."

"What is a two-week-old unrefrigerated pie?"

He frowned.

"It's in the song. I was confused."

"It's a buttery pastry with beef filling—you haven't lived until you've had a hot pie and sauce at the footy."

"What's the footy?"

He grinned. "It's like saying *going to the game*. But in this case, it's the Australian Football League. Australian Rules. No helmet, no pads, full contact. You'd lose your mind."

"Maybe. Or it could be fun. Sounds like backyard football with my brothers. I really like your accent. But you only pull it out when you talk about Australia."

"Yeah, we came to the US when I was ten, and I worked hard to drop it. No one understood me." A knock came at the door, and he got up.

"I'll get it," she said, but he grabbed her arm.

"Nope. You hide in the bathroom."

"What? Do you think Black Widow is going to come through the door disguised as a waiter?"

"My Avengers team hasn't chatted lately, so who knows?" He pushed her inside and toward the bathroom. "Lock it."

"For the love—" But she closed the door. He waited until it clicked, then went to the door and peered through the peephole.

A man, dressed in the uniform of the resort, holding a wide tray of food under silver covers. Another man behind him held a tray of drinks.

"What's for breakfast?" Hud asked.

No answer. Here went nothing. He opened the door a crack, left the chain on.

"Sir? Your breakfast?"

He glanced over the man. No obvious weapons. "Just leave it on the floor."

The man frowned.

"I'll leave a tip with the front desk." He motioned to the floor.

The waiter slowly lowered it, and the man behind him did the same.

"Thank you," he said and closed the door. Watched as the two looked at each other, then walked away. Waited a full two minutes and then opened the door again.

He scooted the tray inside, then the second and shut the door.

"So, Thor, any trouble?"

"You were supposed to stay in the bathroom."

"And you were supposed to not be a crazy person." She walked toward him.

"Have you been asleep over the past twenty-four hours?"

She stared at him then. Sighed. "You're right. Sorry. I'm hungry. And the game is on."

"The game?"

"Barcelona Dragons and Vienna Vikings?"

"That's today?"

"No, it was last night. But I caught the rerun in the bathroom." She walked over to the television and grabbed the remote. Turned it on.

And there it was, on the flatscreen. His team, sallying forth without him.

"It probably shouldn't give me satisfaction that they're losing without me."

"Only because the replacement official missed an interference call. Sheesh." She carried one of the trays over to the sofa and set it on the coffee table. Lifted the lid. "I've died and gone to heaven."

"It's not a burger, but it'll do." He set the other tray down. Coffee, tea, water, and a couple more umbrella drinks, probably mimosa.

She'd fixed him a plate, and he picked it up, blowing on the warm spanakopita.

Watched as his quarterback, Jackson Ernst, threw a pass over West's head, the tight end from Brown landing in the dirt.

Head Coach Clay from the Vikings called a time-out, and the team ran in.

"My crew is on the field," she said, sipping her coffee. "I wonder who Yannick got to sub for me." She leaned forward. "Abe's at ump, and Zach looks like he's in my position as back judge."

"Which one is Abe?"

"He's the big guy, darker skin."

She pointed him out. He'd gone to the sidelines, grabbing a drink from the trainer. "Looks like they put in one of the subs as a line judge. Good kid—young. From Spain, I think."

Yannick blew the whistle, and the teams came off the sidelines into huddles.

"Coach is going to tell them to do an end-run fake, and then Jackson will throw it out into the flats to West, who will dance it in."

"That's a long throw."

"Jackson Ernst is from Minnesota—" He glanced at her. "They make them tough there."

She grinned at him. Glanced back to the screen.

Stood up. "Oh no."

He turned back. The play had stopped as Abe fell to his knees on the grass. The camera centered on him as players rushed around him. He started to shake, collapsed and seized hard, on camera.

In a moment, the crowd hid him, but Iris got up, moved to the television as if she could part the crowd. Hud got up also, watching in silence.

She put her hand over her mouth.

Trainers ran from the sidelines, and the crowd parted.

Only briefly did they spot him, lying still.

"Is he breathing?"

Iris looked at him. "I don't know. I..." Her eyes brimmed with tears.

And just like last night when the cave began to fill with water, when he realized he'd trapped them both, when Iris looked at him, fear in her eyes, and yes, most definitely, despite her protests, began to unravel, he reached out and pulled her to himself.

He simply held her as he tried to make sense of the tragedy on the field.

And wondered, in his gut, why he couldn't shake the sense that somehow, their nightmare was bigger than they thought.

They watched in silence as trucks came out onto the field and Abe was lifted, fitted with oxygen and an EMT delivering CPR, onto a gurney and then loaded onto an ambulance.

"I have to call Yannick." She detached herself from Hud. "He's our crew chief. I have to know if he's okay."

"Iris."

"No." She pushed away from him. "No, no. No...no."

"He didn't look—"

"No!" Her eyes filled. "Abe is a good man and..." She swallowed. "I need to get back to my life."

He cocked his head at her. "Iris."

"Fine. Then I need to get to Barcelona." She met his gaze. "I need to go to Barcelona."

A beat.

"You do mean *we* need to go to Barcelona, don't you?"

"Hud. Look at you. You're exhausted. And hurt. And hungry and...I got you into this."

"Oh goody, we get to have this argument again."

"You can't keep protecting me."

"Really?"

"I mean...you shouldn't." She sighed.

He stepped up to her. "There's a lot of things I shouldn't do."

She pressed a hand to his chest—maybe to stop him, maybe to hold him back. And it sort of slowed him down because, yeah, after five days on the run with her, and the last twenty-four hours, he suddenly had things in his head that probably wouldn't work once their life righted itself.

So, Hud, no more brilliant ideas that could get them in trouble.

Instead, he touched his forehead to hers. "Let's call a truce on the blame, okay? You may call the shots on the field, but I made promises."

She blew out a breath, gave him a wry smile. "I just hope those promises don't get you killed."

Right back atcha, baby.

19

Two

The boys weren't telling her something, and it wasn't that they'd finished off the lasagna.

Jenny Marshall stood in the bath of light from the open door of the refrigerator and pulled out the empty glass 9x13 pan. A layer of crust remained around the edges, the rest of the container empty save the litter of cheese and tomato sauce.

They'd probably scarfed it down early this morning on their way to the Minneapolis airport at oh-dark-hundred—as Fraser or Ned, her military sons, would say.

She put the container in the big farmhouse sink, then glanced at her watch. Oops—*yesterday* on their way out of town. They would have already landed in Paris, probably—she thought Ned had mentioned their flight routing through Charles de Gaulle International Airport.

Please, Lord, let them find Iris.

Don't worry, Mom. We'll find her. Ned's voice last night as she'd stood at the door, watching Ned and Jonas pile into the truck. Not boys anymore. Even Ned was a grown man—dark hair, steely eyes, a Navy SEAL with a look about him that suggested business. So much like his oldest brother, Fraser.

Ned had a firm grip on his fiancée Shae, too, whom he wasn't letting out of his sight. She wasn't sure exactly what had happened between them, but no one had had time for Ned's story after Jenny mentioned she hadn't heard from Iris.

She'd simply *mentioned* it, and suddenly Fraser had disappeared, then returned with a decree that they—the precise *they* to be determined—were going overseas to find her.

What?

Jonas had even returned from Montana where he'd been visiting his girlfriend—Jenny hadn't seen that one coming—and decided to go with them.

And at the head of the pack was her husband, Garrett. Not that anyone was overreacting, but the fact that he had decided to helm the trip—or maybe tag along with his sons?—to track down his only daughter felt a little like everyone might be overreacting.

Way overreacting. Hello, the woman traveled constantly.

Jenny couldn't quite put her finger on why the panic, and maybe that was the most unnerving of all.

Something was up, and no one was talking. At least Fraser had stayed home, so maybe the sky wasn't completely falling in, but still. Iris was probably just jetting around Europe and hadn't had a chance to call.

Jenny ran water into the lasagna pan, then added soap to let it soak and walked over to the sofa. Pulling an afghan from the top, she sat down and spread it over her.

How she hated jet lag. Three weeks home and still every night she woke at three a.m., wide awake, restless, something dark nagging inside her she couldn't put her finger on.

So she got up, came downstairs, grabbed her Bible, and prayed.

Now, she opened to the Psalms.

Listen to my words, O LORD, consider my lament.

Hear my cry for help, my King and my God, for to you I pray.

In the morning, LORD, you hear my voice; in the morning I lay my requests before you and wait expectedly.

That's what it was—a cry inside. One she didn't want to

name. But she had a request all the same, and now looked out the window, to the heavens.

Please. I need more time.

The after-midnight starlight fell into the windows of the family room, casting an ethereal glow across the old sofa, the overstuffed chair, the stack of pictures on the mantel.

Maybe it was nothing. Maybe the fatigue really *was* jet lag.

Maybe she'd spent too much time on Google, on WebMD, and cancer-survivor boards.

Please.

A board creaked on the stairwell, and she looked up to see Pippa, royal bodyguard of the House of Blue from Lauchtenland, venturing down the stairs, wrapped in a fuzzy bathrobe, her dark hair pulled back in a ponytail, her golden-brown eyes missing nothing. She came over to the sofa. "I thought I heard you down here."

"Thinking about the boys," Jenny said.

Pippa settled herself in an overstuffed chair. "They'll be okay. And so will Iris. I don't know your family well, but what I've seen of them, they're not the kind to fold easily. I've never met Iris, but my guess is that she's made of the same stern stuff."

"She is. She's a professional referee with the European League of Football—one of the few women, and she started as one of the few women in the NCAA, so she's not easily pushed around." Jenny smiled at Pippa. "Reminds me of you."

Pippa leaned back, folded her arms. "And you. What's going on? I heard you a couple of nights ago, in the bathroom. Were you sick?"

"Oh. I'm sorry I woke you. I used the hall bathroom because I didn't want to wake Garrett. The chicken casserole didn't sit well with me."

Pippa made a face, nodded. "That was the third time in two weeks."

Jenny arranged the blanket on her legs. They'd been so restless lately, and occasionally her hands too. "I'm fine. I might have picked up a bug overseas. And when I'm worried, I don't eat well."

"I'll make you some tea." Pippa got up and headed to the kitchen.

"Oh, no, Pippa, it's okay."

"My mother used to make it for my father when he'd come home on leave. He was so used to night shifts that he'd prowl the house. I bought some for Imani when we first arrived, but she prefers hot cocoa. Such an American."

Jenny laughed. "I don't know how you put up with us Yanks. And especially Fraser." It wasn't lost on her that her oldest son had a terrible crush on Pippa. Probably more, the way they spent long hours walking the perimeter of the security area. Jenny hadn't been a fan when she returned to discover that Fraser had turned the winery-slash-farm into a top-secret bunker for a runaway princess, but she was hardly going to turn Imani and Pippa out into the street. Besides, she liked the way Fraser had softened, laughed more, become less dark, angry.

"It's easy, ma'am. Frankly, I've never been around a family like this before. I was an only child, so this is a little..."

"Overwhelming?"

"Comforting." Pippa set the pot on the stove to boil.

Jenny turned on the sofa. "Not too loud?"

"Extremely." Pippa folded her arms over her chest. "But in a good way. Like a rugby team on a pitch, all working together."

"All worrying together, clearly. I'm not sure why they all dropped everything and took off for Europe. Like it might be a road trip to Florida or something. Europe! And yes, Iris calls me nearly every day, but...she's busy."

"How many days has it been since you last heard from her?"

"Five. I mean, please. Five. I don't know—"

"I'm sure they're just worried. Especially after what happened to Shae."

Jenny stilled, looked at Pippa. "What happened to Shae?"

Pippa had frozen like a deer, wide eyes. "Oh. Um. She got into a bit of a fray, I believe, but I'm afraid I'm not the one to ask, ma'am."

A fray. How she hated it when her boys kept things from her.

But perhaps turnabout was fair play.

Jenny got up, draping the afghan around her shoulders. Went to the window. Outside, the big barn where the Marshall Fields wine sat in barrels loomed dark against the night. The vineyard lay barren, the vines gnarled and bare.

"I hope we have snow before Thanksgiving."

"That's right—the American escape-from-England holiday. When is that?"

"The end of the month. I was hoping..." She forced a smile. "Nothing."

A beat. "They'll find her, ma'am. Fraser says that he got a lead from a woman his friend Ham works with. Or maybe Logan Thorne. Fraser says he's a former SEAL, from your hometown. Fraser says he doesn't remember him, though."

"He went missing for a few years. Everyone thought he was dead. Showed up in town one Christmas a few years later. Funny to think he's the head of some government special ops agency."

"I don't think we're supposed to know that." The water had started to boil on the stove, and Pippa took it off. Jenny turned back to the window. The wind tossed a few curled, dead leaves across the patio.

Please, let her live until spring. She loved the spring, with the budding of the vines and Garrett's excitement for a new varietal. He'd hauled her out to the barn a few days ago just to smell the must of the fermenting La Crescent Gold, his newest creation.

"Here you go."

Jenny turned around, and Pippa held a cup of tea, doctored with milk.

"It's chamomile with a touch of cream, just like my mother used to make it."

Jenny determined to enjoy it, regardless of what it tasted like. She sat again on the sofa, crossed her legs. Sipped.

Tangy, the bitterness softened by the cream. Could use sweetener, but she didn't need any more toxins in her body. "Delicious. Thank you."

Pippa nodded. "I'm just going to check the security system in the den." She headed over to Garrett's office, where she and Fraser had set up shop.

More creaking on the stairs, and this time she spotted Creed descending, his leg still in a brace. Her youngest wore his dark hair tousled, a pair of pajama bottoms, and a T-shirt. He moved his bad leg down, then his good leg, one step at a time.

She got up, unable to stop herself, and went over to the stairs. "What are you doing up?"

"I couldn't sleep." He glanced at her cup of tea. "Pippa's brew?"

"Yes."

"She made it for me a few times after we got back from Europe."

"You had trouble sleeping? Pain?" She helped him over to the sofa, then covered him with the afghan. Poor boy. He'd been through so much in his young life. Of course, he'd turned into a hero, rescuing Princess Imani from some murderer—at least, that was the sketchy story she'd gotten that went along with the explanation of the security perimeter. That and the fact that her oldest and youngest sons had been shot at and injured by said murderer.

The thought of it still kept her staring at her popcorn ceiling sometimes.

"Mostly worried about Imani."

Jenny sat in the wingback chair. "You really like her, huh?"

Creed was darker than her other children—darker skin, darker hair, darker eyes, and sometimes darker demeanor. But Imani had brought a lightness to his countenance—so many times Jenny heard them laughing together as they played video games or even stayed up late engrossed in a board game.

"I do. But you know, she's a princess, so..." He lifted a shoulder.

"And that means?"

"I'm not a knight or anything. I don't think I qualify."

"I think you're a knight."

He laughed. "Yeah, well, all this sitting on the sofa, playing video games, and praying my leg heals is getting old. And Dad's winterizing the vines alone...it's getting under my skin. I can't just sit here much longer."

"Physical therapy will start soon, and then you'll wish you were sitting on the sofa."

"No. PT means I'm that much closer to walking again. And then, maybe, running."

She nodded but didn't comment. With a pin in his femur, the idea of him running again, at least competitively... But then again, he was a Marshall. And Creed didn't have much quit in him, so... She got up and tousled his hair, even though he was twenty-one, nearly twenty-two. "Tea?"

"Thanks, Mom."

She'd never get tired of hearing her adopted son call her *Mom*.

She was pouring water into the teacup when her phone vibrated on the counter. Unknown number. Still, she scooped it up, a feeling cementing inside her. "Iris?"

"Hey, Mom. Sorry it's been so long."

She closed her eyes, something unleashing inside her.

"Is that Iris?" Creed said.

She nodded. "I've been...we've all been a little concerned."

Maybe that was an understatement given the search party landing on European soil.

"I know. It's a long story, but I'm fine. But I lost my phone, and it took me a few days to get another one. Sorry."

"Where have you been?"

A beat. "I was in Greece. With...um, anyway, I'm in Paris. It's so terrible, Mom. Abe Bartmann, our ump, dropped dead during a football game. No one knows why."

"Abe. He was the American from Georgia Tech, right? Has a daughter?"

"Yeah. And now I'm headed to the funeral. I just...I don't even know what to...say. Or do or—"

"Take a breath, Iris. You just say you're sorry. And you listen. And you help. And you remember that you can't fix it. Only God can. But you can offer compassion."

Pippa had walked out of the room, was now standing at the end of the counter.

Iris was crying, maybe, by the sound of her voice.

"Honey, are you going to be okay?"

Another beat, and this time it stuck inside Jenny.

"Yeah. I...yes. I gotta run, Mom, but I'll call you later. I love you."

"I love you too."

She hung up. Pressed the contacts and added Iris's new number. Then she forwarded the number to Garrett's phone with a text. *Iris called. She's in Paris.*

Her hand shook as she put down the phone.

"She okay?"

"Yes. No. I mean—one of her crew died. Sounded sudden."

Pippa drew in a breath, nodded.

"How?"

She looked over, and Fraser stood in the landing. He too was dressed in his pajama bottoms, a T-shirt, his wrist and hand in a cast. She hadn't been thrilled when he'd taken off with Ned two weeks ago—or that he'd had to have his hand recasted when he returned. But at least the old fire was back in his eyes.

Her oldest son always looked a little on edge, capable and unwavering. At least, until this summer, when he'd been rescued from the Boko Haram. And then he'd become quiet and brooding, secretive and not just a little grumpy.

Now, he walked up to the counter. "Was he murdered?"

Jenny stilled. Stared at Fraser. "*Murdered?* What aren't you boys telling me?"

He drew in a breath.

Aw, she knew it. Just *knew* it. Right in her bones.

And right then, Her Royal Highness Princess Imani came down the stairs. She wore a pink bathrobe, her dark hair in a night bonnet. "What's going on?"

Jenny pinned Fraser with a look, then turned and pulled out her cast iron skillet. "I'm making pancakes. And then I want some answers."

HE DIDN'T WANT TO DO ANY HIGH-FIVING YET, BUT THE fact Hudson had gotten Iris to Paris still alive felt like a win.

And how terrifying was that?

It used to be that a good day was a ninety percent completion rate and a frothy Vienna lager at the end of the day. Now he was running around Europe, one eye over his shoulder, hoping that he didn't step out in front of a speeding car, Iris in tow.

He gripped her hand as they reached the metro stop, a reflex of protection more than affection, although—

Nope. They were just friends. *Only* friends.

And if he just kept telling himself that, maybe he'd figure out a way to believe it. Because back in his real life, the one where he played football for the ELF and she worked on a crew of officials...

He dropped her hand.

She gave him a thin smile, maybe reading his mind.

She wore a pair of black pants, a white shirt, a black jacket, her blonde hair pulled back, bare makeup, and fatigue around her blue eyes. He probably looked the same, really, having spent the night in the Athens airport for their six a.m. flight to Paris. He'd wanted to mention that they could have stayed at the hotel with the view in Santorini just one night, maybe taken the morning flight to Paris, but there'd been no reasoning with her after she'd gotten the news from her crew chief, Yannick Mayer, about Abe's death.

She'd barely slowed down to purchase winter attire and a jacket for the memorial service of sorts at Abe's flat in Paris, before his body was shipped back to Georgia.

She had, however, bought a disposable cell phone as soon as they'd landed in Paris.

"Everything okay at home?"

"Yes. My mother was worried, and I would have liked to talk to her longer, but I'll call her later. I still can't believe that Abe is *dead*."

She looked away, and he wanted to reach out, pull her to himself when moisture whisked her eyes. But they were back from never-never land, and who knew if he'd run into a fan.

Oh, who was he kidding? If he was a footballer, maybe, although Paris had added an American-style football team to last year's lineup. The Musketeers.

"You know where Abe lived?" he said as they lined up by the doors.

"Yannick sent me the address."

The doors opened, and he got off. She followed him, and they merged into the crowd, taking an escalator up to the street level. Pushing through the revolving doors, they exited through a tunnel and up another set of stairs to the street.

An overcast sky hovered over Trocadero Park, and the smells of croissants and coffee drifted from a nearby café. Around him, despite the dour day, people rode bicycles, mopeds, and scooters, many on foot, all bundled up in warm jackets, scarves. He turned the collar up on his own jacket, picked up at the airport when they'd landed in Paris. A puffy black thing that'd cost about twice what it was worth.

He didn't want to look at his bank account. All the reserve he'd saved for the past two years of living in a rent-free apartment, his only costs being food and wine, he'd done a great job of depleting over the past five days, living like he might be a superstar or something.

He did have his investments, thanks to the lawsuit, but still, he couldn't afford to be dropped by the Vikings.

So really, no more hand-holding, no more flirting with the petite blonde official who now pulled out her cell phone and pulled up the GPS for Abe Bartmann's flat, somewhere near the Eiffel Tower.

Which he spotted through the trees, towering and magnificent on the opposite shore of the Seine.

"I think it's this way," Iris said, holding her phone and orienting herself toward a side street. The ornate buildings rose seven stories high, capped with black mansard roofs, most of the windows hosting scrolled wrought-iron Juliet balconies.

She grabbed his elbow, jerking him away from the tree-lined edge of the sidewalk. A bicyclist zipped by and shouted at him.

"Saved your life just then."

"Thanks."

"I'm not sure we're even, but you're welcome."

"Even?"

"Saving my life? How are your shoulders?"

"I'm fine, Iris." He didn't mean for it to emerge curt—he'd blame it on his lack of sleep, maybe—but the last thing he wanted was to return to that moment in the cave when he'd realized he'd gotten them in over their heads. Literally.

"It's just up here a block."

He didn't know why his stomach had knotted, why he fought the sudden urge to grab her hand, yank her back to the subway.

Get on a plane.

Weird.

They found the building and, in the lobby, she pushed the button to Abe's flat. A voice answered, female, Southern, with a twang.

"It's Iris Marshall."

"C'mon up, honey."

Hud gave her a look as he opened the buzzing door.

She walked in and hit the button for the tiny lift. "Abe is divorced. His ex-wife is some high-powered attorney in Atlanta. She let Abe take their daughter, Genesis, to Paris to attend school here. She lives with his ex in the summer."

The apartment lobby bore the look of ancient days, with ornate columns and a travertine staircase that wound up around the lift in the center. It smelled of age and history, and he imagined freedom fighters from the French Revolution barricading themselves inside the thick walls.

The lift shuddered down to the floor, and the doors lurched open. "You sure this thing is safe?" Hud said as he got on, ducking, squishing himself into the tiny box. The lift opened on the seventh floor, and they got out. A spray of flowers was affixed to a wooden apartment door, and Iris headed that direction.

It opened even before she reached it, and a middle-aged woman wearing a black dress and heels, her dark braided weave pulled back into a ponytail, came out. "Iris."

"Camille." Iris pulled her into a hug. "I'm so sorry."

For her part, Camille looked wrung out, no makeup despite her attire, her eyes reddened. "Thank you for coming."

Iris let her go, then Camille looked at Hudson. "Oh. You're—"

"Hudson Bly, ma'am," he said and reached out his hand.

She ignored it and pulled him into a hug. "Abe liked you. Said you had real talent."

Huh. He hadn't realized that Abe had even noticed him.

She led them inside the flat. Not impressive, it had parquet floors and scrolled crown molding, and giant floor-to-ceiling windows that overlooked an inner courtyard. But the kitchen was tiny, jammed with women—most of them speaking English, maybe Abe's family—and in the main room, a few familiar officials sat on the sofa. A couple coaches from rival teams ate brie and crackers from the spread on the table that had been shoved against the wall.

His gaze fell on Coach Max, his wide-receiver coach, and the sight of the big Austrian loosed a knot in Hud's chest he hadn't realized he'd been carrying. Coach nodded at him, smiled, then turned back to a man Hud recognized as coach of the Berlin Thunder.

"I'm going to check on Gennie," said Iris. "You okay?"

"Yeah," he said. "Just don't disappear out any windows or anything."

"You're no fun." But she smiled at him, and that weird feeling simply wouldn't go away.

He headed toward the table and recognized most of the food—cheeses and meats, but also baked macaroni and cheese, potato salad, and ham sandwiches.

"Feels like a church potluck," Coach Max said as he came over.

"My family weren't church people," Hudson said. "But clearly that was a mistake." He picked up a plate.

Max gave a smile. Said nothing as Hudson loaded his plate, then motioned him away from the table.

"You okay, Hud?"

Hud had picked up a fork, was diving into his macaroni. He looked up. So many ways to answer that question. But, "Yeah. Why?"

"Doc in Athens got ahold of the team doc with some questions. Said you had a seizure a week or so ago?"

Hud put down the fork, then the plate. "I'm fine."

Max raised an eyebrow. "Is that why you called in sick for the last game?"

"It was supposed to be an exhibition."

Coach held up a hand. "Yes. It was. Is. But with the game in Lauchtenland coming up, I thought you'd want to get all the practice time in—especially after the call from your agent."

Hud just blinked at him. "Waylen called the Vikings?"

"Asked how you were doing, physically. Said your completion

rate had caught the attention of a couple of professional US teams."

Good thing he'd put down the macaroni and cheese. "What teams? The NFL?"

"I don't know. He said he tried to call you, but you weren't answering."

"My phone took a bath." He didn't add that it was also on a boat that had gone up in flames. "Had to pick up a new one in the airport." He pulled out a simple flip phone.

"Text me your new number. Then call Waylen. And show up for practice tomorrow. We added another game next week with the Berlin Thunder. The team has been invited to help with a fundraising event for the German Children's Cancer Foundation. Come to the event, shake a few hands, and then show off what you can do at the game, okay?" He clamped Hudson on the shoulder. "Can't let Felix get all the grabs, right?"

Felix Wolf, the young and eager wideout from the Danube Dragons. He'd been four for seven in the exhibition game—not a terrible showing given the velocity that Jake fired off his missiles. Left a guy's hand nearly broken if he didn't catch the ball right.

"Right."

Max considered him. "You'd tell me if the TBI was starting to be a problem, right? Another bad hit and—"

"I'm good, Coach. I promise."

Max considered him, then pointed at his food. "That mac and cheese is to die for." He patted Hudson's arm and walked away.

Hudson stood at the window, staring at the courtyard, and beyond, the top of the Eiffel Tower. The sun had started to burn through the gray, tipping the tower with light.

The NFL.

"Are you sure?"

The question, not directed at Hudson but overheard, came from Yannick Mayer, Iris's crew boss. The man easily stood six foot four, blond hair, built—no one messed with Mayer when he made a questionable call. He talked with another official, also built, this one clearly American the way he stood, arms folded, his mouth a grim line. Reminded Hudson a little of one of Iris's bossy brothers.

"According to the report that Camille got, yes. It looks like poison. They're trying to nail down what kind."

Hud must have made a sound—no wonder he'd failed at being a spy—because they looked at him. And, oh well, he took a step toward them and cut to the chase. "Abe was *poisoned*?"

Yannick glanced away, toward a woman who carried cake to the table. Could be Abe's mother. But Hud wasn't stupid—he'd kept his voice low.

"It's not official," the other man said. Hud remembered him now—Zach Warton, fellow American, mid-forties. "But Camille said that she's hired a private investigator. Apparently, if it's murder, the insurance company won't pay out life insurance."

"Murder. You think Abe was murdered?" This, a whisper, because, well, *murder.*

And then there was the whole "hit on Iris" thing, so maybe...

Maybe it wasn't about her personally, but her as a football official.

"I don't know," Yannick said. He turned, however, to Hudson. "You were with her, weren't you?"

Hudson stilled. "Um..."

Yannick pulled out his phone. Scrolled and opened an app. Instagram. "I have a fan account?"

"Apparently, and someone in Athens spotted you in a restaurant. With Iris."

He took the phone.

Not a great shot—but that had been about two minutes before he'd gone down, his head pounding, his brain short-circuiting. They sat at a table, reading menus.

"You know the rules, Bly. I don't care if you're old grammar school pals—the last thing she needs is a hint of scandal." He put the phone away. "Stay away from our crew."

Hudson just stared at him. Drew in a breath. And the words

nearly—*nearly*—left his mouth. *What if I told you someone was killing off ELF officials?*

But no. Because that sounded crazy, even in his head.

So he nodded. "Excuse me."

He headed down the hallway in the direction Iris had gone. A bathroom, a master bedroom—and at the end of the hall, a room decorated for a child, with a mural of an enchanted forest, an ornate makeup table and mirror against one wall, an overstuffed single bed with a pink comforter, a massive plush bear in the opposite corner and...

And no Iris.

He stepped into the room, his chest empty. "Iris?"

A beat, during which his imagination had a good run at him, and then, "Out here."

Two doors opened to a balcony—who thought that was a good idea for a child's room?—and on it sat Iris with a little girl in a faded blue dress, maybe twelve or thirteen years old, her dark hair pulled back with a band, creating a puffy halo intertwined with gold clips. She looked up at him with golden-brown eyes, then wiped them with her hands.

"Sorry. She just needed some space," Iris said. "This is Genesis. Gennie, this is Hudson."

"Hey there," Hud said and held out his hand. She gripped it.

"Daddy liked you," she said. "You play for the Vikings, right?"

He raised an eyebrow. "Right."

"Gennie knows all the team. And she knows the rules, don't ya, Gen."

"Yeah. I watch all the games my dad umps." Her eyes widened. "Umped."

Uh-oh. Hudson crouched next to Iris. "Do you remember a play, a couple weeks ago, against the Prague Lions? I missed a pass—should have been called. The guy was all over me."

He glanced at Iris. She rolled her eyes.

"That pass was uncatchable," Genesis said. "He was in your

face, but it was thrown way over your head, so..." She had folded her arms and now shrugged her shoulders.

"Smart girl." Iris put her arm around her. "Someday, maybe she'll be an official."

Now, Gennie pulled up her legs, tented her dress over them, and put her head down into her arms. "I don't want to go back to Atlanta. I hate Atlanta."

"What's not to hate? It's hot and—"

"Hud!" Iris glared at him. She turned to Gennie. "Listen. First, you'll be with your mom—she loves you. And that will help. And then, you know, sometimes we just gotta be tough. Even if life feels unfair." She eased up Gennie's chin, met her eyes. "When I was a kid, I wanted to play football more than anything. My dad and I would watch the games together—just like you and your dad did. And he'd yell at the television and show me the penalties so I started to figure out the game. But I was a girl, and they didn't let girls play football in my hometown. And it was unfair, because I was fast, and I could throw a great spiral."

Hud smiled at that, imagining her as a twelve-year-old, going back to pass with her long blonde braids. Probably there was another reason the coach hadn't wanted her to play, and it had everything to do with his team not paying attention to the football.

"But since I couldn't play, I became the manager of the team. I was really good—so good that I started calling out the penalties during practice. So he let me officiate—at least, some of the practices. Pretty soon, I was working on the weekends at middle-school games. Then I went to college and..." She sighed, swallowed. "And did the same."

Huh. Hud had the sense that she'd left a great deal out with that swallow.

Not the least, the game in which she'd destroyed his future.

Except she didn't know that, and it had sort of stopped stinging over the past few days. So maybe he should just swallow and go on too.

"So yeah, it feels unfair right now. But you keep studying, you keep working for what you want, and you stay tough, and someday, you'll end up right where you're supposed to be."

Genesis's gaze affixed to Iris, caught in her words.

"You'll be okay, kid," Iris said quietly, then pulled her into a hug.

Sheesh, now even Hud felt better.

Except, "Iris, I need to talk to you."

Iris let Genesis go. "Do you need anything?"

"No. Thank you, Iris."

"Let me know if I miss any penalties."

"You don't miss anything." Genesis grinned.

Iris winked at her, then held out her hand for Hud to help her up. "'Sup?"

He took her arm and pulled her into the room. "I think you're in bigger trouble than we thought. And we need to get out of here."

IT JUST DIDN'T MAKE SENSE.

"What do you mean you think Abe was murdered?"

He held up his hand, but they'd locked themselves in a bathroom about the size of a Tardis—without the magic inside—and now Hudson leaned against the door, his arms folded over his impressive football chest, wearing a grim expression.

Gone was the Greek god, and now she faced a tired, just-a-little-bit-frayed, self-appointed bodyguard who apparently wasn't going to let her out of the room.

And maybe she didn't want to go anywhere either, so there was that.

"According to your boss, or maybe it was the other guy, Abe was poisoned. And yeah, Ziggy said that she thought the assassin after you was this guy Alfonzo that you met—"

"Alan Martin, according to Ziggy. Ex-CIA spy."

"Right. Him. But she wasn't sure, and she said there was no way to track down who did this until after the hit was done, right?"

"Where are you going with this?"

"Well, maybe—maybe it's not Alan."

"Then who?"

Outside in the hallway, voices hummed in conversation, most of it in English, although she heard some French, some Spanish, maybe some German. Abe had been well known and beloved as a line judge before he moved to umpire.

"Well, that's the thing—what if Abe was on the hit list too? And now that he's—"

"Dead? Now that he's dead, we can figure out who wants *me* dead?"

He made a face. "Well, yeah."

"That's horrible."

"Sorry."

She turned, grabbed some toilet paper, and pressed it against her eyes. Oh brother. She wasn't a crier, but something about losing Abe... "He was just about the nicest man I knew. Besides my dad." She lowered the tissue. Perfect. Now she had black smudges. And then... "What if this is my fault?"

She looked up. Hud had narrowed his eyes at her. "I don't think—"

"I mean. This happened after...well, the thing in Prague, right?"

"You mean the thing where your cousin nearly bled to death, right before my eyes?"

And for a second, she saw it all in his eyes—the rainy night, the dark outline of Tate, his contact, the moment when an assassin stabbed him. She'd seen it all.

She'd also seen Hudson run out from his secure position and save Tate's life, so there was that too.

"Yes," she said softly. "I keep asking myself—why would Alan want me on that bridge?"

"I sort of thought it was because he wanted to frame me for Tate's murder."

She looked at Hud. "Oh. I hadn't thought of *that*."

"Why else? You were supposed to take pictures, send them back to him, right?"

Right.

"Why would he want to frame you?"

"I don't know. Take me out of the picture? I have no idea."

"Maybe he didn't know Tate was about to be stabbed."

Hud raised an eyebrow.

"Right. Okay, frame you—maybe frame me? Because he had to know that I wouldn't just let someone die out there on the bridge."

He smiled at her then. "You would have helped me, even if you thought I was a traitor?"

"I wasn't sure you weren't until I saw Tate."

"Oh."

"But no, Hud. In my gut, I knew you weren't that guy."

She met his eyes, and something warm settled in her chest. Okay, it had been there for about two days, since he'd taken her hand in the water and helped her swim to safety. And then yesterday, at the hotel room, when she'd seen Abe go down.

He'd hugged her. And for a long moment, she hadn't wanted to leave, so...yeah, that was a problem. Because...well, just because.

The list was long. And started and ended with him being a football player.

Only part of it was because she was an official.

So down, girl. They were just friends.

The kind of friends who apparently nearly died together. And now... "So, what? You think they're after officials?"

"Maybe, yes." He met her eyes. "What if this is bigger than you? What if your whole crew is in danger?"

Her whole crew.

"We should call Ziggy," she said.

Banging on the door made her jump. "Lemme in! I gotta go!" Genesis.

Iris shrugged, and Hud moved away from the door, opening it.

Genesis looked at Hudson, then Iris, and put a hand over her mouth.

"Stop, kid. We're just talking," Hudson said and pushed out of the room.

Iris followed him, and Genesis stepped inside.

Half the guests, however, stood in the hallway, which had gone sort of quiet as they emerged.

Oh. Um...

Yannick stood in the hallway, his arms akimbo, and raised an eyebrow.

"Excuse me," Iris said and headed past Hudson, toward Yannick.

He followed her into the family room, where she headed to the food table, suddenly ravenous. Macaroni and cheese—finally, some comfort food. She picked up a plate.

"Is there something you want to tell me?" Yannick came up next to her. "I already talked to Hudson—he says that—"

"Nothing is going on," Iris said. No silverware, but she picked up a napkin. "Really. We just...happened to..."

"Need the bathroom at the same time?" This from line judge Zach Warton, who came up beside her.

"What is this, a blitz? Back off."

She muscled away from them, but they followed her into the kitchen. "Okay, what?"

"We saw an Instagram picture of you and him in Greece," Yannick said.

She pulled out a drawer, searching for a fork. "Yeah, well, we... happened to be there. At the same...time. Where is the silverware!"

Zach reached over to a drying rack, where silverware poked

out of a slot. Grabbed a fork. "The macaroni needs salt. And at the same hotel?"

She swiped the fork from him. "Fine. Okay. We...there was..." Her mouth tightened. "Can't a lady have a few secrets?"

"Not if it's going to disqualify her from the crew. Listen, even cheerleaders have a no-dating policy, and that's when they're on the same team," Yannick said.

"I'm not dating him!" Her voice rose, and she wanted to jerk it back when she spotted Hudson standing at the door.

He didn't flinch, however. Just came in, crowding the room even more, his hands in his pockets. "She's right. We're not dating. We're barely friends. But we did run into a bit of trouble together."

She stared at him.

"We have a mutual friend that...was in trouble, and we both ended up in Greece, helping her out."

Oh, that was a long stretch from the truth, but it had shades, so she nodded. "Yes. And then...we..."

"Ended up on a boat in the Aegean sea—sort of an excursion. And...it—"

"Ran out of gas. And we were adrift?" She met Hud's gaze. One side of his mouth quirked up.

"Yes, adrift. And then we washed up on shore in Santorini and came straight here. You could say we were sort of like hapless travel companions. Like Steve Martin and John Candy."

Yannick frowned at him.

"*Planes, Trains, and Automobiles*," Zach said. "My parents love that movie."

"It's a classic," Hud said, and smiled. "Those aren't pillows."

And then it was okay. He'd sort of charmed away all Yannick's snarl, and somehow, in the next moment, had Zach laughing at his pillow reference.

What. Ever.

"If you'll excuse me, I have some macaroni to rescue," Hud said and moved away. Yannick turned back to her, as did Zach, but she spotted Hud in the doorway, glancing again at her. And then he lifted his hand and made a finger walking motion.

As in, he was leaving?

Oh. Uh.

Right.

Probably that was for the best, right?

But she couldn't ignore the hollowness in her stomach. Sheesh, she'd come to depend on him way too much.

Just. Friends. Although she didn't know what he meant by *barely friends.*

Okay, maybe that had been true a week ago. She could barely stand the arrogant wide receiver before that moment on the bridge.

Sort of hard to remember, really, the way she'd hated his swagger, the way he'd acted like the whole world belonged to him. The way that, ever so briefly, she'd believed the lie that he could be a traitor.

"So, you're ready to come back, right?" Yannick said as she downed the macaroni and cheese.

Hud's words swooshed back to her. *What if your whole crew is in danger?*

"Are you sure it's safe to...I mean, Hud said that maybe Abe was...murdered."

Yannick blinked at her, then looked at Zach. Back to her. "What?"

Oh. "I thought...I mean..."

"Listen, we don't know anything," Zach said. "Camille said the hospital thought he'd been poisoned, but it could have been anything—food, or maybe an allergy. He'd gotten sick between the quarters, I remember that. And was acting a little disoriented, but no one knew anything until he just stopped breathing and dropped dead. So, yes, she thinks it might have been poison, but that's a leap, don't you think?"

She gave a slow nod. Because her other option sounded a little cray-cray, and as the only female member of the crew, she didn't want to be the one dubbed nuts.

"We have two more games added to the roster before the event in Lauchtenland in December," Yannick said, "and I need to know if I can count on you being there."

She blinked at him. "Yes. Absolutely."

"We had to put Zach in your spot."

"He missed a pass interference call." She looked at Zach.

"I know, sheesh."

"He'll get it, Iris," Yannick said. "But more importantly...we need you at ump, Iris."

She stared at him. "Abe's spot."

"Yes. We know it's the most dangerous spot on the field—"

"Please."

Yannick held up a hand. "But we know you've got the eye for the illegal movement, illegal blocks and holds, and line of scrimmage infractions. And you're the only one who's worked Abe's position."

She folded her plate of macaroni and moved past Yannick and Zach to put it in the nearby, overflowing trash. Then set her fork in the sink, her back to the door. "I never thought I'd take Abe's place for good."

Silence, all around.

"Where are the games?"

"Berlin next weekend, and two weeks after that, a tryout game with the Amsterdam Admirals. They've put together another team and are hoping to get into the ELF."

Maybe by then, the nightmare would be over.

"We're all going to Berlin early to watch tape and get ready for the game. You'll need to be there by Wednesday." Yannick had turned now and waved to someone behind her. His gaze returned to her. "I'll see you there?"

"Yes."

Yannick pushed past her, but Zach stopped her. "You sure you're okay?"

She frowned.

"I know you and Abe were close."

Oh. "Yes. He was a mentor. It won't be the same without him."

Zach's mouth tightened, and he nodded. "If you ever need to talk...or just...whatever, I mean, you know..." He blew out a breath.

Wow. Her voice lowered. "Thanks, Zach."

"Mm-hmm." He smiled and walked away.

She washed her fork, then dropped it in the container.

"So, you and Zach, huh?"

She turned and Hudson leaned against the doorframe.

"No. I mean—I'm not sure what that was, but..."

He sighed, folding up his plate. "I didn't mean to get you in trouble." He shoved the plate into the trash, then pulled up the edges of the plastic back and knotted it. Pulled it out of the container. Another bag lay inside, and he affixed that in place.

Such a helpful guy. Probably his babysitting of her had fallen into that category. Something she needed to remember.

Barely friends. Right.

"I thought you were leaving."

He stood up, holding the trash bag. "Uh, I thought maybe *we* should leave."

"We?"

"I mean...not together, but...um..." He ran a hand behind his neck. "Okay, so, I'm still thinking that maybe I need to get you home, safely."

"Hud."

"I made a promise to your brothers."

"I think you did your part."

"Not until we know—*I* know—that nothing is going to sneak up on you in the middle of a dark alley."

"That's a little creepy."

"Too many horror movies as a child. My brother loved them. But now I can't get it out of my head."

"Maybe we're overreacting."

"Boat. On fire. Boom!" He made a little hand gesture to go with it, his fingers opening. "And then shooting." He made the appropriate gun symbol, along with sounds.

Shoot, he was cute.

"Okay, Bourne Identity, you can drive me to the airport. But if you get on the plane to Milan—"

"Deal." He held up his fist. "But you won't mind the little surveillance camera I add to your luggage, right?"

"You're hilarious." She went to push past him, but he grabbed her arm.

His smile had fallen. "In all seriousness—I know I'm not one of your Navy SEAL brothers, but promise me that if you get scared, if something happens, you'll call me."

"And you'll fly in with your hammer and save me?"

He said nothing, his eyes in hers.

Oh. And the heat, the warmth was back, sweeping over her to her toes.

Then he smiled again. "I was thinking more of my cool new axe, Stormbreaker, but...that's the gist."

"What do you want me to call you?"

"God of Thunder?"

"For the love."

He grinned. "Okay, so here's the plan. I'm going to leave, take the garbage out, and I'll meet you outside in five."

"Should we sync our watches?"

"If that makes you feel better."

"What would make me feel better is a decent dinner, a glass of wine, and a bath."

"I can do two out of three." He winked and picked up the trash. Headed for the door.

Sorta made a girl want to quit her job.

What? No. She'd worked too hard to throw down the flag.

She briefly searched for her jacket and found it in Gennie's bedroom. Gennie was sitting on her bed, watching her tablet.

"You going to be okay?" She gave the girl a hug. Then a fist bump. "Big girls can cry, but then they wipe their eyes and keep going, okay?"

She nodded. "Oh, by the way, your phone rang."

Her phone. Iris put on her jacket, then found the phone in her pocket. Unknown number, not the Marshall Field Winery she'd called earlier. She debated calling it back, then dropped the phone back into her pocket. Didn't want to keep Bourne waiting.

Oh shoot. She was so in over her head.

"See you in a couple days," Yannick said as she lifted a hand to him.

Camille met her at the door, gave her another hug. "Keep in touch."

Iris nodded, then stepped out into the hallway and called the lift.

The sun had peaked, then arched overhead, falling toward the backside of the day. Maybe Hud was right about dinner, but she'd like to take a red-eye to Milan.

And suddenly, the danger of the past week seemed ages away, despite the boat, the bombing, the bullets, and now Abe. With her conversation with Yannick, and even crazy teasing by Hud, it all seemed...

What if they were just overreacting? What if all of this was coincidence, that no one wanted to kill her? Maybe the stove in the boat had overheated, and the bullets had simply been debris from the bomb, and Abe had simply eaten bad fish.

Really bad fish.

The lift opened on her floor, and she got on, then closed the door and pushed the button. It shuddered its way down to the bottom floor, and she stepped out.

Garbage bins would be not on the street but in the back of the building, near the courtyard and the parking area.

She turned and found her way through the building to the back and stepped outside.

No Hudson. Walking through the courtyard, she found the

trash, but the bins were locked. She turned, then spotted more trashcans through an alleyway.

She headed toward them, picking up her pace.

And maybe because thick shadows fell across the courtyard, and maybe because she could still hear the echo of Hudson's voice—*What if this is bigger than you?*—whatever the reason, she picked up her pace.

Started into a jog.

And of course, that's when a voice lifted, carrying across the cobblestones, bouncing off the buildings and following her down the alleyway—

"Hey—there she is! Don't let her get away!"

Iris didn't look back and simply ran for her life.

THREE

No, Hud wasn't going to just drop Iris off at the airport, but she didn't need to know that.

Right?

Hudson threw that thought around his brain as he fiddled with the garbage bins around back of the courtyard. He'd tried the ones by the entrance, but they were locked, so he'd spotted more down the street.

Then he'd rounded back to the front of the apartment to wait for Iris.

Sync their watches.

Okay, that was funny, and the thought of leaving her at Charles de Gaulle to go back to Milan, where someone could be waiting to poison her, sat like a fist in his gut.

Nope.

Although, he didn't exactly know what to do with Coach Max's words either.

A shot at the NFL. It seemed like something he'd dreamed of only to have it wisp away in his grasp.

The sun had fallen behind the horizon and, from where he stood, cast shadows onto the street. Cars honked as they entered the circle around the park down the street, and the café smells caused his stomach to growl. The cold macaroni and cheese, along with a ham sandwich, had done nothing to soothe the beast inside.

He could go for a pizza. And a heaping bowl of spaghetti. Maybe some hot French bread—

He checked his watch. Five minutes, for sure.

Bicyclist sped by in the bike lane— *Saved your life just then.*

He smiled. No, he wasn't ready to let her go quite yet.

His cell phone buzzed in his pocket, and he pulled it out. He'd texted Coach Max his number earlier while Iris had been chatting up her future with her crew boss.

Unknown number.

He answered. "Hudson Bly."

"Hud! How's Paris?"

The Texas drawl of his agent poured through the phone. "Waylen?"

"Where have you been, kid? I've been searching for you for a week. Living large in the Greek isles, according to Instagram."

"Yeah, on my oh-so-massive three thousand euros a month salary. If I re-sign with the Vikings, you gotta negotiate for more. Did you see the sacrifice I made for the team in the game against the Panthers?"

"I did, and I've got you slotted for a walk-on tryout with the Minnesota Vikings in the spring, if you want it."

"The Minnesota Vikings?"

"They just lost their starting receiver—high ankle break—and are shallow on the bench. And they're not the only ones. Seattle is looking lean too. I think we could get you a number of tryouts. Too bad the trade deadline just passed, but your showing in the ELF Super Bowl put you back on the radar here in the States. Stay in shape, and don't get hurt in these exhibition games, and I'll see if I can't wrestle you up a deal."

He was nodding before he realized he hadn't said anything.

"Hud, you there?"

"Yeah. You got it, Waylen."

"You got grit, kid. I always liked that."

"Thanks—"

"Hey—there she is! Don't let her get away!"

He heard the shout in English, and for a second, it registered in the back of his head, something that felt—wait.

Where was Iris?

He turned, closing the phone, and spotted—*what?*

Three men were running hard after Iris, who was just disappearing around the end of the courtyard.

What—

He took off in the opposite direction, around the end of the building where he'd left the trash, into the alleyway between buildings, and sprinted.

He caught up to her just as she passed by him. He turned, ran hard, and grabbed her, scooping her up against him.

She screamed, elbowed him in the gut, and he gasped, nearly dropping her.

And then she screamed again, pushing away from him, just as someone jumped him.

He flew forward, but he'd learned how to take a hit and turned just as he landed, rolled and found his feet.

Then he rounded and hit the man who'd tackled him square in the jaw.

The man tumbled back, and another man grabbed him around the waist.

"No! Stop!"

Iris's voice rose above the ruckus but did nothing to slow anyone down.

The man rammed Hud back against the building, and the breath whooshed out of him. But he turned and got his knee up into the guy's gut, and the man jerked back, off him.

Hudson turned to Iris. "Run!"

"No!" She rushed toward him, just as the first man came at him again, a little fire in his eyes. She stepped in front of Hudson, her arms out, a tiny spitfire of fury. "Jonas, stop!"

The man called Jonas stood in front of her, his eyes pinned to Hudson, breathing hard. Then he bent over at the waist and spat out blood.

Yeah, well, that's what he got for—wait. She *knew* him? "What's going on?"

The other man came up to him, holding his nose, blood trickling out. Oh no, because now recognition clicked in. "Ned?"

"Hudson." Ned held out his hand.

"Don't shake hands!" Iris slapped Ned's hand away. "You scared the life out of me. How about a simple, 'Hey, Iris! Stop running'?" She stared at Ned, then at Jonas.

"We didn't want to lose you."

The voice was deeper, and came from a man who was breathing hard, had run up after the other two.

Iris turned, clearly following the voice. "Dad? What are you doing here?" But she ran up to him, threw her arms around his neck. His curled around her waist.

Her father? Tall, dark hair, blue eyes. He was an older version of his sons, although with something sterner on his face that unnerved Hud a little.

"What's going on, Iris?" Hud said.

Iris turned away from her father. "I have no idea."

"And why does every time I meet your brothers result in a punch-up?"

"Maybe you're the one who needs to stop hitting people!" This from a blonde who now handed Ned a cloth from her backpack. Looked like a sock.

He pointed to Jonas. "He tackled me!" Then Ned. "And so did he!"

Ned held up one hand. "He's right."

"Sorry." Blood reddened Jonas's teeth. "I think you loosened a tooth."

The blonde shook her head as Iris's gaze fell on her. "Shae. You're okay."

51

Shae. Ned's fiancée who, last Hudson had heard, was lost in Russia. Clearly not anymore.

Shae nodded to Iris's statement, then, "Are *you*? You've been missing for five days. Your mother was completely freaking out."

Oh. Hudson looked at Iris, who looked at him. Whoops.

Gone for five days, and the Marshall family had sent out a *search party*. Across the ocean.

Overkill, much?

But as Iris hugged Jonas, then Ned—who then shook Hudson's hand—he couldn't help but feel a little like maybe he'd been benched.

"What are you guys doing here? And how did you find me?" Iris stepped toward him, and he fought the urge to take her hand. Like, what—asserting his spot in her life?

He had no spot in her life, really.

"Mom texted us your phone number," Jonas said. "Said you'd called and were in Paris. And we just landed, so then Fraser sent us an address. Said that Coco had hacked the GPS position off your phone."

Coco, as in her cousin Coco? Huh.

"And please—why were you on a plane to Paris? Or wherever?"

"Lake Como, actually," Jonas said. "We thought we'd check your house first."

"For what? A dead body?"

Jonas made a face. Ned's mouth tightened in a grim line. Hudson looked at her father, who drew in a deep breath.

"We prayed not," her father said. "But after Shae's abduction and Jonas's crazy radioactive weather balloon story, and, well, even Fraser and Creed's race through Europe, I think we might have jumped to conclusions."

And any hope that Hudson had of quarterbacking what happened next died with Iris's words. "You're not wrong."

He wanted to turn and bang his head against the plaster and concrete.

"Hudson and I have been on the run since last week."

Silence, and Hudson drew in a breath. Then Ned looked at him, met his gaze. "Tell us everything."

Oh. Because he'd been assigned her babysitter way back then. By Ned.

So, okay. "Let's get something to eat."

"I'm on board with that," Shae said and took Ned's hand. She didn't seem undone by her kidnapping ordeal, so maybe that had been overblown too.

Or maybe that's just what this family did—rolled with the crazy of their lives. Except for the night in the cave where they'd nearly drowned over and over again, Iris had held it together pretty well.

What had she said to Genesis? *You stay tough...*

They found a table at the nearby Café du Trocadéro and sat outside under the expansive white awning. They all—even he—looked like American tourists, with their puffy black parkas and hiking boots. Except for Iris, who wore a wool jacket and a pair of dress shoes. She also ordered tea and the sea bass fillet with fennel, while the rest ordered fish and chips or cheeseburgers and french fries.

He asked for the tartare, with carrots and mushrooms and a side of fries.

No one did french fries like the French.

Her father finally introduced himself—Garrett Marshall—and Hudson returned with, "Hudson Bly, wide receiver for the Vienna Vikings, formerly from Montana."

Good grip, and he met Hudson with a thorough once-over. Then he sat next to Iris, and Hud didn't know if he'd passed inspection. Garrett put his arm across the back of her chair.

Maybe not.

"Okay, so please clarify what you meant about 'on the run,'" Ned said after they'd handed over their menus.

Again, he wanted to reach out and take her hand, but she

dove right in. "Nearly two weeks ago, I stood on a bridge and watched someone stab our cousin Tate."

Okay, he might not have started *there*.

"I was there because a couple weeks before that, I was asked by what I thought was our government, aka the CIA, to deliver a package to a Berlin train station. Since I travel a lot, they told me that I could be useful. And stupidly, I said yes."

The waiter brought them their coffees and teas and tiny cups of espresso. Iris doctored her tea with milk and sugar.

"I came to my senses pretty fast—I'm not a spy, and I don't want to be one, ever—so I met with my...I don't know, handler?, and told him I was out. He told me that I needed to do one last favor"—she took a sip of the tea—"and help them find a mole. Which involved going to the Charles Bridge in Prague to take a picture of a handoff between a courier and said mole."

Hudson raised his hand. "Courier."

Garrett raised an eyebrow.

"For the record, I too was recruited by the CIA, but as it turns out, we were working for opposite teams."

Thankfully no one asked him why he'd said yes to the CIA. Looking at Iris, maybe the answer didn't matter anymore.

"The man who sent me to the bridge was actually a rogue spy named Alan Martin. We're not sure why he wanted me to take pictures of Hudson and the so-called mole. But I never did, because the mole turned out to be our cousin, Tate Marshall."

"Tate is involved with the CIA?"

"Not exactly," said Ned. He had leaned back, his arm around Shae, his back to the wall, his focus on the street. His gaze flickered now and again to Hudson. He leaned forward. "Tate, according to Fraser, works for a private security group attached to the government. And that's who Hudson here had hooked up with." He looked at his dad, then Iris. "As it turns out, the information Hudson was passing off had to do with the whereabouts of Shae."

He squeezed Shae's hand. She smiled at him, then looked at

Iris. "If you hadn't completed Tate's mission and passed on the information, then I still might be stuck in a gulag ship in Siberia."

And that shut down the table. A beat, then another.

"What did you say?" Jonas said, leaning back in his chair. "You didn't tell me that."

"No time. Fraser called me in Montana and told me that Iris was missing. Asked me to come home," Ned said.

"And I wasn't letting him out of my sight," Shae said.

"He told me the same thing," Jonas said. "And I'm not sure why, but after the scare we had in Slovenia, I thought—what if they found out that I had been instrumental in taking out their biological weapon?"

"Who is *they*?" Iris said.

"A Russian group called the Petrov Bratva," Ned said, then turned to Jonas. "And they did. Or at least figured out that my SEAL Team helped with the mission. We're not sure why they took Shae, but it got complicated. Still is."

More silence around the table.

Then, finally, Garrett leaned forward, his hands folded. "That doesn't explain why Iris was on the run for five days."

Hudson looked at Iris, and then he did take her hand, under the table. "After we met Ned and Fraser in Paris—just a little ways from here, at Napoleon's grave—and handed off the information, they asked me to make sure Iris was safe." He met Ned's gaze. "I flew her back to Milan and left her there."

"I didn't need him babysitting me," Iris said now, and let go of his hand.

"Or maybe you did, because you didn't show up at your house for three days, and Ziggy showed up in Vienna, at my apartment, in a panic."

"Who is Ziggy?" asked Shae.

"She's with the Caleb Group," said Ned. "I met her in Slovenia on the op to intercept the dirty bomb. Jonas met her too."

"Scary woman," Jonas said.

No doubt. "She was also *my* handler," said Hudson. "And she told me that there was a hit taken out on Iris and I needed to find her."

"A hit?" Jonas said, then cut his voice down. "As in someone wanted her *dead*?"

"That's what Ziggy said."

"By who?" Ned asked.

"Alan Martin," said Iris.

Ned shook his head. Leaned back.

The waiter appeared with the first plates of food and set them on the table. He wanted to dive into his tartare like a beast, but he sat back and waited for the next plates.

"Are you sure it was Alan Martin?" Ned asked.

"No," said Iris. "It was a theory, because apparently she couldn't be sure until the hit was completed and the assassin collected his bounty." She leaned forward to smell her sea bass. It sat in a sauce of fennel, turmeric, and lemon juice.

A raw egg sat in the middle of his tartare, seasoned with anchovies, capers, Worcestershire sauce, and sriracha, and surrounded by pickled red onions.

Shae made a face at his food and turned away.

"It's delicious," he said. "And frankly, I could use the protein. I'm wasting away."

This got a laugh from her and seemed to put a pin in the horror of Iris's story.

The waiter brought the rest of the plates, and he picked up his fork.

The rest of them bowed their heads.

Oh.

Garrett's voice was low, earnest. "Lord, we thank You for keeping Iris safe. And the rest of our children as well, including Shae. Thank You for watching over us even when it feels overwhelming. You are our firm foundation. And thank You for sending Hudson to protect Iris. Please bless him in his career and future. Thank You for this food. May we be strengthened by it."

"Amen," said Iris and a couple others.

Huh. But, "Amen." Hud glanced at Iris.

She was smiling at him. Then she winked and picked up her fork.

So, maybe not benched after all.

The story fell quiet as they ate their food, but Iris picked it back up after a moment. "After Hudson dropped me off in Milan, I went shopping for a few days—I called Mom, I remember that. But when I got back to my house, Hudson had broken in."

"Did you do the door trick?" Jonas asked.

"The sliding door trick?" Ned said.

"I remember teaching you guys that," Garrett said.

"No. The door to the house was open," Hudson said. "And the house was ransacked."

Garrett put down his hamburger. "Ransacked."

"As if they were looking for something," Iris said. "Which freaked us both out. So after I nearly clobbered Hudson for sneaking into my house, he convinced me to go to Greece with him and hide for a few days."

"Without your phone?" Jonas said.

"The phone was a casualty of our sailboat being blown up."

"Now I'm not hungry," Ned said. "*Blown up*?"

"We weren't on it at the time," Iris said. "You sure you don't want some of my sea bass? It's delicious."

"I'll have a bite," Shae said and reached over with her fork. Iris cut her off a piece.

"We hid in a cave for the night, and the next day were picked up by a fishing boat." Hudson ignored the way Iris looked at him. Well, he didn't need to freak them out more with the details, right? "We were watching the exhibition game on cable when Iris saw her friend Abe collapse on the field. She called Yannick and found out Abe died, which put us on a plane for Paris." He had broken the egg and was now working it into his tartare. Took a bite.

Heaven. Tangy and fresh, with a hint of vinegar bite. He took a bite of his crostini to wash it down.

Iris finished her sea bass. Set her fork and knife on the plate. "Okay, so please, tell me why you put the whole team in, Dad. I mean, it's nice to know you care, but this feels a little over-the-top."

Hud raised an eyebrow. Was she not listening to the story?

Garrett gave her a look. "Okay, truth is I'd like to blame it on your mother, but the fact is, I was worried too. And what everyone left out of this story is that about a month ago, after we all saw each other at Creed's international meet, Creed got mixed up with an incident involving a princess from Lauchtenland, and Fraser had to fly over and help him get untangled. And now said princess and her bodyguard live at our house, and ever since then my children, one by one, have been embroiled in some kind of danger, and frankly, I just needed to know my only daughter was safe."

Okay, that was...well, even Hudson wanted to tear up.

Garrett took her hand. "I know you're tough, Iris. As tough—maybe tougher—than your brothers. But you're still my daughter, and if you think your mother worries about you, well, let's just say she wasn't the only one who realized you hadn't checked in."

"Aw, Dad." Iris leaned over and hugged him.

He let her go. "I don't suppose we can talk you into coming home for a couple weeks, now that the season is over?"

"I can't. I have a game next week. And one a couple weeks after that."

"You're going back to work?" Ned said. "What about"—he lowered his voice—"the hit?"

Right. What he said. "Especially after Abe."

"What about Abe?" asked Shae.

Iris's mouth tightened. "They think he was poisoned."

"Murdered?" Jonas had finished his meal too. "Seriously?"

"No one knows for sure."

Garrett leaned back, folded his arms. "So, she's still in danger."

No one had an answer for him.

"Well, that settles it. I'm not going anywhere until we stop whoever wants to kill her." This from Garrett. Ned nodded. Jonas folded his arms.

Shae reached out and squeezed Iris's arm.

And maybe Hudson should have felt relief, a loosening of the knot in his chest. But he was doing the math.

If her father intended to stick around, then Hud was officially relieved of duty.

And then Garrett confirmed it by turning to Hudson. "Thank you for everything you did, Hud. I'm sure you're ready to get back to your life."

He nodded. Smiled. But his tartare turned to a lump inside his gut, and he lost his appetite. "Yeah, can't wait," he said.

And really, this was for the best, right?

It wasn't like he was giving up football. And she wasn't giving up her career.

Besides, if he wanted a run at the NFL, he needed to listen to Waylen.

Focus.

Iris wasn't his life—football was. And probably it was time to shake off his weird inner babysitter and get back to his life.

"I need to run," he said and pushed away his chair.

"We'll pick up lunch."

Iris looked up at him, her face suddenly drawn. "You're leaving?"

"I need to get home, hit the gym and get ready for my next game." Oh, he wanted to reach down, pull her into his arms. Instead he swallowed, forced a smile.

She got up, however, and put her arms around his neck. Oh, she was a small thing next to him—he had to lean down. "Thank you."

"Call me anytime," he said softly.

"Thunder."

He let her go, met her eyes. "See you on the field." And then he walked away, forcing himself to forget the last five days.

It was for the best. Honestly. Really.

Iris had told herself exactly that as Hudson had walked away, toward the metro, back to where they'd come from only a few hours ago.

When he'd been her, what—partner on the lam?

Babysitter?

She blew out a long breath through the knotting in her chest and refused to let it rattle her.

Just friends. No, *barely* friends.

"I think we should find an Airbnb and hunker down here while we figure out what to do," her father had said as he'd finished off his french fries.

Jonas had gotten out his phone then and found them a gigantic five-bedroom, five-bathroom townhouse steps from Saint-Sulpice, Saint-Germain-des-Prés, and overlooking the Jardin du Luxembourg.

Now, as the sun set over the skyscape of Paris, Iris sat on the rooftop deck that overlooked the mansard rooftops and towers of the two churches, listening to her brothers argue about what to do next.

Ned wanted her to go home and let him and Fraser figure out who was behind the hit. Jonas wanted her to return to Lake Como and to set up a perimeter there.

No one had asked her, really, what she wanted to do.

All her answers, pitifully, included Hudson.

Shoot, she'd depended on him too much.

"Glass of wine, honey?"

Her father stood in the doorway. "I cracked a bottle of Côtes du Rhône chard." He held the glass by the stem and swirled it. "It's good. Dry, but complex. Peach and pineapple tones. Probably good for the ramen noodles your brothers are cooking up."

He walked over and gave her the glass.

"How was your wine tour?" She took the glass, swirled the wine, and took a sip. "Mmm, that is good."

He sat down on one of the lounge chairs on the deck. Miniature cedar trees lined the edge of the deck in boxes, and a long table hosted dried hydrangeas. Iris sat with a blanket from an inside basket over her, the chill in the air biting.

"We had to cut it short when Creed was shot."

She lowered her glass. "How is he doing?"

"He's getting around."

"And Fraser's hand?"

"He messed that up a little during his escapade with Ned, rescuing Shae." Her father sat with his hands tucked between his knees, wore a flannel shirt. She still couldn't believe he'd come looking for her.

Reminded her a little of the days when they'd watch football together, just them.

Her gaze cast to Shae in the kitchen, dicing onions. "How is she?"

"Quiet. Won't talk about it much. But I'm sure it'll come out when she's ready. She reminds me of you—strong and silent."

"Maybe I shouldn't be so silent. I'm sorry I worried you."

"I called your mom. She said you two were due a long talk. I think you should do it face-to-face." He raised an eyebrow.

"Dad. I know you want me to come home, but...well, Yannick promoted me to ump, in Abe's position—"

"Ump." He drew a breath. "That's the most dangerous position on the field. That's right behind the line of scrimmage—it's where the blitz happens and most of the plays develop. Last year alone, there were three concussions and a number of shoulder and knee injuries—"

"Seriously? How do you know that?"

"Your *Referee* magazine subscription still comes to the house."

"Don't worry. I'm fast—probably the fastest official on the field. And I know how to stay invisible and out of the way. I'll be fine."

"I know. Mostly. But your mother worries." He winked.

"Right."

He got up and pinched her toe through the blanket. "She's been under the weather a little since we got home. Can't quite seem to shake the jet lag. Call her more."

"Okay."

He stopped at the door. "And by the way, I'm not done with nagging you about coming home. Ned called Fraser and he's getting ahold of this Caleb Group, trying to find out more, but if there really is a hit out on you...I might have to pull the dad card."

"I'm nearly thirty."

"You say that, but I see a four-year-old in pigtails talking to me."

She lifted her wine glass and sipped it.

He rolled his eyes and went inside.

The sun had sunk to just above the roofline, spilling orange across the dark rooftops. Paris was such a gorgeous old city, every building, every winding street pulsing with history and significance.

She would have liked to explore it a little with Hudson. Maybe get some gelato—

Stop.

She took another sip of wine. Tangy, bright, it warmed her through.

The door opened, and Shae came out. She carried a glass of wine and a wooden board. "I found some Manchego cheese and cut up some bread."

"Fancy."

She set the board down on a small table and sat on the lounger where Iris's father had been. Shae had her blonde hair back, wore a pair of cargo pants, an oversized Montana Grizz sweatshirt. She might have even gotten it out of Iris's closet, back in Minnesota.

"Is that a *bruise* around your eye?"

Shae's hand went up to touch her eye. "Yeah. I forgot. It's almost gone, but—"

"What happened?"

"I was in fight." She reached for the cheese.

"A *fight*?"

"In gulag. On the ship. It was an escape tactic."

So much to unpack in that sentence. "Did it work?"

"Yep." She grinned. "But enough about me—I want to know everything that happened between you and Hunk."

"Hud."

"Hunk." Shae cupped the bowl of the glass with her hands. "Spill."

"First of all, don't hold your glass like that—you'll warm the bowl, and white wine needs to be chilled."

"Oh my gosh, you Marshalls. So many wine rules."

"Can't help it. When you grow up with a vintner for a father, it's in the blood."

"Stop dodging. You spent five days with the man, and he just walks away? No looking back? No kiss goodbye?"

"We *are* just friends."

"Sure you are. Or rather, are you sure you want to be?"

Oh.

And suddenly, she was back in the cave, the night thick around them, his arms, his body, her only anchor to safety.

"You're blushing, even in this light." Shae had repositioned her hands to hold the stem. "You do like him."

"He's...surprising. I told myself I'd never date a football player."

"Why? Because they're so consumed with the sport?"

Well, she was consumed with the sport, so no, but the real reason felt too much right now, so, "Yes."

"I can see that. Who ditches the woman he loves to go home and lift weights?"

"Hud doesn't love me, I promise."

"Maybe that's overstated. Let's go with really likes, with a dash of protective warrior in his gaze when he looks at you."

She laughed. "We just—had some adventures together is all."

"Adventures?"

"I did mention the boat blowing up, right?"

Shae's eyes widened. "I thought you were kidding—like the motor went kaput or something. You mean it *blew up*? With fire and smoke?"

"And left us stranded at sea. And then there might have been bullets."

She didn't know why she felt the sudden need to confess all this to Shae. Maybe her inner competitor—topping Shae's escape-from-gulag story. Or maybe she just needed to air it out, get a good look at it.

Decide for herself if the feelings that had consumed her that terrible night were real or just adrenaline.

"Someone was *shooting* at you?"

"I don't know, but Hudson grabbed my hand and pulled me under, and then he practically pulled me to safety in this coral reef. We hid there for a while and then kept swimming. We were too far from Santorini to swim, so we took shelter in this cave for the night. It sort of faced the island, and we could see the lights, but then the tide came in. We were sitting on this ledge, but with the tide, it was a good ten feet under water. And by this time, the opening was completely under water, and it was dark, and we couldn't see anything, even if we wanted to swim out and...I was pretty scared."

"Water. Darkness. Yeah, I get it."

"There was this little pocket of air near the surface, about a foot, maybe, of space, and the walls were brutal—coral, or maybe lava, I don't know, but it hurt to hold onto them. And it was hard to get a hold. Hud managed to get a grip on something above him, but I couldn't reach it. I was exhausted, treading water, scared, and then this swell just hit the cave, and for a second, we were underwater. The current took me, and if it hadn't been for Hudson grabbing me and holding onto me, I might have been bashed against the rocks. But he did—he just reached out and pulled me against him, and I was terrified, so I...held on."

"To all that manly muscle."

"I was thinking more about not drowning."

"What a shame."

She laughed. "Well, after the swell died down and we found ourselves breathing again, I did notice the manly muscle. The bad part is that the swell had slammed him against the lava and scraped open his skin on his shoulders and back. So he was bleeding and trying to hold on to the rock, and I was holding on to him, and the salt water was in his wounds...it wasn't romantic."

"Sounds a little romantic. If you were writing it in a book. Or watching it on the big screen. His strong arm around you, saving your life—"

"Six hours. That's how long it took for the tide to go down. Six hours, and that wasn't the only swell."

Shae nodded, took a sip of her wine.

"Okay, after a while it might have been a little romantic. I mean, he refused to let me go—not that I wanted him to—but then we just hung out there, trying to keep each other from drowning, talking in the night. He told me about his favorite plays, and I told him about epic calls. He talked about his future and how he wants to play for the NFL. I told him about my house in Lake Como and the remodel I did. We talked about the winery, and I told him about how I got into officiating—at least, most of it. And he told me about his life in Australia."

"Oh, that's the accent. I wasn't sure."

"He moved to Montana when he was ten. His mom got sick and his dad lost their farm in the outback, so he moved them back to Montana, to live on his grandfather's ranch. Only his grandfather died heavily in debt, so they had to sell it, and now his dad works as a cowboy on some cattle ranch. He has a brother named Harry—Harrington—who is some search and rescue guy and works for a team in Glacier National Park."

Shae had turned silent, watching her, lifting her glass now and again. The sunset glinted off the golden wine.

Iris reached for a slice of cheese. "Manchego. Good choice with the wine."

"Your dad suggested it." She met Iris's eyes. "You more than like him."

Iris looked at her glass, swirled the wine. "I'm an official. He's a player. Any fraternization between us would be the end of our careers."

"And you've worked too hard to give that up."

She leaned back. "Hud wants to play for the NFL. It's his dream. I can't compete with that."

"So, you're out before he has to make that choice."

"Seems easiest."

"Except for your poor heart."

Iris gave her a look. "My poor heart is fine. There's no room for romance with a football player in my world. And yes, for a whole minute there, I did let myself hold onto him. But that was panic and desperation, and I'm back to myself now. I got this."

She raised her glass. "To the strong. To the survivors."

Shae touched her glass to hers. "And to the men who try and protect us."

Yes. She owed him that much. She took a drink. *Promise me that if you get scared, if something happens, you'll call me.*

She looked back out to the sunset, now winking out into the darkness.

Thank you, Thor.

The door opened and Ned popped his head out. "Dinnertime."

She got up, along with Shae, and they went into the apartment.

The boys had set the table with bowls, candles, and glasses of wine. A regular party.

"What is this?"

"Ramen noodles extraordinaire," Jonas said. "Ramen with egg, green onions, cheese, and bacon."

"I'm in," Shae said.

Iris sat down, drew in the smell. Refused to wonder what Hud was eating.

Probably he was back in Vienna by now. Or just about—

Stop.

Her father said grace again, and Iris picked up her spoon.

Ned slurped noodles into his mouth. "Okay, Iris, Jonas and I have been over and over your story. And if we could figure out why someone wants you dead, maybe we could figure out who put out the hit."

Jonas had opted for a fork and was winding the noodles around them. Now, he slurped them into his mouth, then wiped it with a napkin and set down the fork. "What stands out in your story is three things—the phone you were given to take pictures, the ransacked apartment, and your trip to Germany."

"I gave the phone to Ziggy. She was supposed to try and contact Martin."

"Have you heard from Ziggy?" Ned asked.

"No. Hudson tried to call her a couple times."

"Okay, so we have the ransacked apartment. Do you think they were looking for the phone?"

"Maybe. We can't figure out why he'd want pictures of Hudson on the bridge, although Hud thinks maybe Martin was going to frame him for Tate's murder."

"And you kept the phone, so he could be after that."

"Except I don't have it anymore, so that's a problem."

Ned stirred his Ramen. "Let's talk about the drop in Germany. What was that?"

"Just a manila envelope. I dropped it at a train station. Took the key."

"Do you still have the key?" This from her father.

She stared at him. "Um...yes. No—I had it on me when I got back to my house in Lake Como, but I left it there. Hidden in my closet."

"So it could still be there," Jonas said.

"Yes. And they wouldn't have known that I had it on me, so maybe that's what they were searching for."

"What was in that envelope?" Shae asked.

"No idea."

"You weren't supposed to drop the key anywhere?"

"Not to my knowledge."

"Those lockers have master keys to them," her dad said. "They wouldn't need her key to get in."

Silence, some slurping.

"Maybe we get the key, go back to Germany, see if the box is empty," said Ned.

"I have to go to Berlin to prep for a game in two days," Iris said.

Ned had picked up his bowl to drink the broth. Now, he put it down, wiping his chin with a napkin. "I haven't been to Berlin for a whole week."

She frowned at him.

"Long story."

Her dad touched her arm. "Don't worry, honey. We're going to figure this, make sure you're safe, and get your life back."

Perfect. Just perfect. That's exactly what she wanted.

FOUR

Three more reps, rest, then one more set. Hudson readjusted his grip on the weight bar sitting heavy on his burning shoulders, sweat running down his spine, and slowly lowered himself down into a deep squat. Held it there, then slowly pressed back up.

Eight.

Around him, music blared in the Vienna Vikings' gym, an old factory refurbished into a modern practice center. Massive windows were cut into the galvanized roof that let in the morning light, although today, rain plinked against them. Long-stemmed fans extended from the ceiling, stirring the air, thick with the scent of disinfectant and rubber.

The massive open-air gym and indoor turf field ran nearly eighty yards, so it felt like a field. The smaller area, once used as offices, contained the weight equipment. A sauna and showers extended past the weight room, with adjoining rooms for massages and cold baths.

Inside the gym, motivational quotes plastered the cement walls, most of it in Austrian, but Coach Clay had had some American phrases added too. *All progress takes place outside the* comfort zone! Or, *If it doesn't challenge you, it doesn't change you!* Or, *Your only limit is you.*

Good thoughts, the kind that should probably keep Iris from tiptoeing back into his brain.

Maybe she was back in Lake Como—

He shook the thought away. It didn't matter where she was. He'd walked away, back to his life.

Where he belonged.

Metallica played over the speakers in the corners of the room—metal that was supposed to inspire sweat, although Hud had never been a fan of the screaming. And it wasn't so loud that it overpowered the conversation between groups of players positioned around weight machines or mats, some spotting, some resting while the others lifted, grunted, blew out breaths of stress and triumph.

The players had arrived over the last two hours, most of them spending time with the weights, squatting or lifting. Some worked with the strength coach on explosive techniques like box jumps—one legged jumps to a high pad. Some simply did calisthenics—good old-fashioned push-ups and sit-ups, although many added a weight belt to their efforts.

Nine.

Hud's chalked hands repositioned on the bar, his weight belt tight against his straining muscles. The wrist guards kept his hands from falling back.

"One more, Hud." This from Toby West, their third American, a big tight end out of the University of Idaho who'd played on the practice team for the Green Bay Packers before getting cut and landing over the pond. At two-ten, and six foot one, he was just a little slower than Hud on the forty, but still managed to cause trouble for the wideouts on the opposing teams.

He also happened to be the one person who knew Hud's story—besides, of course, Coach Max. Probably saw it on the game tape, over and over again.

Hud lowered himself once more, took a long breath, and forced himself up.

Toby and his other spotter, big safety Luis Spiegel, took the bar and set it back on the rack.

Hud unstrapped the wrist braces and stepped away, breathing hard. Caught a view of himself in the warped wall mirror. Gray wells under his eyes betrayed last night's sleepless wrestle with his sheets, and a few of the scratches remained on his shoulders, fading but still reddened. He'd worn a T-shirt today, and the cutoff arms revealed the wounds from that night.

Shoot, if he let himself, he could be right back in the cave, feeling Iris's arm around his neck as she treaded water next to him.

"Hud? Give me a hand?"

Toby waited to add more weight onto the bar, then helped lift the bar onto Luis's back.

No more Iris! "Right. Sorry." Hud pulled the pin, added another five pounds onto the bar, then resecured the weight and helped position the bar. He stood to spot as Luis readied himself for back squats.

"You okay?"

He glanced over at Toby. Behind him, on a large turfed area, Coach Max was drilling Felix on catches. The wideout lay on the ground, eyes up, while Max tossed footballs over his head.

He had missed quite a few, and Max had started to yell.

"Yeah. Just, you know, focused."

"I hope on the game this weekend against the Thunder. I know it's an exhibition game, but rumor is that you have a tryout with the MN Vikings lined up."

Luis blew out as he stood up, then grunted and started back down.

"Of course. What else would I—"

"The whole team saw the Instagram picture with that official." Toby raised an eyebrow. "Seriously? Iris Marshall, of all people? Hud, what are you thinking? That girl nearly wrecked your entire life."

"She doesn't know."

"Don't know what?" Luis stood at the top of his squat, breathing hard.

Hud shook his head, but maybe Toby ignored him, because, "Iris Marshall was the official who caused Hudson's TBI."

"She didn't cause it. It wasn't like she was the one who targeted me."

Luis was mid-squat now, paused at the bottom. He pushed up, breathed out. "You got targeted?"

"Head-on collision," Toby said. "He lost his helmet and hit the deck, hard. Had to be carted off the field. That's five. Give me five more."

"That's whack, man." Luis went down again, grunting.

"He missed Combine because of it. He would have gone first or second round, for sure."

Luis came back up. "I'm shot."

"Gimme one more," Toby said. Luis stood, panting.

Behind Hud, Felix was still missing catches.

Luis lowered for the last squat, his legs shaking.

"She really doesn't know? Even after the lawsuit?"

"She wasn't involved. I'm not sure she even knows about it."

"It was a groundbreaking lawsuit—no one had ever sued the NCAA for a targeting hit."

"I wouldn't have, but I was in a coma for a week. The hospital bills were brutal. They settled out of court, so my guess is that they didn't even contact her. She was just a back judge, anyway— the responsibility fell on the referee, and ultimately Bryce Smalls, the guy who hit me."

They both helped Luis up, holding the weights so they didn't slip off his shoulders. They racked the weight, and Luis leaned over, grabbing his knees. "That's the guy who hit you?"

"Yeah." Hud tossed Luis a towel. "He had targeted the wideout a few plays before, and the guy went down with a dislocated shoulder. Smalls should have been tossed."

"But Marshall didn't call the penalty."

"I don't know how she missed it," Toby said. "He was like a bull to a red flag. But she just called an incomplete pass. And Hud went in for the injured receiver. Two plays later, they were carrying him off the field on a stretcher." He looked at Hud. "Was she paid off? It was a championship game."

Now that he knew Iris? "She wouldn't do that."

Toby raised an eyebrow. "Really. You know her that well? Something going on between you two?"

"No. We're—we're just...listen, she's a good official. And that was a long time ago."

"Dude, what are you talking about? You still have headaches, and everyone here knows that one more bad hit—"

"I'm over it. Listen, I gotta help Max with Felix. The kid is a disaster." He turned to jog away.

"But we have another rep!"

"Take a look at Luis and say that!"

Toby took a couple steps toward him. "And you're not over it—you're in denial because she's cute!"

Hudson looked back at him and drew his hand across his neck. C'mon, bro. The last thing he needed was shade thrown his direction about the lady official.

Especially since she was out of his life, thank you. No turning back.

Toby shook his head and threw his towel down.

Hudson exited the gym, the big doors open to the field, and ran over to where Felix still lay on the ground, his chin up, eyes on Coach Max, who stood ten feet away, parallel with his head.

Felix was getting antsy, slamming his fist into the ground when he missed another pass.

"Find the nose, then watch the pass all the way into your hands," Hud said. He lay down next to Felix. "Watch."

He looked up, then gestured to Coach Max. "Bring it!"

Max fired off a bullet. Hud caught it in his vision, followed it, then at the last second, brought up his hands and nabbed it.

"Nice catch," Felix said.

"See how I snapped up my hands, at the last second?" He sat up. "When you're running, you need to pump your arms. If you have your hands outstretched, it'll slow you down. Plus, the safety will see you coming. He'll be all over you. Let's go again."

He lay back. "Shoot it at me, Coach!"

Again, the bullet. Again, Hud shot up his hands, caught it. "Laces." Then he tucked it.

"Why did you say *laces*?"

He tossed the ball back, then sat up again. "I want my brain to register that I got it, so I name the identifying mark on the ball—the laces, the stamp. I hold it for two seconds, then tuck. In a game, it'll be reflex. But it forces you to see the ball into your hands before you tuck."

"And keeps you from fumbling," Coach Max said, coming up. "Good coaching there, Bly."

Hudson got up. "Don't forget to extend to the highest point—when you're standing, it'll keep you out of the way of the defender. I'm hitting the mat for the box jumps."

He walked over to the mat where the running backs were jumping with one leg to a high mat. Coach Clay was watching, arms folded.

"Hey, Coach," Hud said. "Who's this?"

"Berker Rennich. Transferred from the Panthers just this week. We're giving him a tryout in this week's game." He motioned with his head toward the door. "Someone wants to talk to you."

And right then, as he turned and spotted the blonde hair, something inside him just lurched. Blonde hair, petite, she stood with her back to him, wearing a pair of jeans and boots, a black wool coat.

Iris?

No, how—

And then the woman turned, and he tried to ignore the terrible clattering of his heart. Not Iris.

"Who is she?"

"Reporter with the *Red Zone* magazine. They want to do a feature on you and some of the other American players for the game against Lauchtenland."

He sighed, set his back teeth, and headed over to the woman.

"Hudson Bly. Glad to meet you." She stuck out her hand. "Brette Remington. I'm working on an article for the *Red Zone* magazine about the growing interest in the ELF as an alternative for players post-college, and I was hoping I could follow you around for a few days."

A few days? "Are you going to Germany for the game?"

"And the charity event."

He raised an eyebrow. "I don't...this isn't—"

"Oh! No. My husband is with me. We travel a lot for my job, and he doesn't like me to travel alone. And it's not just you—I'm going to interview Tobias West and your quarterback too. But when I googled you, your name came up the most."

Perfect. "Because of the TBI."

"And the lawsuit. And I'm from Montana, so of course I had to look into it."

"Whatever. For the record, I'm not allowed to talk about it with reporters."

She smiled. "I see that you're working out, but I was wondering if you could meet me afterwards, maybe for coffee?"

He sighed. "Sure. Why not?" See, Waylen, look how he was cooperating.

Heading back to the box jumps, he did three sets, ten jumps on each leg, then angled jumps, and had worked himself into a sopping mess by the time he finished.

Then he set up some cones and worked on his double move, changing directions in a second on the inside arch of his feet. He did five sets of thirty seconds, both legs, then switched to a longer pattern, working on keeping his hips straight as he turned his upper body, keeping his toes in.

"You look like a duck," said Toby, coming over with a towel around his neck.

"It helps me change directions, stay explosive," Hud said. "Wanna run a couple routes with me? See if you can interfere without a penalty?"

"I'm not safety, but I got this. Let's call Jack over," Toby said. "Make it interesting."

Hud grinned and whistled, motioned for Jack, who was working on handoffs with the running backs.

Jack came running over. "Yeah?"

"Coach, okay if Jack throws me a few?" Hudson shouted over to Coach Clay, who stood on the field, supervising the linebacker coach.

He waved and Hud lined up across from Toby.

"I stop that catch, I get the girl."

Hud stared at him. What?

Jack snapped the ball.

A half second, but Hud was late off the snap. Toby read his juke, was on him like glue, and when he went up to catch it, one-handed, Toby smacked it away.

He landed, Toby on top of him.

The safety rolled off him. "My win. My girl."

Hud got up, stared at him. "She's not your girl."

"So, she's *your* girl."

"She's not my girl. She's...we're...friends. Or maybe not, I don't know. But listen, just hands off, okay?"

Toby frowned at him, then suddenly began to laugh. "Wait—dude. I was talking about the woman by the door. The blonde chick. And I was just kidding. But methinks someone is lying to himself."

Hudson glared at him. Then looked at Jack. "Again."

This time he exploded off the line. Beat Toby by two steps, jumped and snagged the ball one-handed. Brought it down into the pocket, landed, spun and jerked away from Toby.

He ran into the end zone. And then, just for fun, spiked the ball.

Then he put his hands on his hips, stared out of the windows at the cityscape around them, the rain and the thunder in his heart.

And tried not to call himself a fool.

"WITH A VIEW LIKE THIS, I DON'T KNOW WHY YOU'D ever leave."

Ned stood in the guest room of Iris's Lake Como apartment, the third-floor, double bedroom where Fraser and Jonas had stayed a month ago while she'd been, um, dropping off spy stuff in a Berlin train station.

Stuff that hopefully was still there and would lead them to some clues as to why this nightmare had started and how to end it. At least, that was Jonas and Ned's goal.

Iris just wanted to get her life back. "I'm not leaving." She tucked the fitted sheet onto the mattress of the twin bed, one of two in the attic room. Her dad would stay in her office-slash-bedroom, and probably Shae would sleep with her in the king bed.

And tomorrow, they'd head to Germany. "I worked hard to renovate this place and make it what I want. This is my home."

"A messy home. Sheesh."

"You're hilarious. But thanks for the help. I'd sort of forgotten that I left the place a disaster."

"Or rather, whoever tossed it left it a disaster. You sure nothing is missing?"

"No, but none of my jewelry was taken, and really, that's the only thing of value I have."

"Don't discount those Larry Norman vinyls. I didn't know you were into Jesus music."

"Remember when grandpa used to listen to him? And Love Song?"

"That was a you and grandpa thing. But I remember the

albums. They're still in your room back home, I think. Where, by the way, you should be if we can't figure out who is trying to kill you—"

"Okay, just stop there." She'd finished pulling the sheet onto the single bed, and now picked up a bare pillow and a case. "What if all this is in my head? I mean, I've been thinking about it, and who would want to kill me? I'm nobody."

"And your friend Abe?"

She yanked the case over the pillow. "I don't know. I'm just tired of letting fear control my life."

"It's been a grand total of six days, Iris. It's not like you've been holed up in a prison, zombies surrounding the gate, waiting to eat you."

She just stared at him. "What are you talking about?"

Ned made a face. "Oh, right. Maybe you...okay, so Shae and I are in the middle of *The Walking Dead*—"

"Why? It's about zombies."

"It's about survival, although yeah, each episode is about the same—get food, stay away from the zombies."

"Isn't your life exciting enough?"

He sighed and ran a hand around the back of his neck. "Shae's having some trouble sleeping. Especially after gulag. So we stay up and watch it on my phone until she falls asleep."

Oh.

"Maybe you could try something less...gross? Like *All Creatures Great and Small* on PBS?"

"I think the point is for her to watch something unbelievable to escape the reality of her memories."

"That's rather insightful."

"That's me, Mr. Feels."

She threw him the pillow and grabbed the comforter. "She still doesn't want to talk about it. It was bad?"

"Yep." He came over, set the pillow on the bed, helped her with the other side of the comforter.

"And now you're not talking."

"I think sometimes denial is our friend. And with Shae, the more we don't talk about it, the more she can get some distance. She'll talk when she's ready."

"And you?" She walked over to the other twin. "You were pretty scared when I last saw you."

"I was scared because my big sister showed up to deliver highly secret information like she might be a spy."

She cocked her head at him.

"Okay, and my fiancée was being held in a Siberian gulag." He walked over, yanked the sheet up the bed. "And I was helpless. And I don't like being helpless."

"No one does. But worse is having someone tell you that you can't do something." She pulled up the twin sheet. "Did you know there are only five female officials in the ELF? And three in the NFL. I've worked really hard to get here, and now I'm an ump. Which is huge. A few more years and I'll have my own crew."

"And then what? The NFL?"

She tossed him the other end of the comforter. "No. I'm happy here. No NFL for me."

He pulled up the covers. "Sis. You gotta come home sometime."

"I come home—"

"You haven't been home in years. Not since—"

She tossed him the pillow. "I'll come home as soon as the season ends. But no, I'm not going to try out for the NFL. Not when...well, not with that video still out there."

"Your lawsuit had it taken down."

"My guess is that it's still up on some dark web sites. My naked body being ogled by named and unnamed men. Yeah, no. I'm not interested in becoming the laughingstock of the officiating community again."

He finished pulling on the pillow cover, then tossed the pillow on the bed. "No one was laughing."

"No one in our family. I mean, I know if you could, you

would have personally handed Darren Pike his backside. But it wasn't your fight."

"He's still winning if you don't go back."

"Maybe I've moved on. You did mention you liked the view." She turned and walked to the window. Indeed, from here, the sun spilled twilight gold upon the waters of Lake Como, the peaks to the west covered in blue snow, the glory of the heavens turning a deep magenta with the late-afternoon hour. "I love it here. And I love my job. And I'm going back to my life."

"What if we find something...I don't know...incriminating in that locker?"

"Like what?"

"I don't know—like your photo and pictures of your life."

"Spoken like a SEAL who's had too many op packages or whatever they're called put together."

He shrugged.

"Okay, if we find a picture of me and my itinerary and a blueprint to my house, then yes, I give you permission to freak out. Until then, I'm packing my uniform and going back to work."

He held up his hands. "I'm not the one you have to convince."

"Dad."

"Just saying. It was his grand idea to jump on a plane." Ned came over to her. "No one is trying to boss you around. We do know better than that." He kissed her forehead.

Sure they did.

But maybe she was wrong, because twenty-four hours later, as they disembarked in Berlin's Tegel Airport and got on the S-Bahn for the Hauptbahnhof, her father let her lead the way, her German directing her to the right train stops, finally pulling into the central train station.

The soaring glass ceiling let in the wan sunlight from an overcast sky as they pulled into the station. She slung her backpack over her shoulder and lined up by the door, flanked by her way overprotective brothers, and disembarked into the massive train station. The platform surged with travelers, and she pulled out in front, weaving through the crowd, past a couple holding hands, a mother and her children, countless students. Someone bumped her and she turned, frowned at him, but the man wore headphones.

Shae caught up to her. Oops, she hadn't realized she'd been walking so fast.

"I've never been to Berlin," Shae said. "I heard it was destroyed in World War Two."

They emerged from the massive glass tunnel into the station. "The bombing of Berlin destroyed almost the entire city," Iris said. "Which is why Berlin is a modern, hip town, while the rest of Europe is steeped deep in its history. Aside from a few miraculously saved buildings, like the Kaiser Wilhelm Memorial Church and the Brandenburger Tor, most of Berlin was either reconstruction or rebuilt after the war."

The others caught up, and they got on an escalator, which brought them up from the platform to a massive shopping plaza, with a McDonald's and other restaurants. Above them, on the next level, another platform led to the trains into the city.

"I could go for a burger," Jonas said.

"After we find the locker," her dad the general said. He'd been brutally quiet since arriving at her apartment yesterday, and Iris guessed that probably he'd been more than traumatized at the state of it.

And what might have happened to his daughter if she'd been there.

She fell in beside him now. "You know, I've lived overseas for a while now. I do know what I'm doing."

He wore a flannel jacket and shoved his hands into the pockets. "I know. But it feels like that time I showed up at football practice to see you out in the field. The ball was snapped, and you were nearly mowed over by a defensive tackle, and it was all I could do not to run out into the field."

"As I remember, you did cross into the plane of the field. And I was fine."

"Scared me to death. I still have a hard time seeing you out there."

She glanced up at him.

"Not that I'm stopping you." He held up a hand. "I am aware of your stubborn streak. Got it from your mother."

"Yeah, right."

He smiled, but then turned his voice low. "Just don't forget that you're not alone. And it's not weakness to let other people protect you. You have a team."

"I'm not a SEAL, Dad."

"No, you're a Marshall."

She knew he meant it as encouragement, but sometimes, being a part of this over-the-top family felt just as suffocating as... okay, yeah, being in a cave filling with tidewater in the middle of the night. And maybe that was overkill, but really.

Everybody just calm down.

"The lockers are this way," she said, pointing to a ramp that led to the parking garage. Big windows overlooked the river on one side, the city on the other. "Near the garage entrance."

Ned stepped up to them, cutting his voice low. "Someone is following us. He's in a red jacket and has been hustling up behind us since we got off the escalator. I'm going to cut away and watch him."

Iris glanced at him. "Seriously?"

"Just keep walking. Act normal."

She wasn't sure this family could do normal.

Jonas came up beside her. Ned took Shae's hand and pulled her away with him toward a shop. He wandered inside and started looking at a display of purses.

Oh. Hence why he'd needed Shae.

Iris cut her voice low too. "What do I do? What is normal?"

"I don't know," Jonas said. "I'm not a SEAL."

"Just keep walking. Which locker is it, honey?" She glanced

at her father. He still walked with his hands in his pockets. Ahead of them, the hallway with the banks of lockers cut off on both sides.

Jonas had gone stiff-faced, moving just his eyes.

"Oh, for Pete's sake, I'm sure no one is—"

Scuffling sounded behind her, and she whirled around.

To her horror, Ned had grabbed a man and shoved him up against a locker, his arm twisted behind his back. A big man with blond hair, he wore a black sweater, black pants, but no other identifying marks.

"Ned!" Shae stood back her hands over her mouth.

"What are you doing following us?" Ned said.

"Weg von mir! Ich bin ein Polizist!"

Oh no. "Ned—he's a cop!" Iris ran up to him. "Let him go!"

"Prove it," Ned said.

"Lass ihn gehen!"

She froze and put her hands up even as she turned around. Oh no—two German security officers wearing black sweaters, black vests, black pants strode up to Ned.

"Ned, let him go! It's the cops!" Jonas shouted.

Ned pushed off the man, then turned, his hands up.

Shae screamed as the two men—the word *Polizei* written on their sweaters—came right up to Ned, grabbed him, and sent him to the floor.

The other man turned and landed on Ned, his knee in Ned's back.

"Get off him!" Shae screamed and ran toward him.

Jonas grabbed her, his arm around her waist, pulling her back.

"He thought you were following us!" her dad said, but Iris grabbed his arm.

"Er ist mein Bruder. Er ist unbewaffnet!" She'd probably said it badly, so just in case, "He's my brother—he's unarmed. He thought that man was following us!"

A small crowd had formed.

Perfect.

"C'mon, we didn't do anything," Ned said, his face against the cement floor.

Just stay down, Ned.

The first man, who Ned had grabbed, finished searching Ned and stood up. Motioned to the other two to let him up. Ned practically launched to his feet. But he held out a hand, palm up, to Shae.

Weirdly, it reminded her of something Hud might have done.

Thor, where are you? But Hud wasn't here. And clearly this had gone too far.

"Passport," the man said, and Ned held up one hand, used the other to unzip a pocket in his cargo pants, then pull out his passport.

"Military," said the man. He wasn't wearing a Polizei designation.

"Navy," said Ned, leaving out the rest. Probably for the best.

"Do you want our passports, too?" Iris asked. Maybe if she was helpful—

"You don't have a passport, ma'am," the man said.

She stared at him. "Yes, I do."

The man handed Ned's back to him, nodded, then turned to her. "No, it was pick-pocketed in the station. We got it on camera, but I happened to be standing nearby." He reached into his sweater pocket and pulled out her tidy blue passport. "I was trying to catch up with you without making a scene." He glanced at Ned, then handed her the passport.

"Oh. Thank you. I…" She reached for her backpack. Sure enough, the outside pocket where she'd shoved her passport was torn. "He broke the webbing."

"Probably hoped for money, or better, a phone."

"He'd be sad with my phone." She unzipped her pouch and showed him the tiny disposable phone. "Already stolen."

"Be more careful, miss," he said, then looked at Ned. Gave him nod.

Ned nodded back.

The cavalry left them standing there, staring at each other.

"Well, that was exciting," her dad said. "You okay, Ned?"

"I told you we were being followed."

Iris rolled her eyes.

"At least you didn't lose the key, right?"

"I was pick-pocketed, Shae. I didn't *lose* my passport." But just to make sure, Iris checked her backpack and pulled out the key.

Ned reached for it, but she pulled it back. He held up his hands.

She was really starting to miss Hud.

The locker was still secured, the third from the top, number two-thirteen. "Please let it be empty." And she didn't know why she wished that, because that would put them back at nil, but maybe it would be easier to believe that maybe all this was in her head.

But the manila envelope that she'd left was still propped up against the side of the locker.

"I have to admit, I thought it would be empty," Jonas said. "Why go to all that trouble to drop it off, only to never have your contact pick it up?"

She stared at it. "I should have looked at it."

"I would have totally looked at it," Ned said.

"Let's find something to eat and open it," her dad said. "Preferably without causing an international incident."

"Where's the love? I was *right*! Someone was following her!" Ned shook his head.

They found a booth at the McDonald's, and while they waited for their order, Iris opened the envelope.

She half expected it to explode, or puff out purple powder or something, but the only things inside were two pieces of paper.

"No microfilm? I'm brutally disappointed," Jonas said.

"What is wrong with you two? This isn't a *game*!" Shae said. Their number came up on the screen, and she left to get it, along with Ned.

"Sorta feels like a game," Jonas said.

Iris grinned at him. He met it.

Her father reached over them and picked up the papers. "This one is a list of places and dates." He handed it over to them.

Just that. A piece of paper with places and dates. She turned it over, but no other identifying marks.

"And this is a blueprint for what looks like the Colosseum, sketched out by hand."

He set that down too.

He was right. The drawing depicted a historical building of some kind, with turrets flanking a massive staircase leading up to a grand entrance.

"It looks like the old Wembley Stadium," said her father. "Before it was demolished."

"There's a drawing on the other side too," Jonas said.

She flipped the page over. "It looks like a horse track."

"Or a soccer pitch, although it's round instead of square."

Shae and Ned returned with their food. "So?" Shae said as she set the trays on the table.

"So," Iris said as she reached for a fry. "You guys are going home. Clearly, whatever this is has nothing to do with me. And I have a life to get back to."

"Honey—"

"No, Dad. Listen, I promise to be careful. I'll stay with my crew, I'll put a hanger over my hotel room door, I won't eat any smelly fish, and most of all...I'll come home as soon as the season is over."

Silence. Her father's mouth tightened. "You'll call us every single day?"

"I'll call Mom every single day."

Ned slid into the booth next to Shae. Opened his sandwich.

"I'm okay with that," Jonas said.

"Shae and I are staying," Ned said. He looked up at Iris. Smiled.

Perfect, just perfect.

"How about this? I'll call Hudson and see if he's heard from Ziggy, okay?"

She pulled her phone from her pack. Hud had put his number into her phone when she first got it, and now it rang.

And rang.

And rang.

And finally flipped to a voice that said he hadn't yet set up his mailbox.

So, there was that. And she didn't know why she was so disappointed. Barely friends. Yes, apparently.

"Does this mean we get tickets to the game?" Shae asked.

Iris folded her arms on the table and sank her head onto them.

Ned pushed his fries toward her. "Could be worse."

"How's that?" She looked up and gave in, grabbing a fry.

"You could have Fraser staying with you."

FIVE

See, she was back in her life, and everything was fine.

Everybody calm down.

"I love these open-air stadiums in the fall. I know it's just an exhibition game, but it brings me back to NCAA football. There's a smell in the air." Iris walked the field of the Friedrich-Ludwig-Jahn-Sportpark, in the borough of Pankow, in a northern suburb of Berlin. The air held a nip, but the sky overhead cast blue and wispy.

The scent of fall hung in the air, not so different from the autumn husk of Minnesota, and for some reason, the craziness of the last week had sort of fallen away over the past two days of being back at work.

Watching tape, talking through angles of viewing, slowing down questionable moments, and talking through the regulations.

It helped that she'd put Jonas and her father on a plane yesterday, even if Ned and Shae had stayed behind. She had a feeling that her brother had more on his brain than protecting his big sister with his insistence on sticking around. He'd been on the phone in the second bedroom of their Airbnb for the better part of a half hour last night, pacing.

Shae had mentioned it had something to do with his SEAL team, but it was all hush-hush and clandestine.

Today, he and Shae had set off to see Berlin, so maybe this was a getaway of sorts for them, the replacement of the one that had been cut short weeks earlier when he'd been deployed suddenly.

And right about the time Shae had been kidnapped, so yeah, Iris would give them a little room.

Fact was, maybe if they could all just keep moving forward, they could forget the past two weeks had even happened.

"That smell is called smog," said Zach, walking the field with her.

"Oh, please. Germany is about the cleanest country I've ever been in."

Zach grinned, and his eyes probably sparkled under his Oakleys. Once upon a time, she'd harbored the smallest of crushes on Zach. But he was too much like herself—driven, bossy, maybe a little hard to get to know.

Huh. She'd never considered that about herself before, but maybe. She thought of it more as being independent.

Zach put his hand to shade his eyes, turning in the field. "The field runs almost north-south, and they've moved the game up to one p.m, so tomorrow the sun should be right about..." He turned and indicated a point in the sky just a little higher than the sun's current position. "Could be a lot of missed passes over the left shoulder."

"That's not my job anymore," she said, and glanced at Zach. "Get ready for the wideouts to come at you for missed pass interference calls. You have all the fun."

He laughed. "Oh, you'll miss fighting with Hudson Bly, don't try and deny it."

She shook her head, trying not to let the words find soil.

But he hadn't called her back yesterday, and maybe that hurt a little.

Barely friends.

Maybe she should wake up and face the truth. Just because

they'd spent a couple days on a sailboat and one harrowing night together didn't make them secret pals, or anything else.

Just two people caught up in circumstances beyond their control.

But this job, this position, she knew how to do. "Bly is a player. And I mean that in every sense of the word. He has plenty of women to hang out with."

Zach glanced at her. "Bly? I see him alone in the pub after games, without the cheerleader accoutrement."

"You keep track of Bly's dating habits?"

He lifted his hands. "No. I was just saying that yeah, he drives a nice car, but you don't see him in the news like you do some of the other American players. That's why your Instagram picture with him was so viral."

"It was *viral*?"

Oh brother. Because that's just what Darren Pike and his ilk would like—for her name to be circling scandal again. "It was a moment in a restaurant where we happened to be sitting together. Never going to happen again."

"Calm down, Marsh. I believe you."

Her back teeth tightened.

A whistle blew down the field, and the huddle of Berlin Thunder players broke. They jogged down the field, others filling the sidelines.

"Ready for this?" Zach held out his fist.

She met it, then jogged into place in the offensive backfield. Ref Yannick placed the ball, and she counted the players, then kept her eyes on the lineman, looking for holding or illegal blocks.

The quarterback snapped the ball, dropped back. She saw him out of her periphery, her gaze on the linemen, watching the tackle, and the guard, the center—

"Marsh!"

She turned a second before the running back charged into her, having received the handoff. He jerked, spun, and still managed to clip her.

The blow shucked out her breath, threw her to the ground. She landed on her hip with an oof.

Yannick blew the whistle.

"Stay out of ze way!" This from the running back, but as he helped pull her up, he wore more concern than anger on his face.

Still, he was right. She brushed the grass off her pants, grabbed her hat, and tried to ignore the throb in her hip.

"Marsh!" Yannick came over. "You're lucky they're not practicing with pads. He could have been going full speed—"

"I know. I know. I got this."

"You gotta keep your eye on the lineman while still seeing the play develop in the backfield. Invisible but omnipresent, right?"

"Right, boss."

"I can move Zach to this position—"

"I got this!" She blew out a breath. "Sorry. But really. I'll be fine. That's why we have practice, right?"

Yannick studied her for a moment, his blue eyes pensive. Reminded her a little of Aragorn, from the *Lord of the Rings* series, except with shorter hair. Deep angles to his face, his countenance at once sweeping and authoritative. "Okay then."

He blew the whistle, and the players lined back up.

She again counted the offense, eyes on the line. But this time, when the ball snapped, she peddled back, keeping a wider range of vision, not unlike she had when playing back judge. See the field, only now she couldn't zero in on the ball but had to feel the play develop, her gaze on the blockers.

There, a hold by the offensive guard. She threw down her flag just as the running back swept by her. He was stopped at the line of scrimmage, and she signaled to Yannick the penalty, offering up the number with her fingers.

He called it off and moved the ball fifteen yards.

She got a look from the offensive player as he went to the huddle, but ignored it because, *bam*, that's how it was done.

They ran three sets of downs, and she started to feel the play, see the rhythm. Sure, she'd officiated as ump before in the NCAA, but only once in the ELF.

Really, she loved this position. From here, she watched the play develop, saw the potential, felt in the middle of the gritty scrimmage-line action. Brutal, with grunts and shouts and nothing like the open field ballet of wide receivers. Reminded her, in a way, of high-school football, and being right there on the sidelines, listening to her team fight it out.

The Thunder broke for a water break, and trainers ran out onto the field.

The teams usually provided officials with their own water personnel, but today she walked over to the side and picked up her water bottle. She preferred her own bottle, sanitized before every game. The last thing she wanted was a bottle slurped by the men. Hers was pink, so that helped them stay away too. She opened it and drank.

"We're done here," Yannick said as he walked up. Zach and the other four officials joined them—the sub now and side judge, Roque Franco from Spain, the line judge, a Hungarian named Milos Sallali, the down judge, a German Arne Fischer, and their field judge, a Czech named Jakub Janota. "The Thunder need us to clear off the field—but they are expecting you all tonight at the charity dinner."

She lowered her bottle and managed not to spit out the water. "What?"

"Yeah. It's black tie—or black dress, if you want." He shot at look at Iris. "But it's for the International Children's Cancer Society, so it's must-attend. The ELF wants to see all their people there, and for some reason, that includes the zebras."

Great.

Fine.

Perfect.

Zach looked at her, and she narrowed her eyes at him.

Maybe Hudson wouldn't even be there.

Zach grinned, and she capped her water bottle and walked away.

"There's a limo picking everyone up from the hotel at five!" Yannick shouted after her.

She turned. "I'm not at the hotel. I'm staying in an Airbnb."

"Text me the address. We'll pick you up."

Apparently, she was going. Inside the officials' locker room, she gathered up her gear just as Zach walked in.

"I don't want to hear it."

"What?"

"Whatever snarky quip was on your lips about Hudson being at the dinner."

"What quip might that be?"

"You know, the one about how maybe I should wear a dress and see if this 'barely friends' thing is true, to which I'd just say it doesn't matter because, hello, conflict of interest, but yes, the season is over, officially, so maybe we could go on a date, but how is that going to end up anywhere but tragic, because I'm not quitting my job, and last I checked neither was he, so come June, when the season starts back up, it's quitsville for us, even if we did get along, which maybe we don't, because maybe this was all some sort of weird, off-the-hook circumstances, so no thanks, I'm not interested in getting a dress. Or heels. Or whether or not he might be wearing some awesome-looking tux."

Zach nodded. "Yep. That was the quip."

"Really, I'm not wearing a dress."

"That would be crazy talk."

She picked up her backpack. Looked at him. "Promise you'll be there?"

"I wouldn't miss it for the world."

She didn't know what she was all riled up about. So what Hudson was going to be there?

They were barely friends.

But she spent the next four hours with Shae (Ned grumpily in tow), shopping in the massive ALEXA Berlin mall, trying on dresses.

Dresses.

And shoes.

And this was never in her contract. But she managed to find a one-shoulder black dress with a not-too-high slit up the side, and a pair of black pumps with a little shimmer on them, and what was she *doing*?

Shae applied her art degree to Iris's face and hair, putting it up in a French twist, and at five p.m., Iris stood in front of the mirror and didn't recognize herself.

"You clean up well, sis," Ned said after he knocked and Shae let him into the bedroom. He added a whistle. "Hoping to impress someone?"

"Not even a little," she said and grabbed the tiny bag that held her wallet.

Shae leaned close, spoke into her ear. "He'll notice, I promise."

She met Shae's eyes and wrinkled her nose. "I'm trying not to care."

"Oh yes. That outfit has *I don't care* all over it." She winked.

The limo arrived and Iris grabbed her wool coat and left the apartment before she lost her nerve, ripped off the dress and donned her sweatpants and a T-shirt.

Yannick and Zach had piled out, holding the door for her.

One of the guys inside started with a whistle, but Yannick shut them down with an upheld hand.

She looked at Zach, then Yannick. "Thank you. What, did you guys kill a bunch of secret security agents? Or join a top secret intergalactic agency? What's with the black suits?"

"There was a sale down at suit supply," Zach said, and she wasn't sure he was kidding.

She somehow managed not to fall as she got in in the ridiculous heels Shae'd had her buy. Arne, Roque, Jakub, and Milos were inside, and she sat next to Milos on a long sofa.

Zach and Yannick sat opposite her.

Suddenly, she very much missed Abe. "Any word on Abe's autopsy?" she asked Yannick. "Confirmation of his poisoning?"

He raised an eyebrow. "Um, now?"

"Sorry. I just..."

"No word yet, Iris." Yannick gave her a tight-lipped smile.

The limo driver turned on some classical music, as if they might be going to the opera, and they drove through the city a short way, over the river starting to sparkle with light, to what looked like a giant warehouse. Other cars—limos, Bentleys, Rolls Royces—were pulled up to a massive lighted portico entrance.

They pulled up like they might be royalty. Or celebrities.

The door opened, and a valet ushered them out.

A couple stood by the door, greeting everyone, a gorgeous blonde in a shapely gold dress—Iris recognized her, with a start, as the General Manager, Deborah Saint. Next to her stood the Director of Football, a German-American who had played back in the early days, a Warner Burgmann. She shook their hands, then received a program and headed inside.

The venue had perhaps been a former warehouse, because the ceiling soared five stories, with balconies that ran overhead, open pipes, and massive cement columns now decorated with tulle and chrysanthemums.

Paintings to be auctioned off sat on easels at the front of a room crowded with round tables and yellow-and-red floral centerpieces. Gold place-settings, templed white napkins, and at the front of the room, a chamber orchestra played a waltz.

An impressive congregation of players milled around the tables, accepting fluted champagne glasses from white-gloved waiters. She took a glass and moved with the officiating crew to their designated table.

"Clearly we're trying to keep up with NFL," she said and pointed to a photographer taking snaps of players standing with what she assumed were donors. A few players stood in tight circles, scarfing down the appetizers—black bread with beer radish dip, smoked trout on cucumbers, German pickled eggs. She set down her glass, not sure what sounded good.

Running, maybe.

Because that's when she spotted Hudson.

He took her stupid breath away in a form-fitting teal blue suit that made his eyes practically glow and his shoulders look a mile wide. He cut a powerful form as he stood talking with, aw, of course, a beautiful, petite blonde who wore her hair back in a high, elegant ponytail and a black dress that stopped above her knees. She was smiling, nodding, probably enraptured by his words.

Next thing out of his mouth, he'd tell her that she was targeted for danger, take her hand, and run off to Greece—

Oh, *stop*.

The woman was probably a smitten cheerleader or something. And there were rules about dating cheerleaders. Not unlike the rules about dating officials, although, technically, there was nothing formal in the regulations.

Still.

"Ah, I see you have spotted the prey," Zach said into her ear as he came back from somewhere with his plate loaded.

"Please stop talking," she said and sighed. "Where did you get the food?"

"There's a buffet past the pillars. And the doors are beyond that."

"I'm not running away."

"You had a look."

"That look is I-think-I-hate-you-for-making-me-wear-this-dress."

He opened his mouth, but she held up her hand and walked away.

She spotted Toby, the tight end from the Vikings, at the table. He glanced at her, then again, and smiled. "Please wear that to the game."

"One word out of you and I'll throw a flag."

He laughed. "Nice to see you, Iris." Then he shot a look at Hud. Back to her.

And what was *that* about?

"Ready for the game on Saturday?" She picked up a plate and perused the offerings.

"I think so. It's really just practice for the Vikings game in Vienna, but with the NFL looking at Hud, it's a big deal for him."

The NFL was looking at Hud? Oh, and she didn't know why that nearly took her out at the knees. But of course they were. Good for him.

Good for both of them. Get him out of Europe and away from—

She wasn't watching him, really she wasn't, but for some reason, she spotted him when he took the blonde by the elbow and herded her past the pillars.

And then out the side doors.

"Entschuldigen Sie mich, bitte."

The voice jerked her out of the crazy tightness of her chest and back to the food. No, to the waiter who waited to fill the pickled egg tray.

"Sorry." She stepped back. Then walked over and set her plate on a discard tray.

Then she walked over to the table, slipped off her stupid shoes, and sat down.

Yannick looked over at her. "Quitting already?"

"Bench me, Coach."

He laughed. "My guess is that you'll have a good time."

"Wanna lay some bets?"

"I'm in," said Zach.

"Me too," said Milos.

"I hate you all," said Iris, and they laughed.

Hud returned before the first course and took a seat next to the blonde at the table. Laughed with her the entire meal. Bid on a piece of art that he didn't get. Ate two bites of his dessert, a delicious cheesecake with raspberry. Iris cleaned her plate.

Finally, the orchestra came back. She turned to Yannick. "Can we please leave?"

He checked his watch. "Limo isn't due back for an hour."

"I'm grabbing an Uber." She got up.

"I'll go with you," Zach said.

"I don't need you to babysit me." But she wobbled as she got up, and he caught her elbow. She grabbed his arm, steadied herself.

"Clearly not." He picked up her coat. "Don't forget this." But he carried it for her as they moved away from the tables.

Last she saw of Hudson, he was posing with the blonde as another man took their beautiful picture.

AND JUST LIKE THAT, SHE WAS GONE.

"Thanks, Hudson, for everything. This has been really fun." The words came from Brette Remington, the reporter who had followed him—okay, not followed, since she'd been invited—to the charity event. In Germany. So it sort of felt like following. And of course she'd ended up at his table, right next to him, and what was he going to do? Be a jerk?

Besides, he'd been not-on-purpose but maybe-just-a-little dodging her since that day at the practice stadium in Vienna, not really interested in pouring out his life to her.

Then he'd found out that she knew his brother, Harry, and apparently that's how she'd gotten the gig in the first place. Harry had dropped the tidbit of news to her husband, Ty Remington, that his brother played for the ELF. With the ELF and NFL game coming up in Lauchtenland, and her being a freelance journalist, she'd pitched a story to the *Red Zone* magazine.

"Besides, we're headed to Zermatt ski resort in Switzerland for some fresh powder," Ty had said when they'd arrived to the field today to take more pictures. "We're meeting my buddy Gage and his wife there." So, okay, Hud posed for a few shots, then agreed to an interview tonight.

He'd had to step outside with Brette to get some quiet, but she wasn't a brutal interviewer. Mostly questions about life in the ELF.

"Why don't they have more Americans?"

"They're only allowed three A-team foreigners. We have a couple Brits, but they're B-teamers."

"And you're considered A-Team, even though you never played in the NFL?"

Ouch, but he'd smiled and reminded her he'd been a contender in the draft back in the day.

"But the TBI set you back."

He allowed it. "Just a year. Then I was itching to play and went to arena ball for two years before the Vienna Vikings reached out."

"And you like playing in the ELF?"

"It's a growing sport here. It's not soccer—or European football—by any means, but we have a tidy group of fans, and our games are gaining traction. This year the Barcelona Dragons played to a stadium of twelve thousand. And our stadium holds seventeen thousand. We're not at capacity yet, but we will be once we win the championship again."

"The Super Bowl?"

"It's not called that, but yes, essentially."

"And you won it last year."

"Made two touchdowns."

"Impressive."

Okay, he liked her. But a couple times, his gaze had drifted back inside to where Iris sat at a table, her shoes off.

She'd blown the breath right out of him when she'd walked into the room at the beginning of the night. He'd been talking with Brette and had to turn his back to Iris to keep focused.

When he turned back, she'd disappeared, and he'd suffered a moment of panic. But he'd spotted her by the buffet, and that's when he took Brette by the arm and headed outside for their interview.

Which was over by the time dinner was served. He'd walked back in after a question about his future, which he'd deflected, and noticed Iris sitting at the table, slowly rotating her champagne glass. She'd done something spectacular with her golden hair, pulling it back, then looping it over—it was elegant and revealed her jawline, all the way to her to sexy bare shoulder, and wow, he needed to focus. He'd nearly bought a painting he didn't want while trying to figure out what to say to her after dinner.

Hey, Iris, you look great.

No, that would imply she never looked great. Which she did.

Nice to see you. How've you been?

What, were they old school chums?

I've been desperately worried.

Too much. Way too much.

I'm sorry I left.

That's what he *wanted* to say. And sometimes he still couldn't figure out why he'd gotten up from the table in Paris, really, except maybe his stupid pride trying to wrap his brain around the fact that he was no longer needed.

So maybe that had been a giant temper tantrum. And that's how he'd start. *Sorry I was a jerk.*

Yes, that.

"Thanks again for dinner," Brette said as the orchestra came on and waiters came to clear their dessert plates. Hud had no room for the cheesecake, trying to look-not-look at Iris. "Do you mind if Ty gets a picture of us?"

He found a smile and put his arm around her.

When they finished, he spotted Iris rising from the table.

"Have a great time skiing, and let me know when the article runs." He was shaking Ty's hand and looking over his head as he spoke.

Everything inside Hud stilled when Iris reached out and grabbed fellow official Zach Warton. Jerk. He was at least a decade older than her too. The man put his arm around her, and she looked over and laughed.

Hud's chest nearly exploded.

Warton grabbed her jacket, then carried it as he followed her out.

His breath turned to glue in his lungs.

"Hud, can you come around early to practice tomorrow? Jack and I want to go over the game plan with you." Coach Clay had come over.

Hud blinked at him a moment, then, "Yeah, sure."

Fellow American Jackson Ernst pointed to him, grinning from across the room. He had his arm draped over some lovely brunette who Hud didn't recognize.

They might not get paid like NFL players, but over here, they were big dogs in a small pond. Hud had tried not to let it go to his head.

Maybe hadn't succeeded.

Iris had left the building.

"I'd like you meet someone, by the way."

Aw— "Coach—"

"It'll just take a second." He motioned him over to his table, where a man stood talking to Clay's wife, Veronica. Gorgeous, with long auburn hair and piercing golden-brown eyes, she made Clay look like he belonged with the big leagues.

"Hudson," she said, and gave him an Italian kiss. "You clean up."

He'd worn this suit for the MVP banquet last year. "Thanks."

Coach slapped him on the shoulder. "Hud, this is my brother-in-law, Gripe Carlson. Coach of the Seattle Kraken." Handsome man, dark-brown hair, fit, mid-fifties.

"The *what*?"

"It's a new league in the US—the USFL. First run was this year, and Seattle is putting together a team. Gripe needs a wideout, and he's got his eye on you."

Hud just stared at him, then at Coach Clay. "I...are you not renewing my contract?" This had suddenly gotten awkward.

Gripe looked at Coach and then patted Hud on the shoulder. "I'll give you a call after the game this weekend. Nice to meet you, Hudson."

He shook Hudson's hand. Hud managed to grip it.

The Vikings were letting him go?

Coach moved his brother-in-law over to other people, and Hudson just stood there.

A beat. Then, *Iris.*

He took off for the door, moving around the tables, scooting around people, groups of conversation, past greeters, and outside.

A sedan was just pulling away. And maybe it wasn't her, but how crazy would he look if he took off after it, down the sidewalk, waving his hands?

Probably crazy enough to be another Instagram hit.

Shoot.

He drew in a breath, standing there, feeling like he'd just taken a hit by Luis.

Calm down. It wasn't like she was in danger, right? He'd see her at the game on Saturday, and then...

Well, then he'd use the words. *I'm sorry I walked away, Iris. I know you had your family, but...I miss you. And I can't sleep knowing you might not be safe. And...*

Maybe this was for the best. Especially if his future was back over the pond.

He should leave things as they were. She seemed to be moving on just fine. And really, moving on from what? Her harrowing adventure with Hudson? Probably she'd like to keep that in the rear view mirror.

Besides, they were just friends.

Yep.

He headed inside, was standing by the door, not sure what to do, when his phone vibrated. He pulled it out but didn't recognize the number.

He'd gotten a call a couple days ago that he'd missed from an unknown number. Maybe—he flipped open the phone. "Iris?"

"No, it's Ziggy."

Ziggy. The woman who'd gotten them all into this mess. Oh, he'd like to reach through the phone and— "Where have you been? I've been calling for days." He cut his voice low and stepped back outside. "We were nearly blown up. And almost drowned. And did you know that one of Iris's fellow officials *died*? They think he might have been poisoned! How big is this thing, Ziggy? What have you gotten us into?"

Silence. And for a terrible second, he thought she'd hung up.

Then, "Sorry, Hudson. I really am. I've been trying to track down the person who killed your friend Abe, because yes, according to my contact with the Orphans, there was a contract on Abe. He was murdered."

"Assassinated, you mean."

"I think that's the same thing."

"It's not the same thing. Murder is...personal. Assassination is a job."

"Point taken. Okay, assassinated."

And her saying that aloud only made it weirdly worse.

He was getting looks from people emerging from the event, waiting by the valet stand for their cars. He leaned against the building, breathing in. Out. In.

The last thing he needed was a heart attack. Or an aneurysm.

"So, before or after Iris's?"

"What?"

"Was Abe's contract listed before or after Iris's?" And he couldn't believe he was asking this. What world did he suddenly live in?

"Abe's contract was listed and bidded out after you went missing."

He stilled. "What does that even mean? Is the same person after Iris?"

"I don't know. And the bounty on Abe hasn't been picked up yet, so we don't have a name."

No name. He stared out into the dark city, where her car had vanished.

"Hud?"

"I've made a terrible mistake, Ziggy. And I have to figure out a way to fix it."

Six

A glorious afternoon for a football game, and the familiar fire had already lit inside Iris.

She emerged from the private bathroom, gave herself a once-over in the mirror. Her uniform wasn't made for the curves of a woman, but on the field, she was simply an official, neither male nor female, one of the crew that kept the game fair.

Which meant that Hud wasn't even a blip on her radar.

Zach sat on the bench, lacing his cleats. Roque and Milos had already left for the morning meeting, Jakub and Yannick walking the field for any anomalies before the game.

She grabbed her cleats, then slammed her locker door. "The Vikings have a new running back, transferred from the Panthers. He's a little sloppy, so keep an eye on him with the short passes."

"Stay up all night doing homework?" Zach said, picking up his water bottle.

"Maybe." She sat on the bench and pulled on her cleats. "I just want to make sure we have a clean game."

"The meeting with the NFL officials got under your skin, didn't it?"

She finished tying her shoes. "It just irks me a little that they have to 'approve us.'" She finger-quoted the last words. "We're every bit capable of reffing the Lauchtenland game, and just because it's against an NFL team doesn't mean we're not going to do a stellar job."

He held the door for her. "Agreed. But with the NFL refs supervising in the booth, my guess is that they don't want any controversy."

"Reviewed plays are always controversial. When I was officiating for the NCAA, over ninety percent of our plays weren't reviewed. But the ones that were were almost always upheld."

"Didn't you officiate a bowl game?"

She glanced at him, stilled. Wait—did he... But Zach just kept walking, not a hint that he knew— Breathe. "No. It was an All-Star game. The Senior Bowl."

"I heard that the NFL is on the hunt for better substitute officials. Maybe they're scouting."

She stilled in the hallway. "Really?"

"Why not? There are still people angry about the games played during the 2012 lockout—remember the Green Bay, Seahawks game?"

"The double caught pass? I watched it with my dad. Golden Tate totally pushed the Packer cornerback—I saw it even before the replay. Should have been offensive pass interference, Packer's victory." She walked down the hall to the official's office. "I think it's what led to the end of the lockout."

"The NFL has a new program to help non-NFL officials be ready for the show."

"I know. The Mackie Development Program." She reached the office door, where Yannick leaned against the front of a desk, working the remote for the flatscreen. "I'm not interested."

She left Zach standing in the hallway, maybe a little undone by her words.

She, herself, couldn't believe they'd issued from her mouth.

But maybe his reference to the All-Star game had raked up a knee-jerk response.

Because really, who didn't want to officiate an NFL game?

"I just wanted to run over a couple last minute formations the Berlin Thunder sent me," Yannick said as they came in. She sat on a chair in the cramped room, still holding her hat.

"They're going to run the single back formation. Watch for the running back—he's about five yards behind the QB." Yannick looked at Iris as he said it. "It's a wide-receiver play, but look for the RB coming around behind you."

She gave him a thumbs-up.

"And, Zach, you'll remember this one. The pro set—the Vikings might run that. It's a pass-heavy set, so you might see a lot of activity. And Milos and Arne, keep an eye on the D-backs and corners for holding and defensive pass interference near the line of scrimmage."

He fast-forwarded the tape, paused it. "The Vikings are probably going to stay with the 5-2 defense, but keep an eye out for the occasional blitz. And since the Vikings are heavy on the passing game, look for the 3-3 stack from the Thunder. That's a lot of one-on-one on the line, so that's you again, Iris."

He stopped the tape. "This might be a fast game, a lot of passing plays with these two quarterbacks. The Ernst-Bly connection is hot, given what I've seen in practice, so keep your eyes on the Thunder's safety."

Zach nodded, as did Roque and Jakub.

"Zero mistakes. Stay safe. Let's get out there," Yannick said, and the crew got up. Iris put on her hat, pulling her ponytail through the hole.

"Iris, stick around for a second."

Zach glanced at her, an eyebrow up as he left. But he closed the door behind him.

"If this is about the—"

"Coach Clay called me. Apparently, Hudson Bly is trying to get ahold of you."

"—scouting, my mind is on this game. Wait, what?"

His mouth opened. "You know about the scouting?"

"Guessed. What does Bly want?" And shoot, even his name lit something inside her. No, no—*focus.*

"Dunno. Coach just said that Bly wants to talk to you before the game."

"Nope. I got a job to do." She picked up her water bottle. "Whatever he has to say can wait."

Yannick worked on his white cap, then grabbed the door as she opened it. He followed her out onto the field.

Yes, a glorious day. The afternoon sky arched blue, no signs of rain in the wispy, high clouds. A slight chill bullied the air, but it smelled of loam and cut grass and raked up memories of Friday night games in Minnesota, back in her high-school days.

Indeed, Friedrich-Ludwig-Jahn-Sportpark resembled a high-school field, with a track that ran around the outside, and seating circling the track. Fans had already jammed into the covered stands on either side of the fifty-yard line and now spilled out into the open-air seating. Quite a few for an exhibition game, but then again, it was a charity event.

The teams had already warmed up, their gear on the sidelines.

She'd done some stretching in the locker room before dressing, but now set her water bottle on the officials' bench, then did a few stretches as she watched the stands fill. Gold-red attire for the Thunder, purple and white for the Vikings. With the countries so close together, it wasn't unheard of to see fans travel to away games.

Bly wants to talk to you before the game.

The thought pulsed in her head. If he wanted to talk to her, he could have done it at the dinner. Besides, what was he trying to do—get them both fired?

She shook the thought away, grabbed her whistle, and joined Milos and Jakub on the sidelines. The Vienna Vikings were taking the field, some running, others meandering on. In a real game, the hype would have them congregating in the tunnel, bursting out in triumph.

Hudson wasn't hard to spot. Sure, all the guys were big, but he carried himself with an energy that usually had him stretching or high-stepping before a game. He'd probably been out on the field with Jackson running routes earlier.

She pulled her cap down, deliberately looked away from him in case he did something stupid and waved at her or something.

Or maybe to keep herself from wishing.

Oh brother. *Focus!*

The Berlin Thunder took the field, to a warm greeting from their fans. Both teams lined up on the sidelines, then a pregame chat before sending their captains out to meet with Yannick and toss the coin.

Vikings won and elected to defer, giving the Thunder the ball.

She jogged onto the field while the teams were in their final huddle, then lined up with the Vikings defense to ensure they were lined up correctly.

Yannick's whistle signaled play, and they were off.

The kick sailed high, deep inside the twenty, but because it was a practice game, the receiver signaled for fair catch, and the Thunder lined up on the thirteen-yard line.

The sun was to her right side, just barely in her eyes, but the cap helped, and she stood a few feet back from the quarterback, her eyes on the center and guards for false starts.

The first play was daring—a long pass, a sunrising blitz by the D-end, and no holds. Pass incomplete, and no flags on the play.

One play down, about one hundred and fifty to go.

Yannick placed the ball and she set up again. She met Yannick's eyes just as the guys came out of the huddle. He nodded at her, smiled.

Zero mistakes. Stay safe.

The thought hung in her brain as she widened her periphery, dodging the Thunder running back a couple times, and once, nearly getting tangled in a pitchout play that went south, the running back being chased down by the outside linebacker.

Loss of ten yards—and her hat as she tripped and went down.

No harm, no fowl. She got up, brushed off some grass stains.

Five holding calls in the first quarter, and only two possessions by the Vikings, both of which she managed not to catch eyes with Hudson. Seemed his focus was also on the game.

The Thunder scored once, and the Vikings came back with a vengeance in three plays when Bly grabbed an impossibly high catch with one hand and scampered into the end zone. Seven catches out of ten tries—if the NFL scouts were here for players, Bly was having a stellar day.

At the quarter break, she grabbed a drink of water, then jogged back out into the field. The first handoff, Thunder's ball, ended up in a fumble, chaos behind the line of scrimmage, and she had to wade into the pile to determine possession. She got an elbow to the thigh but ignored it, as the player had been pushing himself up.

"Vikings' ball!" She held up the ball and indicated their direction on the field. Yannick made it official, and she tossed him the ball.

The Vikings ran onto the field. Hudson slowed his jog onto the field near her, fixing his glove strap. "Iris. I need to talk to you."

She glanced at him. He wasn't looking at her. The other players had hit the huddle.

"Huddle up, Bly."

"Iris—" He looked at her now, big eyes through his helmet, and she frowned at him, then walked away.

What on—

And maybe the encounter had shaken her, because the very next play, the Thunder's D-end came around and nearly flattened her on a blitz. But she'd also been focused on the center, trying to get a fix on his possible hold.

She threw the yellow flag just as the D-end clipped her, and she spun, hit the ground, one hand down.

The blitz failed, the pass incomplete to Bly, and Yannick blew the whistle, came running over. "You okay?"

She was already on her feet. "Yeah." She pulled her yellow flag. "But we have a holding call on the Vikings."

She stood, called the hold, but now her hip hurt.

The Thunder held the Vikings to three and out, then the Thunder got the ball and charged down the field in a series of short-run drives that ended with a field goal, and the half was over.

She jogged over to the sideline and grabbed her water bottle.

"You okay?" Zach asked. "That was a hard fall."

"Naw. Nothing my brothers wouldn't dish out when we played touch football at home." She jogged in after Yannick and didn't spare Hudson a look.

But she grabbed an ice pack during the half-time discussion.

Yannick stopped her on her way back out to the field. "Head on a swivel out there, Iris."

"I got this." She diverted and headed to the training room to dispose of her ice pack. Dropping it off, she was heading to the door when—

"Iris."

She stilled. Turned.

Hudson stood in the hallway, holding his helmet, sweat dripping from his hair, and oh, he smelled. But his eyes, they landed on her, and she felt his gaze to her bones.

"Hud," she managed, her voice more shaky than she'd like. "I can't talk to you." She turned.

"Ziggy called!"

She glanced back. "No, Hud. I'll worry about it after the game."

Then she pushed through the double doors, her heart a fist in her chest. So what Ziggy called? What, someone was going to take a shot at her in front of thousands? Hardly.

Running to her bench, she dropped off her water bottle, then stretched again as the teams came out. Hudson straggled at the end, not that she noticed.

Then Yannick blew the whistle, and the Vikings received for the second half.

The Vikings ran it back to the forty, and Hud jogged onto the field, glancing at her once, but she stepped back, away from him, counting the players, watching the line.

The handoff went to the running back, who headed around the end. She peddled back, still watching the line, when in her peripheral vision, she spotted Hud lighting up the defensive end. The man went down.

But the running back was long past the line of scrimmage. First down, and Yannick blew the whistle, but the play rattled her.

Seemed almost like a late hit on the defender. But she couldn't be sure, and they had no replays for the exhibition game, and Arne said nothing, so she shrugged it off.

Four series of downs later, the big tight end, Tobias West, ran the ball into the end zone.

Vikings were up by four.

They lined up for the kickoff, Yannick placing the ball. The Berlin Thunder brought the ball back to thirty-three, and the Vikings defenders came onto the field.

Three downs later, the Thunder were back to punting.

The Vikings came on the field with one minute in the quarter.

This time, Hud didn't look at her. She took her position, watched the line, counted the snap, and she spotted the play developing in the backfield. Two receivers out, the tight end blocking, Jackson bouncing back, looking.

The center and tackle fighting hard on the line, all regulation—wait. The guard had a grip on the defender, threw him down.

Hand on her flag, she jerked it out—

Spotting the defensive end already headed for the QB, fire in his eyes, she backpedaled, tossing out her flag.

She wasn't sure if the player changed directions or if she just moved into his path, but the flag flew out a second before—bam!

The hit stole her breath even as she flew, maybe five yards, or ten, but she slammed into the ground, bouncing, her head hitting the turf with an explosion of pain. Her breath swept from her and then, in a blink—

Everything went dark.

HE WANTED BLOOD.

Hud stood, helmet off, with the other players surrounding Iris and tried not to do something really stupid.

Like push through the trainers surrounding her, grab her hand, and call out her name.

Please, Iris, wake up.

And then there was the other urge—to find Werner Vogel, number sixty-three, and destroy the defensive end. Hud had blown Vogel up a few plays earlier when he'd made a beeline for Iris, and Hud had tried to tell himself he was just edgy and rattled by Ziggy's call.

And the fact Iris wouldn't talk to him.

Because it had to be his overactive imagination that said she'd been targeted, right?

"Make a hole!" This from Coach Clay as he directed the cart into the field.

She still wasn't moving. Just lay there, her hat off, her eyes closed, painfully broken in her stripes.

He'd seen the hit. Just by happenstance, out of the corner of his eye. He'd run the route perfectly, thirty yards down, a bootleg, juked, got free, his hand in the air—*Jackson, I'm open, hit me!*

And then, right behind his QB, there was Iris, backpedaling a second before *bam!* the D-end pancaked her.

Hud put his hand down and took off back up the field.

Jackson threw the ball over his head.

The official whistled the play dead, and Hud caught up with Jackson as the players gathered around her, the other officials yelling to get back.

Trainers ran out from both sides as the players formed a circle. A few had taken off their helmets, dropped to a knee.

He just stood there, his gut churning.

The cart came in, and he stood back as a couple EMTs strapped her onto a board. She roused then, slightly, moaning, and they affixed portable oxygen on her.

Then they carted her away to the applause of the stands, and the head ref called for a time-out while the officials regrouped.

Hud walked over to the sidelines, found a corner behind the bench, leaned over, and retched. Closed his eyes.

Breathed in. Out. In. Out.

"You okay, Hud?" Toby had run up, then taken a step back. Mostly water—Hud didn't eat much before games—but still.

"Water," Hud said, and Toby grabbed a water bottle from the metal basket, tossed it to him.

Hud squirted it into his mouth, washed it out, spat. Tossed it back. "Yeah," he said to Toby's question. "I'm fine."

He put on his helmet. "Let's finish this game."

"Hud." Toby fell in step with him. "Don't do something stupid."

"Did he target her?"

"The DE? I don't—"

"That was the third time he hit her—or tried to."

Coach was pulling them in for a chat, but Hud barely heard the words as he searched the other sideline for number sixty-three.

"Vikings on three," Jackson said as Coach walked away.

He put his fist in. "Vikings!"

"We're going to run that play again," Jackson said as they ran out.

"Nope," said Hud. "Give the ball to Toby. I want to see if sixty-three blitzes again."

"Hud."

"It's an exhibition game, Jack! Give the freakin' ball to Toby!"

Jackson looked at him, then nodded. They huddled up, then Hudson lined up his gaze on the D-end.

Only, it wasn't sixty-three, and Hudson dearly hoped he hadn't been pulled from the game.

Toby drove for three yards, then Jackson got his replay and aired it out to Hudson in the flats. He pulled it in, a gorgeous catch for a stellar throw, landed a stiff arm in the chest of the safety—sent him flying and found himself in the end zone.

He slammed the ball to the ground and prayed for another shot at goal.

The quarter ended, and the Thunder managed a field goal that ate up most of the fourth quarter clock. Hudson prowled the sidelines, his gut in a knot. He finally took the field again, five minutes left on the play clock.

Sixty-three was on the field, cocky as he came out of the huddle.

Hudson barely registered the play. A running play, up the gut.

Perfect. Hudson lined up, his body buzzing, tasting the tackle.

Sixty-three came off the line, sloughed his defender and—

Hudson had never hit someone so hard in his life. He started ten yards back, so by the time he hit sixty-three, he rolled with a full head of steam, a locomotive that lifted the big defensive end off his feet and slammed him into the ground.

Not quite an illegal hit, but maybe—definitely—unnecessary necessary roughness.

The guy lay on the field after Hudson rolled off him. Stood over him.

"Welcome to the rest of the game."

Then he ran back to the huddle.

Sixty-three took a long time getting up.

Hud hit him two more times before he went long for a pass and scored again.

Coach Max came to stand beside him as Hud perched his

helmet on the back of his head and sprayed water on his face. "So, I think that'll do, pig."

He glanced at Coach Max.

"He's sorry. I'm sure he's very sorry," Max said and gestured to sixty-three, now yanking off his helmet and throwing it to the ground. He walked over to his coach, yelling, pointing toward the Vikings sideline.

Hud watched. "Not sorry enough." He wasn't telling Coach Max, but he and Vogel also had a post-game date—one the officials wouldn't be able to call.

Although, interesting that they hadn't called any of his hard tackles.

"Any news on...the official?"

"Nope."

Hudson ground his teeth and walked off the field as soon as the game ended. No high fives and handshakes for him.

He showered fast—a cold shower, just to calm himself down—and was dressed, his hair wet, his body still buzzing, before coach finished his post-game preaching-slash-celebration.

No celebrating until he knew that Iris was okay.

Toby caught his arm as he headed out the door, his duffel over his shoulder. "Plane leaves in a couple hours."

"Don't wait for me."

Toby gave him a look. "Please don't end up in jail."

Hudson narrowed his eyes. Took a breath. "See you at practice Monday." He shrugged out of Toby's grip and headed out the door.

Then he stopped by the officials' locker room and knocked on the door, didn't wait, and barged in.

Most of them were mid dressing. He stood at the entrance and directed his question toward the man he'd seen at the dinner with Iris. Zach Warton. "Where is she?"

A beat.

Then the head ref, Yannick, spoke up. "Martin Luther Hospital. We're going there now—you need a ride."

He checked his watch. "How long?"

"Fifteen minutes?"

"I'll call an Uber." He walked out, pulling out his phone. Two minutes away. He ordered the Uber and met the driver at the curb. "Drive fast. I'll tip you extra."

Inside the car, he dialed Ziggy. She didn't answer. He hung up and called again.

"Hudson?"

"Is there any reason a player would pick up the contract on Iris?" He'd been circling that question through his head for an hour. But it was crazy, wasn't it?

Still, he'd seen the guy, at least twice, go after Iris during the game, despite his hope of staying focused.

Maybe, in a way, it'd made Hud play with more anger, more urgency. More focus. Because in his head was the driving thought that the sooner they wrapped up the game, the sooner he could track her down.

The Uber driver was a man, mid-thirties, driving an economical Fiat, and he motored in and out of traffic like it might be a game of *Grand Theft Auto*.

"Why? Is she hurt?" Ziggy asked, some concern in her voice.

"She was hit, hard, by a player in the Berlin Thunder. It felt like he targeted her."

"Is she okay?"

"I don't know. I'm headed to Martin Luther Krankenhaus right now." His voice shook a little, and he closed his eyes, ran his thumb and finger against his eyes. "I don't know, okay? She went down really hard. Hit her head. And she was unconscious when she left the field, so—"

"Okay, breathe, Hudson. What was this guy's name?"

"Werner Vogel. Number sixty-three, Berlin Thunder."

"I'll track him down, see what I can find out, but I'm not in country at the moment, and I'm sort of in the middle of something, so you might need to do the legwork on this."

"Anything you need." He hung up and it occurred to him that

was the very sentence that'd gotten her—*them*—into this. Shoot, why had he been so terribly gung-ho to be something bigger than he was?

"You a player with the Thunder?" the Uber driver asked.

"Vikings." Although if coach reviewed the fourth-quarter tapes, maybe not for much longer. "Can you go faster?"

The man met his eyes in the rear view. Nodded.

Hud opened the app and tipped him forty percent as they pulled up to a sprawling white complex on the south side of the city. "Thanks."

He got out and headed to the reception desk. And then he played the same game that Iris had played when she'd tried to see him in Athens, right after he'd had a seizure not far from the hotel breakfast bar. "My name is Hudson Bly, and my fiancée, Iris Marshall, was brought in from the Thunder football game."

He even reached into his pocket and pulled out his ID.

The lobby was sparse and sleek, a leather sofa built into the wall, a few red recliners. The woman wore a green uniform, her blonde hair cut short, in her early fifties, maybe. She eyed Hudson. Finally, "Okay. She's in X-ray, but you can wait with her family in the ER lobby."

Her family?

She took his picture, then produced a badge with his name and picture and clipped it into a lanyard which he put over his head. She pointed down the hall to a door. "Scan the code. The waiting room is inside."

He strode down the hall, scanned the code, and the door released.

Family. So, her father, her brother?

It didn't matter. He wasn't leaving.

The doors opened into the lobby. Massive windows overlooked a tree-lined avenue, gold and red leaves still clinging to some of the trees. The wind took them, and they scattered into the encroaching twilight.

Standing at the window, his back to him, stood one of Iris's brothers. Broad shoulders, a little shorter than Hudson, but built like all of the Marshall men. He couldn't remember all their names.

On the sofa sat a woman nursing a cup of coffee, her legs folded.

"Shae?"

She looked up. "Hudson? What are you doing here?"

"How's Iris?"

"We don't know. We just got here." She wore the same lanyard around her neck.

The man at the window had turned. Ned. Right.

"Ned." They'd met, twice in fact, but the first time had been so brief, and all he'd been thinking about was disentangling himself from Iris.

The second time he'd, well, he'd been thinking about the same thing. This time with regret.

"Where's the rest of the family?"

"Dad and Jonas went back to the States a few days ago."

Hudson nodded. Glanced down the hall. "Let's find Iris."

Ned nodded, and Hudson walked over to the man at the nurses' center. Also blond, blue eyes, he wore green scrubs, a stethoscope around his neck, and looked up.

"Iris Marshall? We're her family." He didn't bother to explain. "What's her status and when can we see her?"

"Just a moment," he said, his accent thick. He typed in her name. "She is out of X-ray and in an ER room. Last door on the right."

Hudson didn't wait for Ned or Shae, just headed down the hallway.

He banged into her room with probably more force than needed, so apparently he hadn't left the fury back on the field. He stopped at the edge of her bed.

She lay, her eyes shut, an IV running into her vein, wearing a pulse monitor on her finger, still in her stripes. A nurse was hanging a blood pressure cuff on the wall. "Is she okay?"

"The doctor is waiting to get the X-rays back before they admit her."

Iris's eyes opened. Fixed to his for a moment, then flickered off to Ned and Shae, who had followed him into the room, then back to him. "Hud?"

"Yeah, that's right. Just the one of me, though, in case you're wondering."

"I can see just fine."

"Clearly not enough to get out of the way!"

His own anger jerked him up, and he took a breath, turned away, his hands behind his neck.

"*Ho*-kay," Ned said behind him. "What are we missing here?"

"How did you guys find out I was hit?"

Hud turned, watched as Ned came up beside her. "So, actually, we didn't know you were hit. We got a call from Fraser, who got a call from a guy named Roy, who got a call from someone named Ziggy who said that you were in the hospital."

She looked at Hudson. "You called Ziggy?"

"Of course I called Ziggy. Hello—that guy had your number from the moment the game started."

"Hud—you're overreacting—"

"Does this in any way look like overreacting?" He held out his hand and swept it along her bed, as if presenting evidence. "You could have been killed."

"From a tackle!"

"You're five foot five, a hundred thirty pounds at best. And this guy hit you with the force of a thousand suns! Yes, you could have been killed. What do you think we do out there—dance?"

"No. Sheesh—but I don't think he targeted me—"

"Okay, hold up, I need a brief sitrep here," Ned said. "What are you two talking about?"

"I'm talking about the hit that is still out on Iris, and she's completely ignoring it—"

"I wasn't ignoring it. I just—I want my life back."

"You'll get it back when you're safe!"

"Okay, Hud. Let's take a breath," Ned said. "How do you know the hit is out on Iris?"

"Ziggy called me, two days ago." He turned to Iris, his hands in fists at his side. "And I've been trying to track you down. Why are you not at the hotel?"

"Because, hello—my brother is here. And his fiancée. And maybe, have you thought that if I was staying at the hotel, that would be the perfect place for someone to find me?"

Oh. He drew in a breath. "Fine. But you...you..." He closed his mouth. Ground his molars.

"What happened at the game?" Shae said softly.

Hud had this. He rounded and held up a hand before Iris could start. "The defensive end for the Thunder took her out."

"It was an accident."

"It wasn't an accident!" Hudson roared. "I saw the hit. I saw his route. He wasn't blitzing Jackson. He was blitzing *you*."

Her eyes widened, just a little.

"Thank you. And maybe it had nothing to do with whoever wants you dead, maybe it was just some game rage, but..."

"But we need to find out."

Hud looked at Ned, whose mouth had gone tight around the edges.

"You know where this guy lives?"

"Ziggy is finding out."

"She's not our only resource." He pulled out his phone. "What's this guy's name?"

"Werner Vogel."

Ned nodded, then stepped out of the room.

He turned back to Iris. And then all of it just dropped—all the anger, the adrenaline, the panic—it simply washed out of him. He collapsed into the chair by her bed.

"Hud?" She sat up, then grimaced, leaned back. "Aaah."

"What. Is it your head?"

"No. I have two cracked ribs."

He looked away, his hands tightening on the armrests. Closed his eyes.

Good grief, he almost felt like crying.

"You okay, Hud?"

He looked back at her. Not even a little. But he didn't know how to say that. Yeah, he'd rushed to the hospital like some lovesick idiot. Called himself her fiancé.

But really, what was going on? He just stared at her. "I don't know."

Ned came back into the room. "I got an address."

Hud hit his feet. "Let's go."

Ned nodded, looked at Shae. "Stay here. We'll be back."

"Spoken like a couple of John Wicks." Shae stepped up to Ned, grabbed the lapels of his jacket. "Please don't end up in gulag."

Silence. She raised an eyebrow.

Ned kissed her.

Hud looked at Iris with a frown.

"I have no idea what they're talking about, but, um, don't do something stupid. I know the NFL is looking at you, Hud, and..." She gave him a small smile. "Please, don't screw it up."

Could be too late for that. "Just be here when I get back, okay?" He headed to the door.

Ned followed him but stopped at the door and looked at Shae. "You too." He walked out behind Hud.

"Gulag?" Hud looked at him.

Ned met his gaze. "NFL?"

"Probably not." He opened the door and stepped inside. "I'll let you know after we find this guy."

THE AIR SMELLED OF STORM. BRISK, A LITTLE FERAL, haunting, the wind shivered the trees and surrounded the field, and Garrett Marshall grabbed his gimme cap before it dislodged from his head.

"Let's get a move on, Joe," he said, leaning up from his shovel to cast a look over the vineyard to his second-oldest son, Jonas, working some ten rows over.

Jonas, dressed in a canvas jacket, wool hat, and gloves, lifted his hand in acknowledgment. "I'm starved!"

"Mom will have breakfast ready when we get inside," he said and used his shovel to lift a pile of mulch and drop it on the root bed of the La Crescent vines that stood in sturdy rows that covered nearly an acre of land.

Not backbreaking work, but tedious, and what a blessing to have Jonas and Fraser working with him on a project that usually took a couple weeks. At this rate, they'd have the fields bundled up for winter in a week.

Then he'd work his way across the fields, pruning, taking his time, evaluating each vine even as winter cast upon them. More tedious work, but it gave him the chance to inspect the spurs, choose the right canes to cut back, leaving two healthy buds on each cane.

Now the rows resembled scarecrows, one after another— gnarled, dry vine with gnarled, dry arms stretching across wires three and five feet tall, one to the next, about five feet between each rootstock. And they needed bedding down for winter.

Which, if he didn't hurry, might be upon him before he wanted.

The sky hung low and dour, the cloud cover so thick it blotted out the sun. The early winter breezes stripped the rest of the leaves from the maple and cottonwood edging the property, and this time of year, everything waited, breath held, for the first snow to turn the land to grace.

The hum of the four-wheeler made him look up as he reached the last of his row. Fraser, towing more mulch from the supply barn in the attached wagon. He stopped, pushed up his baseball hat. He wore a slight beard, a flannel shirt under a grimy vest, and on his uncasted hand, a glove. "You sure you're not doing damage to your hand, Fraser?"

"New cast, Dad. Extra sturdy. Besides, I can shovel with one hand."

Once upon a time, Garrett had dreamed of all his sons joining him at the winery, working alongside him like he had his father, in those last days.

But he'd never wanted to put expectations on them, tie them down. And look at what they'd accomplished. Fraser and Ned, SEALs; Jonas, with his PhD in atmospheric science; Iris, one of the few female officials in professional football; and, well, he couldn't wait to see what Creed wanted to do.

Although his youngest son had saved a princess, so there was that.

He couldn't have been prouder of his brood, especially when Fraser got off the four-wheeler and came over. "Dad, it's getting cold out. You go in. I finished my section—I'll get this."

"I got this, son. But see if you can finish up the patch beside the barn. They're younger and need a little more babysitting. You're pretty good at that."

Fraser grinned. "If you're referring to Pippa and Imani, I'm not sure I'm the one babysitting."

"Pippa is pretty bossy. But you two seem to have worked out the kinks." He liked how the royal bodyguard from the House of Blue in Lauchtenland had smoothed out Fraser's rather sharp corners, his rough edges.

Put a light back into his eyes that hadn't been there after his captivity this summer.

"Yeah. She's probably watching us right now on the security system."

Probably. Fraser had wired up the entire house and the surrounding property to be cast to video screens in Garrett's office. Er, former office.

Lately he'd been doing a lot of work at the kitchen table.

"You need a refill of mulch?" Fraser asked.

"Sure." Garrett picked up the wheelbarrow and trolleyed it to Fraser's wagon. From here, the house beckoned, warm and friendly, and he imagined the smell of bacon frying, maybe one of Jenny's egg casseroles, some fresh muffins.

She'd been pampering all her kids lately, what with the full house, and he didn't mind a bit. Although, she had seemed particularly tired, going to bed early.

Getting up early, too, with her Bible open. Clearly worried, probably about Iris.

Both of them, for that matter.

Fraser scooped mulch into the wheelbarrow. "Hear from Iris since you've been back?"

"No. But Ned's there, so…"

"Iris can take care of herself, you know, Dad. She's tough."

"I know." He took off his cap, ran a hand across his brow. "But she's my only daughter, so I'm allowed to worry a little." A lot.

Fraser reached for the water bottle on the four-wheeler and handed it to him. "I remember when she tried to go out for football."

He uncapped the bottle. "She would have, if the rules hadn't been stacked against her."

"And gotten flattened on the first snap."

Garrett wiped his mouth. "Maybe. But she was fast. Could have been a back, maybe. And she was used to playing with you guys. And you weren't easy on her."

Fraser made a face and took the bottle. "Maybe we should have been. She's a little hard on herself. Doesn't take help easily." He took a drink.

"Please tell me one of you boys who does."

Fraser wiped his mouth with his sleeve. "Ouch."

"You get that from your mom." He winked.

Fraser laughed. "Sure we do." He climbed back on the four-wheeler and gunned it.

Garrett went back to the bedding of the vines, working down the row, then the next. His stomach was roaring by the time he finished his supply, dropping it on the last root.

Jonas was already wheeling his wheelbarrow down the alley between crops. "Sibba called and I missed it. I'm heading in to call her back." He tapped his phone, seated in his canvas jacket pocket.

"Is she headed back to Slovenia?" his dad asked.

"I don't know. She'd like to stay in America, just to stay closer to her grandfather."

"Just her grandfather?" His dad smiled.

"Okay, yeah, we need more time together too. I'm not quite ready to propose yet. Fraser and I were chatting about maybe seeing if Ham's security team at Jones, Inc. could use her. Or maybe the Caleb Group, the outfit Logan Thorne runs."

"What you'd like is for her to change professions."

A sigh from his second-oldest son. "I can't ask her to do that. I love her despite her daily job. But yes, in my wildest dreams, she finds something else just as important but way less dangerous. Just don't know what that is."

"So you're going to stop chasing storms for her?"

Jonas pointed a finger at him. "Always have to ask the hard stuff, don't ya."

Garrett laughed. "You'll figure it out, son." He clamped him on the shoulder, squeezed, then dropped his shovel into the wheelbarrow and followed him to the supply barn. They ran their main winery operation out of the refurbished red barn that once held the tractors and equipment. Now it held French and American oak barrels, fermenters, racking tanks, hoses, a forklift, and most of all, wine.

The supply barn sat away from the house, a metal shed that they'd purchased from the neighboring farm years ago. Now it held a spraying system, a mechanical grape harvester, a fertilizer spreader, a rotary mower, shredder and trimmers, as well as an excavator. He parked the wheelbarrow next to one of their work trucks and washed his hands in the sink.

Jonas sat on a swing in the gazebo between the house and the barn, the one they'd built a couple years ago for tastings and other events. A timber-framed structure with hanging lights, in the summer it was stocked with hand-hewn picnic tables and a tasting bar, and they held events on the weekends.

Fraser was still working in the field, although it looked like he was finishing up.

Poor Creed. Out of all his children, Creed, his last and adopted son, seemed the most interested in the winery, and he'd be out here too if not for the accident—not the shooting—that'd fractured his femur. They'd done surgery and implanted pins, but the poor kid was still in a cast, although he'd started PT and was regaining movement.

Admittedly, Garrett didn't love the fact that Fraser had turned the winery into a top secret security compound to protect a fugitive royal from Lauchtenland, but he really liked Imani. And he really liked how Imani made Creed smile, laugh, and made him feel like a hero. The kid'd had too many tough breaks before he'd joined the family, and Garrett wanted him to see the man he'd become.

He walked into the entry and pulled off his boots, his hat, his jacket. No, he didn't hate the fact that his boys had come home, even if they had shown up injured.

He'd really hoped that Iris would come home too. And in his gut, he just couldn't escape the idea that she was still in danger, despite her shrugging it away.

Maybe it was just the father in him. Weird that he didn't worry about the boys like he did Iris.

But today, right now, everyone was safe, and that's all that mattered.

He came into the house, and that's when he noticed the dark

kitchen. No fragrance of bacon frying, no scrambled eggs, no savory morning muffins baking in the oven.

Huh.

But Jenny had been tired lately, going back to bed sometimes in the morning after breakfast. And yesterday, when he'd gotten home from the airport, she'd been napping on the sofa.

He took the stairs up and down the hall, past the boy's bedrooms and Iris's, which was now occupied by Pippa and Imani, the door closed. His door was also closed, so he eased it open, wishing he'd fixed the whine of the hinges.

No one in the bed, although the covers were mussed, as if Jenny had just gotten up. With the sun already cleared the treetops, he put the time at nearly ten a.m.

"Jenny?" He paused. There, from the bathroom, the sound of the shower. Okay, so she had gotten up late. Hopefully she'd leave it running for him, and he could slick off the residue of the morning's work.

He walked down the hallway of their closets that connected to the bedroom. The door hung open, steam puffing out, the wood a little moist.

Weird.

And that's when he realized what he wasn't hearing—singing.

Jenny always sang in the shower. Often hymns, and her current streak was "How Firm a Foundation."

How firm a foundation, ye saints of the Lord, is laid for your faith in God's excellent Word!

"Jenny?"

He pushed the door open, and for a second, his entire body hollowed.

His wife lay on the floor in her pajamas, collapsed, bleeding from the temple.

"Jenny!" He knelt next to her, turned her over.

She was breathing. And the cut wasn't terrible—a wound above her eye that had stained the white throw rug. But her eyes were closed.

"Honey, wake up. Wake—*up*." He fought the rush of heat in his chest. *Please!*

Her eyes opened, and she blinked, trying to orient herself. "Garrett?" Her hand went to her head, but he caught it, then reached for a washcloth and pressed it against the wound. The bleeding had already clotted, but the wound was surrounded by a terrible goose egg.

She started to sit up, and he caught her, helped her. "Oh, wow, I must have fallen."

He looked around and found the bath mat against the wall. "Maybe you slipped on the bath mat."

"Yeah, that's it." She didn't look at him but put her hand to the towel. Winced. "Wow. Did I hit the counter?"

"I think so. Are you dizzy?"

"No more than usual." She smiled at him.

"That's not funny."

"It's a little funny."

Aw. And then the heat just caught up to him, and shoot, but his eyes watered.

"Garrett?"

"Sorry. You spooked me a bit." He kissed her cheek. "Had a little flashback of—"

"Nope." She held up her hand. "We're not going there. Those are bygone days." She gave him a tight smile, but...

Something haunted her eyes. "Jenny, are you—"

"Help me up."

Okay. He got up and pulled her up from the floor. He let her go to turn off the water, and she caught herself on the counter. "Whoa, okay, maybe I am a little dizzy."

"Let's get you back into bed."

"What? No. I have breakfast to make."

"I'll make breakfast."

She gave him a look.

"What? I can make breakfast."

"Just get me an ice pack and a Band-Aid." She patted his

cheek. "And don't worry. I'm fine." She turned and headed to the bedroom.

But as she went, leaving behind the soggy bathroom and the bloody rug and the discarded towel, the old fear shook through him.

Please, God. Not again.

Not yet.

SEVEN

Maybe this was a bad idea. It sort of settled in Hud's gut as night fell around them in the quietness of the Uber, on the way to Werner Vogel's supposed address in the Mittee district. Hud had looked it up, and from the Google street view, it looked like a standard four-story historic building.

And he was going to, what—assault the man? It was one thing to hit him on the field, completely another to bring the violence to his home. It didn't help that Iris's words sat inside him, haunting. *Don't do something stupid.*

Yeah, this might be exactly that—stupid. But they needed answers.

Except Ned was with him, and Ned was a SEAL, and Hud couldn't get past the idea that he'd somehow notched up the stakes by inviting Ned.

Or Ned inviting him. Whatever.

"Don't kill anyone."

Ned looked at him. "What?"

"Just...don't...you know...do SEAL stuff."

Ned just blinked at him. "You do know that we try very hard to distinguish the good guys from the bad and to avoid collateral damage? And Werner Vogel is not a terrorist, yet. So don't worry, Hud. I'm only looking for some answers. Aren't you?"

Hudson nodded. Looked away, his gut still knotted.

Streetlights lit up the roads as the driver wove through old neighborhoods to the northwest corner of the city. They'd passed the impressive creamy-white Brandenburg Gate, then the river, bright with the lights of the nearby buildings.

"But along those lines, what's up between you and Iris?"

Hud glanced at him.

"Are you in love with my sister?"

Oh. Hud wiped his hands on his jeans. "I...we..." He sighed. "I don't know, okay? I just know that I feel like I got her into this mess."

"How is this your fault? I remember Iris telling us that she showed up on the bridge, she inserted herself into this story."

"If I hadn't been there, maybe she wouldn't have been either. And maybe none of this would have happened."

Ned turned quiet. "Then why were you there?"

Hudson looked out the window again. "I think the Vikings are going to release me."

"To the NFL?"

He gave a harsh, bright laugh. "I doubt it. I mean, yeah, my agent called and said he'd lined up a tryout, but I'm five years off the draft, and sure, I've got great hands, and I might be at the peak of my career, but one more hit to the head and...well, I'm already struggling with brain fog and some steadiness issues..."

And shoot, he didn't know why he'd said that. Especially to Ned.

"Sorry, man. Our guys deal with some of the same things— brain trauma from concussive blasts, and other injuries. But yeah, its an epidemic in football."

"Never mind the guys coming out of college ball—they're getting faster and stronger every year. And some team can pick them up and mold them." He shook his head. "I'm not trying to be cynical—just honest. And so when Ziggy approached me a few months ago and asked me to be a courier for the CIA—which ended up being this private security group—I thought, why not? Maybe...I dunno, I can be a patriot."

"I get that," Ned said.

Hud nodded.

"So, what happens when you get her out of this mess? You walk away?" Ned posed the question so quietly, the effect of it on Hud seemed disproportionately lethal. Like a knife between the ribs.

Walk away.

He swallowed. "I don't know."

Silence.

They turned onto a dark neighborhood street.

"I can't seem to shake her out of my brain, and maybe it is just the guilt, but..." He blew out a breath. "We, uh, we were trapped in this cave overnight, and that was my fault too, but I didn't realize that the tide would come in, so, anyway, it just kept rising until we had only a foot of air. And it was deep and pitch black, and I had no idea how to get us out of there, so I just hung on to the rock. And...I don't know. She started talking. Told me about growing up on the winery, about working the farm, about her brothers.

Hudson sighed. "All I know is that I can sort of get stuck inside my head, and Iris kept me going. She's funny and brave and I like being around her. She makes me feel that maybe everything is going to work out."

"I see."

He did? Because Hud didn't see anything.

Ned leaned forward. "Stop here."

According to Hud's map, they were still a block away.

The driver pulled over, and Hud tipped him, then followed Ned out.

A streetlight bathed the sidewalk, illuminating bicycles tied up at racks, cars parked along the curb. Here, four-story buildings connected one to another, bearing a historical facade despite their rebuild after World War II. A cat ran across their path as the Uber drove away, and Ned pulled up his phone.

"What are you doing?"

"Ordering a pizza."

Hud just stared at him. Ned looked up. "I heard your stomach growling in the car."

"You are kidding me, right?

Ned finished the order, then pocketed the phone. "C'mon."

He walked down the street, Hud beside him, then they crossed and stood in front of Vogel's building, out of the pool of light in front of the door. Ned found a spot in the shadows.

After a bit—"I felt the same about Shae. We met during a tornado, and she was absolutely amazing. There was a guy with us who was bleeding, and I was injured too, and she just held it all together. Even now, after two weeks in a Siberian gulag, it's like...I don't know, she's just, maybe, done with letting it tell her who she is."

"What do you mean?"

He looked at Hud. "You know, after everything that happened in America, Iris is done letting it tell her that she's a victim. Or at least I hope so. All I know is that she's one of the toughest women I know. Here they come."

Hud blinked at him, trying to sort through his words, then turned and watched as a car drove up, a pizza delivery sign glowing on the top.

"Gotta love pizza delivery," Ned said and walked toward the door as the pizza man got out. He waited until the man buzzed the apartment belonging to Vogel. No answer.

"At least now we know he's not home," Ned said.

The pizza delivery man buzzed another unit and spoke German. The door buzzed, and he went inside.

Ned caught the door and held it for Hudson.

"It can't just be that easy," Hudson said.

"People are easily duped, especially if they think they're helping out someone," Ned said.

They waited in the lobby as the delivery man climbed the stairs.

A few minutes later, he came down empty handed.

"I told him in my instructions that if no one answered, to leave it by the door," Ned said, then ducked his head and headed up the stairs.

"This a new breaching technique?" Hudson said.

"Whatever works." He stopped on the second floor, pizza sitting on the floor. He picked up the box. Stilled. "The door is ajar."

Hud reached out, but Ned bumped him back. "Just stay here." He handed Hud the pizza box.

In a moment, Ned had pulled out a knife from his boot. Then he pushed the door open with his foot and crept in. Light shone from the kitchen, and farther, a larger room.

Hud wasn't going to stand in the hallway like a child, waiting for Ned to get killed. He pushed in behind Ned, who was already down the hallway.

The place wasn't large, but newly remodeled with wood flooring, the kitchen just a wall of cabinets topped with black granite, a wooden table set with four chairs.

Ned glanced over at him, frowned, then motioned to stay behind him.

Sheesh, Vogel was a football player, not special forces. What did he think was—

"In here." Ned lowered the knife and headed into the main room.

Hud set down the pizza on the counter in the kitchen and followed Ned into the room, past an arched entrance.

Ned's outstretched arm stopped him cold. "Don't touch anything."

On the long gray sofa slumped Werner Vogel, much of his head gone, splatter on the wall.

On the television, muted, a soccer game played. A Heineken sat on the table, half finished.

Hud turned away, winced.

"Could be self-inflicted," Ned said, stepping closer. "There's a nine millimeter on the floor." Ned pointed to the gun, fallen between the sofa and a coffee table.

"Looks like his computer was taken." Ned crouched and lifted the cord to the computer with the edge of his blade. "Hope it has good battery life."

Blood still dripped down the wall. "How long ago was he, did he..."

"Not long. The blood is very fresh and..." He pulled the sleeve down on his jacket, then pressed his hand against the body. "Still warm." He stepped back. "Could be the pizza man interrupted the murder."

Hud stilled, and Ned looked at him. "Stay here."

This time, yes.

Ned put a hand to his lips—not that anyone hiding in the building wouldn't have already heard them, but okay.

Ned crept to the bedroom and nudged the door open. Hud waited in the main room, not sure what to do about Vogel.

Sorry?

Ned returned. "No one in the bedroom or the bathroom. I think they left the building."

From somewhere in the house, a vibration sounded, buzzing.

Ned stilled, but Hud crouched, following the sound. "Under the sofa."

He crawled over and reached for the phone.

"Hud, get your hand off the table!"

He recoiled, even as his grip closed on the phone. The movement moved the table, jostled the Heineken, which toppled and started to drip down the sides.

"That'll take care of your fingerprints," Ned said. Sirens in the distance whined. "Let's get out of here."

Hud pocketed the phone, started to follow Ned to the door, then stopped. "The pizza." He doubled back, grabbed the box from the counter.

Ned waited at the door, cocking his head.

"What?"

"Trying to figure out what's worse—leaving that here and the cops track down the driver, or an interview by the neighbors admitting they let him in, but the pizza's disappeared."

"My fingerprints are all over this," Hud said.

"So are the pizza guy's."

Hud gave him a look.

"Just saying—cluttered evidence means confusion."

The sirens whined louder. Ned shook his head and pushed through the door.

Hud followed him, scampering down the stairs. Above, on Vogel's floor, a door closed.

Ned glanced at him. "Let's hope that wasn't a witness."

Hud had nothing as they hit the lobby then headed outside.

A police car was just pulling up to the entrance. Hud followed Ned out.

"Don't run. Just act normal." Ned stopped and then, crazily, held the door for the cops as they got out and headed inside.

"What are you doing?"

"Hiding in plain sight," Ned said, then let the door close. "Now we run."

Oh, this was fun.

But Ned didn't run—he walked down the sidewalk, even reached over and grabbed a piece of pizza, folding it, eating it like a sandwich. "It's good. Not American pizza, but still, good."

Hud dropped the box in a nearby garbage can. "I may never eat again."

Ned gave him a look.

Two more blocks away, Ned dialed up an Uber. It picked them up, and they headed back to the hospital.

"I don't know how you do this," Hud said. His entire body was a knot.

"Calmly. Gimme the phone."

Hud handed him the smart phone. Ned turned it on. "Thumbprint entry. Shoot."

"Are you suggesting that we should have cut off his thumb?"

Ned looked at him, then the driver. Raised an eyebrow.

Oops. But clearly, he wasn't cut out for this. "Sorry."

"No. There's always a backup." He swiped the phone. "There's a swipe code."

"Does that help us?"

"Maybe. Our cousin Coco might be able to help with this." He turned off the phone and slipped it into his pocket. "If she can crack it, we might be able to see if he was involved with the hit on Iris. In the meantime, I think it's time Iris went home."

"To...Lake Como?"

"To Minnesota." Ned leaned back, ran a finger and thumb against his eyes. "My team is currently OCONUS, and I need to join them. Which means I need to put Shae and Iris on a plane for home so my brother Fraser can keep an eye on them."

"You're not going with them?"

"I'm headed the other direction."

Hud looked at him. "Um, there's only big country that way." He indicated east. "You speak Russian?"

Ned just looked at him. Took a breath.

"Okay, so, just so we're clear, you want to put Iris and Shae on a plane, alone?"

"I'm sure there will be other passengers."

"Have you never seen any hostage flight movies? Seriously— okay, I'm going with them."

"To America."

"To Minnesota."

"That's a long trip."

"Only if you don't go first class." He looked at Ned, his smile falling. "What you don't understand is that I'm not letting Iris out of my sight until she's safe."

Ned smiled. "So that's a yes, then?"

Yes? To what?

Hud frowned at him, but they had pulled up to the hospital. Hud got out, left Ned behind, and stalked inside. He still had his badge, which he now pulled out and slipped over his neck. Buzzed the door open.

Darkness filled the lobby, now shadowed and empty. He didn't stop at the reception desk but strode down the hall to the ER room.

Slowed. The room was dark, the bed empty.

He returned to the desk. Ned was just walking in.

"The woman in the room down the hall—Iris Marshall. Did she get admitted?"

The male nurse had stood up when he approached the counter, and now shook his head. "She was never admitted. She left over an hour ago with her friend."

Ned shook his head, slammed his fist on the counter, and turned away.

"Any idea where they went?"

"Just that they left with some guy. Sorry."

Some guy.

Hud looked at Ned, whose mouth tightened.

"Do you have security footage?" Ned said, turning back to the nurse.

He nodded and reached for the phone. "Why?"

"Because," Hud said slowly, "I think they might be in trouble."

"He's going to kill me." Shae sat at the long dining table in the Airbnb, her arms folded, her head in her arms. "Ned is going to kill me."

"What?" Iris said. "Won't they just come back to the house?" She lay on the sofa, a cold pack on her neck where it had started to ache. They'd given her enough drugs to flatten an elephant, but frankly, she refused to sleep until Hud returned.

Alive, without blood and without the law on his tail. Because no, she didn't worry as much about him as her brother.

Who tended to dive into trouble without looking back.

"You don't understand. We have a history. It includes me disappearing and him having to find me." Shae got up and walked to an arched bay window with a seat.

"Well, this time you're sitting in an Airbnb in the country, south of Berlin, waiting for Zach to make you avocado toast."

"I'm not sure I'm doing it right, but it's almost ready." Zach spoke up from the kitchen, attached to the main room through a glass barn door. The three-bedroom house sported an updated seventies vibe, with hardwood floors, gold and navy blue dining furniture against an oval walnut table, a green L-shaped sofa, a gold petal hanging light, and a standing stove that pumped out heat.

"Yes," Shae said, in response to Iris's comment. "Which is a thousand times better than a Siberian gulag, but still, poor Ned."

"Seriously, gulag? You keep saying that—are you serious?"

"Da. As in I ate black bread and drank watered down tea for two weeks, digging a ditch on a work crew until Ned and Fraser rescued me."

"How did you even...how are you not crumpled in a ball right now?"

She drew one leg up, held it to herself. "I dunno. I...there was this guy named Judah—an American—who was in the container next to me—"

"Container?"

"Let's call it a cell. And we could talk to each other through this hole in the floor, and he was just...like, an angel. He kept telling me that I wasn't alone, that God was with me. Told me not to be afraid. I don't know—he was right. God *was* with me. Judah told me that peace isn't the absence of fear, but the presence of Jesus, and I felt that, you know?"

Iris considered her. "No, I...maybe I don't know."

"Avocado toast and tea," Zach said, coming from the kitchen. "I'm no gourmet, but I think I did pretty good smashing those avocados."

He set a pot on a hot pad. "And tea. Which is disgusting but, since you can't have wine or a shot of tequila, is the best we can do. Here's some milk. And a vat of sugar." He had retrieved those from the kitchen and set them on the table.

Iris tried to push herself from the sofa. Groaned.

"Stop. You're hurting me. Just—stay there." Zach picked up a plate, loaded it with a piece of toast, and brought it over. "How many ribs are cracked?"

"Two. But it feels like a horse tromped my insides."

"A two-hundred-and-fifty-pound defensive end, more like." He set the plate beside her on the wooden coffee table. "Here you go." He leaned down and helped ease her up to a sitting position. She groaned again.

"More drugs?"

"I'm already seeing colors, so maybe not. Just, can you hand me the toast?"

He set the plate on her lap. "Tea?"

"Water."

"Good choice." He walked back to the kitchen. "You think you're a wreck, you should have seen the hits Hud put on Vogel in the fourth quarter. That guy has to be hurting."

She set her toast down. Swallowed. "Really?" Probably wasn't great that the thought sort of filled her with warmth.

But that and the way he'd walked into the ER room with such...*ferocity*...it sort of shook her. Like maybe he'd almost been...scared?

No, that wasn't right.

"Yeah. Hud hit Vogel so hard my teeth rattled."

"Did anyone call it?"

He poured himself a cup of tea, added about a gallon of milk. "Nope. Technically, it was just a block."

"Every time?"

"Mm-hmm."

She'd have to see the tapes. "You know, if there were NFL officials there and they watched, we could be ousted from the Lauchtenland game."

Zach held his tea in the palm of his hand like it might be a bowl. "Same for your man Hud."

"He's not my man."

"He barged into the officials' locker room like he was on fire. Wouldn't even wait to take the Uber to the hospital." He set down his tea, and his phone buzzed in his pocket. "My Uber is here. I gotta go. I'm on a flight back to Amsterdam in an hour. You going to be okay?"

"Yeah."

He walked over to her. Crouched in front of her. "You call me if you need anything."

"I got this."

He stood up and kissed her forehead. Stepped back. "Sorry, but I was overhearing what you guys were talking about, and Shae's right. You don't always have to protect yourself, Iris. You're not alone, okay?"

She frowned, not sure what he was getting at. "I don't—"

"I got this?" He raised an eyebrow. "Maybe it's okay if you don't."

Oh.

He picked up his duffel on the way out and closed the door behind him.

Shae had gone to the table, was drinking her tea. "He's right. Tea is terrible."

Iris laughed, then groaned. "Don't make me laugh."

"Sorry." She set down her tea. "The guys are taking a long time. Did you get a text back?"

"From...who? I don't have any contacts."

"I thought you texted Ned!" Shae got up. "Where's your phone?"

"Maybe my duffel? I didn't have it when I left the stadium." She gestured to somewhere across the great room. She spotted her duffel sitting on the floor near the door.

Shae got up and headed to the duffel.

"It won't matter—I don't have his number."

Shae found the burner phone. "You only have one contact in here."

"I know. It's Hud."

Shae pressed Send, and it rang, then died. "Shoot. Your phone died."

"Sorry."

Shae tossed it back into the bag. "Please, God, let Ned know where I am. Please let him not kill me." She got up. "We should have waited at the hospital and not gone with your friend Zach."

"Listen, we're fine. Ned will figure it out—"

"Ned nearly died in the Bering Sea looking for me!"

Iris stared at her.

Shae put her hand over her mouth, her pale blue eyes wide. "Sorry. I just...maybe I'm worried."

"C'mere. Let me tell you a story about Ned."

Shae walked over.

"I'm sure you've heard the story of Ned and the Russian kid. I can't remember his name—Alexi, or Illya or something like that. Anyway, he was a couple years older than Ned, and a complete bully, and Fraser and Jonas talked him into standing up to the kid. I mean, he had twenty pounds on Ned and razors for teeth—"

Shae laughed, although her eyes were wet.

"Anyway, Ned totally took him on. He got licked, but he stood his ground to this kid. And after that, everybody around him knew that Ned was the real deal. So, you don't worry about him. Ned is going to be just fine."

Shae ran her hands over her cheeks. "I just need to marry the man as soon as I possibly can."

Iris reached out to give her a hug, then groaned.

Shae grabbed her hands, squeezed. "I think Hudson has a thing for you, by the way. So maybe that dress worked."

"Oh, please, please don't make me laugh."

But the thought added to Zach's words, settled into her bones.

What if...

No, it couldn't work. She met Shae's eyes.

"Don't say it. You don't know until you try," Shae said.

"What does that even look like? We live in different *countries*."

"What are you talking about? You guys fly around Europe as if you have commuter jets."

"It's more than that, Shae. I don't...I don't date football players, for one. And for two, I...I don't have room in my life for a...relationship. I travel all the time, and I...I just don't..."

What? The answer pulsed from deep inside her.

Shae just blinked at her. "None of that makes sense."

"It does if—"

The front door knob rattled, and for a second, Hud's words rushed back to Iris. *I'm talking about the hit that is still out on Iris, and she's completely ignoring it...*

Maybe a house out in the country wasn't exactly the right hideout.

She froze.

The door opened.

Ned came in first, and Shae was up, running.

Hud scooted in behind him.

And inside, Iris was also, crazily, running. Also throwing her arms and legs around the man, kissing him.

Okay, maybe not like Shae, but at least she was...

Aw, who was she kidding? Because the sight of him, walking in, sucking all the air out of the room with his presence, just made her want to hold on to him.

Just like she had in the cave.

Oh, she was in big trouble.

Because she didn't hold on to anyone, thank you. Not even her family.

But maybe Hud didn't know that—and why would he? She'd done nothing but hold on to him since...well, since he'd needed her in Athens.

And then she'd needed him right back, at least for a bit and—

"You left the hospital."

Her eyes widened. "Zach picked us up. I..."

He pushed away the coffee table and knelt in front of her, those blue eyes in hers. Even on his knees, he was taller than her. "Are you okay?"

She managed to nod. "Are you?"

He drew in a breath. Glanced behind him.

Ned had disappeared with Shae into the kitchen.

He looked back at Iris. "Not even a little."

And then he kissed her. Just leaned in, his mouth against hers, urgent, almost a little desperate.

Oh. *Oh.*

She was so stunned she barely responded, and by the time she caught up, he was breaking the kiss, leaning back.

And she didn't know what possessed her—maybe the craziness of the past two weeks, the trauma of today, or the very real sense that suddenly...

She wasn't alone, whether she liked it or not.

And right now, hurt and tired on the sofa, she liked it.

So, before he could fully pull away, she leaned in and kissed him back. Hooked one finger in the lapel of his jacket, tugging a little.

And he was right back in the game, a little sound deep in his chest, kissing her hard at first, then slowing them down a little as he cradled her face in his big, wide-receiver hands, turning their kiss languid and delicious.

He was a crazy mix of tough and tender, sweet and scary, powerful and passionate, confusing and yet calming.

Exactly perfect.

At least for the moment. He tasted of the night, smelled of strength and power, and with him, she felt...safe. Right. She settled into the kiss, her heart slowing, and she heard her own sound, one that surprised her.

He pulled away, searched her eyes. Swallowed.

Yeah, her too. She caught her lower lip in her teeth. What. Were. They *doing?*

It seemed Hud didn't have an answer either—just kept staring at her, as if taking her in.

Then, from the kitchen, "You guys about done?"

Her eyes widened, and Hud let her go, used the coffee table to hop to his feet. "Um." He ran a hand behind his neck.

Shae came out, holding Ned's hand, grinning.

Ned was smiling too.

Whatever. Iris ignored him. "What did you guys find out about Vogel?"

Ned's smile vanished. He glanced at Hudson, made a face.

"What?" Iris said, looking at Hud.

He turned too. "So, there might have been a small snafu. I think it's probably best if we all leave the country as soon as we can."

She stilled. "Leave...the country? Um...where are we going?"

She might never sleep again.

Jenny stood in the living room, the room softly lit by the snow peeling from the sky. Not a blizzard yet, but it had potential.

She should be sleeping, but the fact was, Jenny knew when her children were in trouble. More than a fear, it was the sense, deep in her bones—no, in her soul—that something wasn't right, that they were hurting, or suffering, or even in mortal danger.

She'd known it when Fraser had been taken captive in Nigeria. Woken, as if God had spoken to her aloud. *Pray. Pray for his safety.* She'd prayed for nearly two weeks before he'd been liberated.

Then Creed, and Fraser again—she lay awake in France, Garrett snoring beside her, feeling that something wasn't right. Creed had been running around Europe like a fugitive, Fraser on his tail. They hadn't told her until recently, but she'd known.

Then Jonas, although that had been more of an impression, a sense of danger that had woken her early one morning, made her hit her knees.

And now—now Iris. She couldn't shake it.

Iris was hurt.

And currently not answering her phone.

No, something wasn't right.

Jenny drew the afghan around her shoulders and listened to the moan of the wind against the panes, the creak of the old farmhouse with its many cobbled-together pieces, starting with the first homestead in the early 1900s, to the add-on in the '60s, to the remodel in the '80s and the recent kitchen expansion of 2005.

She had spent nearly forty of her sixty-two years in this house. She planned on staying until the end.

Her hand went up to touch the goose egg. The bruise had turned a deep purple, the cut covered with a butterfly bandage. It would leave a scar.

But nothing like the wound of the truth upon Garrett. She'd seen the look on his face when she'd opened her eyes.

Fear.

Sure, he'd tried to blink it away, but it had hung in his gaze, the memories vivid, bright, and ugly.

So she'd lied.

Slipped on the rug. Yes, sort of. But only after the room had pitched, turning, and she'd reached out for the counter to right herself, slipped, hit her head, and then gone down, kicking the carpet away.

So, sort of a lie, then.

Jenny, are you—

Good thing she'd cut him off, because she really didn't want to *directly* lie. And frankly, as long as she simply ignored it all, then maybe it wasn't a lie. Not really.

The clock in the family room gonged, one peal. She'd given up at midnight, tired of staring at the ceiling. A book she'd started a week ago lay facedown, some thriller that kept her awake about an ex-soldier with a K9 dog.

Before that she'd read a romance about a prince who'd found the woman he loved in a small town in Tennessee. Cute book that she'd picked up at the grocery store, on a whim. Reminded her of Princess Imani.

She wouldn't mind if Creed and Imani ended up together. Pretty girl, smart, and she could beat him in a game of horse, although he played one-handed while holding on to his crutch.

Picking up the thriller, Jenny read the page three times before she conceded.

The nagging feeling wouldn't lift.

Fine. The Bible then. She picked it up from the table next to the sofa and let it fall open. Her daily psalm. Today's was Psalm 13.

The words seemed to seep inside her, find her bones, her cells.

How long, Lord? Will you forget me forever?...How long must I wrestle with my thoughts...Look on me and answer, Lord my God. Give light to my eyes, or I will sleep in death.

She closed her eyes, hearing the verse in her head. Yeah, David knew how to lay it out there, stir the cry of her heart. Why was it that she could be a woman of faith for thirty years and still find herself crying out? Alone. Scared.

No.

She opened her eyes and soaked in the rest of the psalm. *But I trust in your unfailing love; my heart rejoices in your salvation. I will sing the Lord's praise, for he has been good to me.*

Yes, that was right.

She closed the Bible, brought it to her chest, her heart. *Lord,*

*help me to trust You for my children. And for my future. And...
wherever Iris is, please keep her safe.*

In the quiet of the night, just the ticking of the clock
sounded. That and her heartbeat, thumping inside her.

Then, suddenly, *Be still.*

She caught her breath, the voice pulsing inside her.

Be still, beloved.

Her hands tremored, and she folded them into fists, pushed
against the Bible.

Know that I am God.

She closed her eyes, the presence suddenly thick in the room,
running through her, touching every cell.

Yes.

Know.

With God came grace. Mercy. Peace.

Hope.

Yes.

She sank into the sofa, closed her eyes, let the wind howl
against the pane. Her heart stopped pounding, her breath
calming.

She must have dozed off, because she didn't hear the door
open. Didn't hear the movement until they were inside the house,
whispering loud enough to wake the dead. Or her. But Jenny sat
straight up and blinked at the entourage stamping off their feet
and shedding their coats in the entryway.

The light flicked on, shone over them, and Jenny gasped.
"Iris?"

Iris looked up, her blonde hair back in a headband, bags under
her beautiful eyes. "Mom. What are you doing up?"

"What—I...praying. For you." She rounded the sofa as Iris
came into the kitchen.

Jenny pulled her into her arms.

"Oh, go easy there." Iris drew in a breath, eased away.

"What is it?"

"A couple broken ribs, Mom," said Ned, who came in and embraced her. "She got hit during a football game."

Jenny clamped her mouth shut. Be still. *Still!*

"What happened to you?" Iris said, her eye on the bruise.

"Oh, you know, slipped in the bathroom." She turned to the blonde coming in behind Iris. "Shae!"

"Hey, Mom," said Shae, and also hugged her. Aw, Shae.

Jenny kissed her cheek. "I'm so glad you're back. I've been worried about you."

Ned put his arm around Shae, his own worry in his expression. "I was going to send her home with Hud and Iris, but..." He looked at his fiancée. "I couldn't let her go quite yet."

"Who's Hud?"

A stranger then stepped into the room behind them. He stood taller than her sons, bigger, wore a pair of jeans and a button-down oxford. "Hello, Mrs. Marshall."

"Mom, this is Hudson Bly. He plays for the Vienna Vikings," Iris said.

Jenny shook his hand. "Do you now?" She shot a look at Iris.

Iris just sighed, then met Hud's gaze and smiled.

And suddenly, for this small blink of time, come what may, all seemed right with the world.

EIGHT

Iris hadn't realized how tired, how tightly wound she'd been, until she woke up on the foldout in her parents' den—her room being occupied by Pippa and Imani—to the smell of pancakes and bacon frying, having slept...well, it was possible she hadn't slept so soundly in years.

Maybe it was the exhausting seventeen-hour trip across the ocean, the four-hour layover in New York City, the arrival in Minneapolis at midnight. Hud had rented a car to drive them to their home, just outside the small town of Chester, Minnesota.

The last thing she'd expected was her mother to greet her at the door. Her chest tightened a bit at how her mother had aged, looking a little run-down, the wound on her head alarming. Just a fall. When was a fall at her age *just a fall*?

Wan light bled through the shutters of the room, and Iris got up, pulling on a sweatshirt over her jammie pants, then went to the window. Her body ached all the way to her bones, her ribs so sore she could hardly breathe.

But outside, a layer of white grace covered the grass, the fields, capping the rows and rows of idle vines in white. The first snowfall, and with it came a magic that meant family and celebration.

Maybe returning home wasn't running. Wasn't hiding.

Maybe, for right now, it was exactly the answer she needed. So maybe she shouldn't have been so hard on Hudson when he'd suggested it.

What about our jobs? Our careers?

You alive is more important than both those things. It was the power of his gaze in hers more than his words that had made her get on the plane from Berlin.

She opened the blinds, and the gray light washed over the computers set up on her father's desk. Four monitors, showing shots of the outside of the house from all angles. She'd slept with her pillow over her head most of the night.

A massive picture of the family winery hung over his desk, an aerial shot of the barn, the house, right after the last addition of the upper-floor master and her mother's office-slash-guest room on the main floor, where her grandparents had stayed when they'd visited, and where Hud had slept last night.

He'd acted a little weird when he'd said goodnight, not kissing her, not even meeting her eyes. But maybe he was tired too.

She tiptoed out to the main-floor bathroom, washed her face, brushed her teeth, and tied back her hair. Good enough for breakfast.

Except Mom had made it into something of a celebration, setting the long table, bringing in extra chairs, adding some dried chrysanthemums to the center.

Creed sat at the island, his leg on a chair, scrolling through his phone.

"Hey, bud," she said. He held up his fist and she bumped it. He seemed about a decade older than she remembered, filled out, wider shoulders, a *grown* man. And handsome, too, with that dark curly hair, chocolate dark eyes. No wonder a princess had followed him home.

She must be the girl laying plates on the table.

"Hi," she said to her. Pretty, darker skin, dark hair pulled back, she looked about twenty and wore a sweatshirt, leggings.

"Hi. I'm Imani."

Yep, the infamous princess that Creed had rescued. "Glad to meet you." She picked up the silverware and followed her around the table, adding forks to folded napkins.

Worship music played from the speaker in the kitchen, CeCe Winans's "Believe for It." Her mom sang along in the kitchen as she stood at the stove, a flat spatula in her hand. "There is power in your name..." She wore a pair of leggings, a sweatshirt, her hair braided, and looked about a thousand times brighter than last night.

"Morning, Mom," Iris said.

"Sweetie. Did you sleep okay?" She handed Iris one of the fresh blueberries she was dropping onto the sizzling pancakes.

Iris took it, popped it in her mouth. "Like the dead. I could go back to bed for another hour or ten."

"Don't," Fraser said. He stood at the sink, washing dishes by hand, still the bearing of a hero despite his longer hair, his smattering of beard. He looked up at her as she came over to the counter, searching for glasses. "You gotta let your body adjust to the new time. Stay awake, no matter what it takes."

"Spoken from experience." She stopped near him and gave him a kiss on the cheek. He returned with a spray of water with his hand.

"Nice."

"Your boyfriend isn't up yet, by the way."

"He's not my boyfriend."

Fraser raised an eyebrow, and then looked over at Ned, who stood at the coffee machine, cup in hand, mentally coaxing coffee to appear.

"What?" Ned said, looking up.

"You told them?"

"I'm sharing a room with him, Fraser, and Joe. What was I supposed to do?"

"What, are you thirteen-year-old girls at a slumber party? Keep your mouth shut."

He grinned, waggled his eyebrows.

"Is nothing sacred?"

"You've met us, right?" The voice, behind her, belonged to Jonas, who appeared in his jeans, shucking off his jacket from the porch.

"Where were you?"

"Checking on the wine with Dad. He's getting antsy to rack the Marquette-based pinot noir he has out there."

Out of the window, she spotted her father, his wide shoulders under a thick flannel shirt, wearing jeans and work boots, headed toward the house from the barn. She still couldn't get past the fact he'd shown up, himself, in Europe to find her.

"Ned, all the flights are grounded."

Shae came out of the den, wearing sweatpants, a T-shirt, her blonde hair back. "I can't get a flight out."

"Where is she going?" Iris asked, joining Ned in watching the coffee brew.

"Back to Montana. I need to deploy with my team, and I don't want her by herself in San Diego."

"You're deploying?" Fraser said. "I thought you were still on medical leave."

"I am, but they're looking for...you know."

"Ah, right," Fraser said.

"No SEAL secrets here," their mother said, then she turned to Shae. "Stay here," she said, adding pancakes to the pile. She looked over at Shae and smiled, so much warmth in it.

Iris's stomach twisted. She hadn't realized how much she missed this chaos, this home.

This safety.

Imani had come to sit next to Creed at the island, and Shae slid onto a stool next to them.

"Maybe," she said in response to their mother's invitation. She drew the arms of her sweatshirt down over her hands. She seemed a little fragile this morning, circles under her eyes. Maybe it had something to do with Ned's deployment.

The front door opened, and into the entryway walked a woman Shae had never seen before. She acted like it was normal to just take off her jacket and her shoes, pull off her wool hat.

Take a weapon out of a holster and set it on the bench.

Iris couldn't take her eyes off the 9mm.

"Hey, Pip, all okay?" Fraser said.

The woman was gorgeous. Dark, almost black sable hair that she wore in a tight ponytail, tall and fit, a sort of no-nonsense air about her as she walked over to the line by the coffee pot. "I don't remember the last time it snowed in Lauchtenland. I love the crunch. And the fact that you can see footprints—or the lack thereof." She turned to Iris. "Hi. I'm Pippa. We stayed at your place in Lake Como. Thanks." She held out her hand.

Oh. Iris shook it. The woman's British accent sealed the name recognition. "Nice to meet you."

"You remodeled it yourself?" Pippa walked over to the pile of clean dishes and grabbed a mug as Ned retrieved the full pot.

Iris held out her own mug, and Ned filled it, then Pippa's, and finally his own. "Yeah. A little bit at a time."

"Brilliant," Pippa said, then walked over to the island and sat on the stool. "So, what's this I hear about someone trying to kill you?"

And with that, the entire room shut down. Her mother drew in a breath. Fraser's jaw tightened, Ned quietly set the pot of coffee back, nearly empty now. Iris looked over, her mouth tight, and Imani set a couple extra plates on the island.

"What? That's why she came home, right?" Pippa took a sip of coffee, then made a face. "Oh, how I miss tea."

"Yes," said a voice on the other side of the dining room, from the hallway leading to the guest room. "She came home because someone is trying to kill her. And nearly succeeded."

"No one nearly succeeded, Hud." He'd showered, his dark-blond hair still glistening, and wore the slightest five-o'clock shadow. His frame filled up the doorway, and she hadn't realized, really, how much bigger he was than her brothers, who had always sort of loomed over anyone in the room. But Hud had a presence that could hold its own with them any day. Even without the heroic monikers.

"Please stop living in denial, Iris," Hud said and walked through the dining room into the kitchen. He looked at Ned, then, "Did you tell Fraser?"

All eyes went to Ned. He shook his head.

Right, because they'd been too busy gossiping about her and Hud. Her mouth tightened. Oh, this would be fantastic.

Fraser turned off the water. "Tell me what?"

Maybe she was in denial, because she sort of wanted to put her hands over her ears.

"We found the guy who tackled Iris dead, gunshot to his head, in his flat," Ned said.

Fraser held up a hand. "Start with *who tackled Iris*." He looked at her. "You were tackled?"

"Not just tackled. Destroyed. Blown up. She left her feet and flew about ten yards," Hud said and walked over to her.

Oy. No wonder she hurt.

Hud looked down at her. "She should have never been officiating that game."

"Whoa, step back there, dude. That's my job. And frankly, we don't know that the hit had anything to do with—"

"Someone is trying to kill you, Iris?" Her mother's soft voice broke through her words.

Oh. "Um..."

And right then, her father walked into the house. "Jenny, it smells amazing in here. What's for breakfast?"

Her mother looked at him, and even Iris wanted to recoil. "Apparently, secrets and lies." She tossed her towel down. "Starting with you. Did you know that someone tried to *kill* Iris?"

"Iris?" He looked at his daughter. "When did you get here?"

"Last night," she said quietly.

"Yes, Iris. Our daughter Iris. Who you told me was just fine and that I should stop worrying." She finger-quoted much of that.

Her father swallowed, took a step toward her mother.

She held up her hands. "Don't." Then she turned to Iris, her boys, and even Hudson. "I am tired of you all keeping secrets from me under the guise of protecting me. I pray for every single one of you every single day, and I have the right to know what is happening to my children. And the people they love." She looked at Shae then, who nodded, eyes wide.

"Isn't it enough that Jonas was nearly nuked, and that Fraser nearly had his hand blown off, never mind Creed's broken leg, and then Shae, poor Shae, got kidnapped? And brought to Russia somewhere?"

"Gulag. I was in a gulag," Shae said.

Jenny looked at her. "Of course you were. Anyone else? Maybe, I dunno, Ned, are you being chased by the mob?"

"Not currently," Ned said. Iris wanted to hit him.

"And how about you, Garrett? I mean, you kill anybody lately?"

"JJ, calm down."

"Mom. Just, take a breath." Fraser, and as the oldest, he might be the bravest. "Even I don't know what's going on with Iris."

"Great. Blow it back on me. Listen, I'm not hiding anything. I don't know what is happening!"

"Well then, let's figure it out," said her dad. "Maybe that's why we're all back in the same room."

A siren started to blare, and her mother turned back to the stove to see smoke pouring from the bottom of her scorched batch of pancakes. She scooped them up and dropped them into the sink.

Ned grabbed a towel and started waving it over the fire alarm, but it blared, undaunted.

Finally, Hud reached up and simply disconnected it.

"Show off," Ned said.

But her mother stood at the sink, staring at her burned

pancakes. "That's...enough. Everybody sit down. We're going to pray, and then we're going to eat. And then we're going to talk."

Silence, and then everyone headed for the table.

"Do those pancakes have blueberries in them?" Hud said as he sat down next to Iris. "Yum."

She shot him a look.

"What? I'm starved."

Her mom set bacon down in front of him. "Thanks, Mrs. M."

Her father made them hold hands—a tactic he'd used when they were young—but having Hud's hand in hers seemed somehow fortifying.

An hour later, Hud had finished the retelling of the events—much of what he'd told her dad and entourage when they showed up in Paris, but now Fraser and Pippa, Creed and Imani listened, rapt, especially when Hud got to the part about the boat and then the night in the cave—which he glossed over—and then the death of Abe Bartmann.

"I should have never left you guys in Paris," he said, which was interesting. "And then Ziggy called me in Germany and told me that yes, Abe's death was an assassination, and that someone was still stalking Iris."

"And you let her go out on the field?" Fraser said. And for a second, it looked like he might come over the table.

"I tried to stop her, but—"

"Fraser. I'm a grown woman. I can take care of myself."

"Clearly not!" Ned said, and now Hud put up his hand, because *she* was going to go over the table.

"Yes, she can. And maybe we're wrong about Vogel. But it just seemed so coincidental when we found him dead in his flat."

"How dead?" Fraser asked.

"All the way." Hud.

"Gunshot to the head." Ned. "We got out of there with his phone though." Ned got up from the table and went out to the entryway. In a second, he returned with the phone. "It died on the way here, but it's an Android. And I'm hoping Coco can get in it."

"I'll call Coco after breakfast," Fraser said.

"Where are you at with the blueprints and itinerary we found at the train station?" Ned asked.

"What blueprints?" Hud looked at her.

"Long story, but they were things I dropped off a month ago—my first courier assignment."

"First?" her mother said. Frankly, she'd been quiet during all of Hud's story, her food largely untouched.

"And last, Mom."

"Whatever possessed—"

"Really? Look around this table, Mom. My entire life, my brothers have been the tough guys, the heroes, the protectors, and I've been...the girl. The one who needed protecting. And maybe I just wanted to prove that I could do cool things too."

"Are you kidding me?" Imani said. "You're a professional football official. That is wicked cool."

Pippa held up her hand. "You ref football?"

"American football."

"Oh. Blimey."

Iris didn't know why, but Pippa's look of esteem went right to her bones. Still. "Listen. I realized as soon as I did it that it was stupid. I don't want to be a spy. I like my life. I don't need to change it. I don't need more."

"It hurts, doesn't it?"

Jonas, quietly, across the table.

"What hurts?"

"Your ribs. You've been holding your arm around yourself for the past ten minutes."

Oh. "Yeah."

"I know. I broke a rib once chasing a storm." Jonas leaned forward. "Everybody take a breath. Let's think. Where are the blueprints?"

"I have them in the office," Fraser said. He got up and disappeared into the office.

"Let's clear the table," Imani said, and stood up. Creed pushed back his chair.

"Sit, son," her father said, and also got up.

They piled the dishes on the island, then cleared the space for the papers that Fraser retrieved. He laid them on the table. "Sorry. I scanned these in and sent them to Coco, but I haven't done much with them since you got home."

Pippa had stood up, was looking over the blueprints. "It's a futbol pitch."

"That's what we thought," Jonas said.

Imani picked up the itinerary.

"Reminds me of the old Wembley field in London," Pippa said.

"That's what I said," her father said.

"You know, when Lauchtenland built Titus Stadium, they fashioned it after this historical Wembley design." Pippa pointed to a box at center field. "But this...this is distinctive. It almost looks like the royal—"

"This is my parents' itinerary," Imani said. "More accurately, the travel schedule of Prince John. My mom has a couple of other events not on this itinerary." She looked at Iris. "Where did you get this?"

"An envelope in my mail, no postage. Then a call from a man who identified himself as CIA—"

"Alan Martin," Fraser said. "Ziggy is pretty sure it's him, at least."

"Yeah. So, I dropped it off coming home from a game—right after I saw you guys in Switzerland, actually."

"So, who was supposed to pick it up?"

Silence.

"This is Titus Stadium," said Pippa. "I'm sure of it."

"I was there a month ago," said Shae. "I can't believe I didn't recognize it." She now stood up. "Yeah. They've done some remodeling though. This section here has been removed for a jumbotron. And there's another box over here for the heads of state." She indicated across from the royal box, on the other side of the field. "I took pictures of it for an upcoming advertising blitz for some event."

"The NFL-ELF matchup?" Hudson said. He looked at Iris. "That's where it is, right?"

"Yes." She looked at Pippa. "Is there any other big event coming up there?"

"Maybe a concert? But futbol is just finishing. I think they had their last match a week ago."

"Is your crew scheduled to officiate the game?" Jonas asked quietly.

Iris nodded.

Her mother got up, went to the coffee machine, and returned with the refilled pot. Started to fill mugs. "Imani, are your parents going to the game?"

Imani looked at the itinerary. "I think so. It's a few weeks away?"

"Yes," Iris said, to Hud's echo.

"Then it's the last event on this schedule." She set down the paper, her finger on the date.

"Whoever is killing the officials, do you think maybe they're hoping to shut down the game? Could be the RECO people. They couldn't kill Imani, so they're going after the game?"

"What do you mean, kill Imani?"

"There was man named Konrad Vogel who was killed after an attempt on Imani's life."

"He's the guy who shot me," Creed said. "Fraser took him out."

"Actually, Pippa shot him," Fraser said.

"Vogel," Hud said, then cast a look at Ned. "Werner Vogel was the player who took out Iris."

"He did not *take me out*."

"I was there. You were out, Iris," Hud said.

She held up a hand. "Okay, so back up. The guy who tackled me was related to the man who shot Creed?"

"Maybe," Pippa said. "I'll ask Gunner, the head of our security. He's still trying to piece together the shooting. His brother, Fredrik, is a RECOist, so maybe they can get information out of him."

"What is RECO?"

"It's the anti-monarchy group in Lauchtenland," Fraser said.

"Hamish Fickle, is an MP aligned with the RECO Party and is our liaison to the delegates of the North Sea Coalition. The RECO party is pushing the country to join with the hopes that by doing so they'll get the protection of Great Britain, the US, and eventually NATO through other various connected treaties."

"I don't understand," their mother said. She'd sat back down, holding her cup with her hands. Iris might have been imagining it, but it seemed like her mother's hands trembled a little. Well, Iris was trembling on the inside, so maybe that was fair.

"Konrad Vogel was the son of the man who killed my father," Pippa said. "My father died protecting the Crown from the RECO faction. They thought that by bringing terror into the country, it would make the monarchy back down. Now they're hoping that they'll look for help."

"What does all this have to do with Prince John?" Imani asked.

"What if the whole thing is a way to get an assassin into the game?" Creed said. "You know, access to the prince."

He'd been so quiet Iris had sort of forgotten he was there.

"What if he's the target? They already failed trying to kill Imani. Maybe this was plan B. Only Konrad never picked up the information because, you know, Fraser took him out."

"Please. Stop saying that."

Creed lifted a shoulder. Sat back, grinning.

The guy had a little hero worship going for his big brother.

"That's not bad, Creed," Jonas said. "It accounts for why the drop was never picked up, and also why a hit went out on Iris.

And when she disappeared with Hudson, why Abe was next in line." He looked at Iris. "Did you get a replacement ref?"

"Yeah. Roque Franco, from Spain. But I know him—officiated with him a couple times. He's a swing official—he's not an assassin."

"I wouldn't have thought Vogel was either," Hud said.

"He didn't try and murder me."

Hud eyed her.

"Fine. But who murdered *him*?"

"He committed suicide," Hud said.

"Did he?" Iris slid her gaze to Ned. "Is that the working theory?"

"No," Ned said. "His computer was taken."

"And we're back to the phone," Fraser said. He got up. "I'll get this phone to Coco. Pippa, in the meantime, let Gunner in on what we know. Maybe he can lean on Fredrik and squeeze RECO's plan out of him."

Pippa got up from the table. As did Iris. "I need to call Yannick and see if Abe's autopsy report came back."

"You can tell him that you're not officiating in the game too," Fraser said.

She stilled. Looked at Fraser. "Seriously?"

"Seriously."

"No. You don't get to tell me how to live my life."

"Great. And we're right back to that, are we? You, diving in without looking, about to get yourself in over your head. Again."

She blinked at him. "Seriously? You're talking about something that happened twenty years ago?"

"If Jonas and I hadn't been there—"

"I never asked you to be there!"

"And you shouldn't try to be tougher than you are!"

Everyone had stilled.

Fraser's jaw tightened. He looked at Iris. "Your pride is going to get you killed. And maybe people you love too." Then he scooped up the papers.

Iris opened her mouth. But Fraser turned to her, something terrible on his face. "I get it, you know? I get not wanting to ask for help. Believe me. But the fact is, it's just fear behind all that pride. And it'll make you forfeit the grace that could be yours. Be smarter than that."

Then he stalked through the kitchen toward the office.

Pippa followed him.

Iris stood there for just a moment. Then she pushed away from the table, walked to the entry way, pulled on a jacket, shoved her feet into boots, and stormed outside.

Ready to run away from home.

So, THAT MIGHT HAVE BEEN THE MOST EXCITING family breakfast he'd ever attended.

Hudson pushed away from the table, stood. Looked at Iris's parents, nodded. "So, thank you for breakfast. I think maybe I should—"

"Go," her father said. "By the way, we're not always this lively."

"I'd be disappointed if you weren't. I just have my brother and my parents. My dad is a cowboy, and the most he says at dinner is *pass the potatoes*, so this was...well, at least we know Fraser cares."

Garrett gave him a half smile. "Yes, he does. I'm not sure what's going on between you two, but thanks for watching over our daughter, Hud. I truly believe that God put you exactly where you needed to be, at the right time to help keep her safe."

Oh. Well, maybe. Because given the theories at the table, maybe he wasn't to blame for the assassination attempt.

And they'd kept each other alive in the cave, so maybe.

But, "I don't know, Garrett. God hasn't exactly been present in my life, so—"

"God has always been present in your life, Hudson. You just

don't realize that he's in every breath you take, every beat of your heart. He is ground under your feet and the air you breathe. And most of all, he's the one that put the love for our daughter in your heart."

He didn't bother to deny the last. Instead, he got up. Pointed at the door.

Garrett nodded and Hud headed to the entryway, grabbed his jacket and shoes—no boots for him—and headed outside.

Cool air, crisp and quiet with the falling snow. He liked it here—reminded him in a way of Montana. The sky hung low and gray, the trees dusted with white. Tracks led to the big red barn with the words *Marshall Fields Winery*.

He followed them and found the big glass door to the building unlocked. He let himself in.

The smell of must swept over him, a little heady as he stepped onto the cement floor. The place held a number of large stainless steel tanks to one side and rows and rows of oak barrels on racks on the other. At one end, hoses ran from smaller stainless steel tanks, and a forklift sat, quiet, in the middle of the room.

"Iris?"

His voice lifted, but the vastness of the room swallowed it. He looked down and realized that her wet boots had tracked in moisture. A little Gretel trail.

He found her in a separate room, sealed off from the main winery. It held a long wooden table surrounded by leather-backed chairs, and on the wall, pictures of her family, of the winery, the accomplishments of the Marshall family. Iris stood, arms folded, looking at the wall.

"This is quite the place," he said.

"My grandfather started it. Actually, he grew corn and started with a small patch of vines. Used to make his own wine. Dad was into computer programming, but when Grandma got sick, he came home and started farming. It was his idea to start the first rows of vines. The rest is history. He loves the winery. I actually think he sings to the vines."

"My dad sings to his horse."

She looked at him.

"He's a day-laborer cowboy for a ranch in Montana. We actually used to have a cattle station in the outback. It had been in the family for generations, and then my dad took it over and, well, it was tough. He's a good man. Hard worker. But he wasn't cut out to be a rancher, and then my mom got sick, and it drained everything they had. He just sort of quit life, and we moved to Melbourne and stayed for months with my mother while she went in for treatment. He lost the station. When she went into remission, we moved to America. I was ten. I missed the cattle station and hated everything, and then I found football. It just felt good to belong to a team, and I was good at it, so..." He shrugged. "I put everything I had into it. Everything I have. It's all I am." He looked at her. "Sorry. I came out here to talk about you."

"I'm sorry about your mom. And for the crazy that happened in there." She looked away. "Fraser's right, you know."

Not what he'd expected to hear, honestly.

She pointed to a picture, the color faded, of the family together, dressed in swimsuits, all of them young and grinning. "This is a picture of when we went rafting down a river near us. It's a little dangerous, and we all tied our tubes together. Mine was in the middle. I kept trying to untie, to go down alone, but Fraser and Jonas wouldn't let me."

"They're older than you?"

"Jonas is a year older. And Fraser is a thousand years older. I used to call him the junior parent."

He smiled at that. "What was he talking about in there?"

"It's stupid." She shook her head. "But he's right. I was stupid." She sighed. "There was this bully beating up Ned, and I was so mad at Jonas and Fraser because they made Ned stand up to him, and Ned got his backside handed to him—well, not really. He got a few licks in, but...I was so angry that I went and confronted the kid. And he...he didn't care that I was a girl, and we got into a wicked fight."

"Please tell me you won."

"Technically? But I was in way over my head. He had me down and had picked up this rock, and I have no doubt he would have used it to do some permanent damage—and that's when Fraser showed up. It was after school, but we'd drawn a crowd, and when I didn't show up for the bus, Fraser got off, along with Jonas, and they came looking for me. They both stepped in, saved me from...well, I don't know. But I was pretty mad. And they were pretty mad. And that's when Fraser told me that girls didn't do things like that."

"Oh no."

"Yeah. I'm pretty sure you can draw a direct line from that to my goal of officiating. But he's not wrong. I am afraid."

"Of what?" he said softly.

She took a breath. "I don't like asking people for help."

"Why?"

She looked at him. Then away.

"Iris?"

"Oh, Hud, there's so much you don't know about me. And I..." She looked at him. "I don't want to wreck your career."

He stilled. And it was right there—*you already did*. But he hadn't thought that about her for a couple weeks, so why suddenly now? So, instead, "What do you mean? You're not going to wreck my career."

She looked away. "I already did, once."

He stilled. What? "Iris, that wasn't your fault."

Her eyes rounded. "You know about it?"

He frowned.

"Shoot. Of course you do. Do all the guys know? Oh, I'm such an idiot. I—"

Do all the guys know? Yes, and about sixty-thousand fans, so, "Maybe we're talking about two different things. Whose career did you wreck?"

She froze. "Darren Pike. He played quarterback for the—"

"Bobcats. Montana State. Went to the Senior Bowl. He was

about three years older than me, but wow, he could throw a football."

"He loved to throw the ball away under a blitz. Lots of intentional grounding, and he knew it."

"I sort of remember that."

"They had a playoff game with SDSU to play in a bowl game—the Celebration Bowl. They were in the end zone after a terrible punt, and Pike scrambled, fell, and eventually threw it away. I was playing ump back then, and I ruled it intentional grounding. Since they were in the end zone."

"Safety."

"They lost that game by two points."

"And that's your fault?"

She blew out a breath. "Pike and I...had..." She looked away. "Pike was from Minnesota. Grew up in Litchfield, a small town near me, and we dated."

"Seriously?"

"When he went to Montana State, I followed him out there. I thought we'd be together forever, you know? But then I asked him to ask the coach if I could start officiating, like I did in high school, and...the coach let me work practices. I decided to major in sports health and started officiating everywhere I could. A lot of Pop Warner games. High school, middle school. The coach liked me and recommended me, and pretty soon I was officiating D-3 and D-2 games."

She ran her hands down her face. "We eventually broke it off, but then I started officiating in the NCAA, and he was a red-shirted senior, so yes, we were on the field at the same time. In an earlier game that year, I'd called intentional grounding. It got him benched, and he was mad."

Hud's gut had started to churn. "And?"

"He said I owed him, I said I didn't, and then he did something...bad."

He stilled.

"He replaced the peephole in my hotel room with a camera and took pictures of me. Without...without clothes."

He turned away, his fists tight.

"And put it on the internet."

He closed his eyes.

"One of the players forwarded it to me. Sort of as a gag, you know, to scare me, maybe. But I was angry, and the next game, I went in looking for penalties."

"And intentional grounding is one of those subjective penalties."

"Yes. After the game, he came after me. We had a loud and angry fight outside the locker room. He accused me of bias and using him."

"It's illegal to come after an official."

"Yes. He was told to stay away from me, and I got a restraining order. Only problem was, I was officiating at the All-Star game, and he was invited."

"And then not invited?"

"Yes. And there went his shot as a draft pick. Last I heard, he was coaching for a college team. But I always felt bad because, you know, maybe...I don't know. Did I cost him his career? Was I that angry?" She drew in a breath. "I hope not. But I realized that I had as much at stake as he did. If he'd proved that I was compromised...there's no way I'd have officiated anywhere again."

She looked at him. "We shouldn't..." She gestured between them. "I mean, I know we had that kiss, and it was—"

"Incredible." He'd taken a step toward her, but now stopped. "Iris. You're not going to cost me my career. Frankly, I'm not even sure I should have a career." He touched his head. "One more bad hit..."

"I should know this, but what happened after college? I know you played arena ball—you didn't get picked up in the draft?"

He looked at her. And he hadn't been sure until this very moment that she didn't know. And it made it that much easier, then, to skim over the truth. "I was hit by a cornerback in a game. Helmet to helmet. Got a concussion, was in a coma, had a TBI."

"What? You're right you shouldn't be playing. Seriously. Who hit you? I hope they were ejected."

"Yeah. But they should have been ejected sooner—it wasn't the first time."

"Oh, Hud, I'm so sorry. We do our best, but we can miss things. I'm sorry I wasn't there. I would have seen it and ejected the guy."

He swallowed, managed a smile.

She stepped closer to him, touched his temple. "That's why you said yes to Ziggy. You needed a backup plan."

"Which I'm going to decline. I'm just a football player, not some sort of international hero."

"With that accent, you can totally pass for an international hero."

He laughed, caught her hand. So maybe she never needed to know, right? He closed the gap between them. "Iris. I'm not going to take advantage of you or hurt you. I'm not going to cost you your career. And you're not going to cost me mine. But"—he touched her face—"I don't want to lose you. Fact is, you're the first woman who's made me think of something besides football for years. You get me outside my head, and I like it."

He put his other hand on her face, cradling it. "I like you."

"I'm not sure why."

Oh, Iris. "Because you're beautiful and strong and smart, and you make me see myself as more than I am. And I'd like a go at helping you see that too." He bent down—

"Hold up there, buck." She put her hand on his chest. "We're on camera, you know. My brother has everything wired."

"I've spent most of my life on camera, honey." And then he kissed her.

If he thought the first time, when he'd been desperate and scared and over his head, had been amazing, this time the kiss lit a terrible fire inside him. She tasted of coffee, sweet syrup, and when she grabbed his shirt to hold him, he picked her up and set her on the table.

She was a little higher then and put her arms around his neck, and he bent down, hands on either side of her, braced them on the table and kissed her with everything he had inside him.

He didn't know what it was. Yeah, she was tough, but the mystery of Iris was that she was also *not* tough. Yeah, she could hold her own, but she also sort of needed him, and it was those tiny revelations that made him hungry for more.

Out of everyone in the world, she chose to need *him*.

To want *him*. At least, judging by the way she clung to him, the way she let him nudge open her mouth, let him deepen their kiss. He finally put his arms around her, pulled her tight to himself, and lifted her off the table, back to the ground. She stood on tiptoes, her arms clinging to his neck as he drew away.

"Probably enough of a show for your brother, I think."

"They're probably gathered around the screen, eating popcorn."

"Oh, that's creepy."

She laughed, but then grew solemn. "Hud, what do we do when—"

His phone rang in his pocket, and he frowned, then fished it out. Answered it. "Waylen?"

"Hudson! Please tell me you're in America."

How did he know these things? "Yes, actually. Minnesota."

"How-dy. Perfect. You know a guy named Gripe Carlson? Coach for the Seattle Kraken?"

He closed his eyes. "Yes."

"Well, Gripe will be in town for a USFL conference, and they're inviting some prospective players and other personnel to the event."

"In town—where in town?"

"You'll have to get on a plane—it's in Miami."

"Hold please." He put his hand over the phone. "Do I want to play football for the Seattle Kraken?"

"The who?"

Right. And even as he looked at her, he heard his own words. *You get me outside my head, and I like it.*

"Hey, Waylen? I think I'm going to pass. I have a job, and I like it." He looked at Iris. "And I'm not going anywhere."

Then he hung up. Pocketed his phone. "Where were we? Oh yeah. You were *not* going to run away. And I was going to hang around, and we were going to let your off-the-hook brothers figure out how to keep you safe while we do this."

"Do what?"

He bent down and whispered into her ear. "Keep you out of trouble."

"Give it a try if you can, big guy."

"Here's to trying." Then he kissed her again.

NINE

Two days of snow, three movies, popcorn, an endless game of Catan, homemade pizza, and a Saturday afternoon of Iris yelling at the television, calling penalties of various college football games, and Hud felt like he might be a legitimate Marshall. Especially when he and Fraser made a run out to the store in the late afternoon for jalapeños so his mother could make poppers.

Fraser had apologized for the fight with Iris, which Hudson had mostly forgotten—or rather, wanted to thank Fraser for not letting her get pummeled so many years ago. Which felt like a weird betrayal to Iris, so he said nothing.

But he got it.

"Any luck with the phone?" Hud asked.

"I dropped it off at Coco's place yesterday, so she's working on it," Fraser had said.

"And who is Coco?"

"Our cousin and hacker—or rather, the hacker that works for the Caleb Group. It's who Ziggy works for, and Roy, who you met in Paris."

He remembered Roy. Tall, dark, a bit of a black-ops feel about the guy.

"She's the one who pinged Iris's phone in Paris, got us into GPS distance. She's married to my cousin, Wyatt, and they have a little boy. He had leukemia, but he's in remission. Wyatt plays goalie for the Minnesota Blue Ox, so they moved to Minneapolis after his treatment."

"I'd like to know who is behind all this," Hudson said. "But really, I just want Iris to be safe."

"You and me both," Fraser said and gave him a smile.

Sort of reminded him, right then, of Harry, his older brother. Who he should call, probably. He hadn't talked to him since before the craziness with Iris.

In fact, being with the Marshalls made him miss Harry a little. The brothers had a camaraderie that reminded him of the days back on the station, when he and Harry rode horses and helped their father with the cattle. Back then, he'd had small, perfect dreams that included his own family running the station.

Funny how life could blow apart those dreams.

They bought every jalapeño in the two grocery stores in the town of Chester and brought them back in time for the University of Minnesota Golden Gophers night game.

The sun had settled over the trees, and outside, Garrett was in the vineyard. From the den, sounds of laughter drifted, along with gaming shots and explosions.

Jonas had gone to the airport to pick up his girlfriend, and Pippa sat in the office, monitoring the cameras.

Iris was on her feet, staring at the television.

"What's up?"

"Snap infraction. The Ohio State center dropped the ball on the snap, and it rolled and Penn State jumped on it. Except the officials ruled that it wasn't a real snap, so it wasn't a turnover but a penalty. They keep replaying it, and I agree with the officials. It needs to be an actual snap, which means it needs to be passed to the QB. And if it's not a legal snap, then it's not in play. Good call."

She picked up the pillow she'd thrown on the floor.

"You can't sit with her in a live game," said Jenny from the kitchen, washing the peppers. "She'll yell penalties from the stands."

"I still think Jonas made it over the goal line in the conference championship." She looked at Hud. "Terrible call."

He laughed. "What's your dad doing?"

She glanced out the window. "Pruning the spurs."

Interesting. He grabbed his jacket and headed outside, pulling on a wool hat as he went. The Marshalls had loaned him a pair of boots from their massive supply, and now he left prints in the yard as he crunched through the snow.

Garrett stood in the vineyard, standing above a plant, inspecting thick branches off the vine that extended like ropy arms along a guide wire between the trunks of the vine. He wore his glasses down on his nose, his breath puffing out in the chill. He held a small pruner in his gloved hand and looked over at the sound of Hud's crunching. "Hudson."

"Sir. Can I help?"

He pushed his glasses up. "I wish, but this is the job of the viticulturist. I have to find the healthiest canes and then prune the canes back to two buds at the base. I try and select upward-facing buds. And then I prune off all other growth. That way, only the healthiest canes survive to produce fruit."

"We used to do that with cattle. Dad would pick the best heifers and keep those, sell the rest."

"Your dad was a cattleman?"

"He ran my grandfather's station for a while. He lost it when my mom got sick. Cancer."

Garrett raised an eyebrow, then sighed. "Yes. We had a scare too."

"Jenny?"

"Breast cancer. Rough fight, but she won."

"You said something—"

"About God's presence in your life."

Hud stuck his hand in his pockets as Garrett went back to

pruning. "Actually, I was thinking about your daughter, and, yeah, I think I'm in love with her."

"Well, when you get past *in love* and are settled on just *love*, let me know."

Hudson frowned. "Yeah, okay."

Garrett nodded but kept pruning.

"What you said about God putting me in the right place at the right time—you really believe that?"

"That God has us all in his hand, yep."

"Even though your wife had cancer?" He hadn't expected to say that, but maybe Garrett could help him untangle the knot inside him.

The one that didn't understand why God had let them lose everything, let his mom suffer.

"Yes, Hudson." He dropped a spur to the ground. "I know without a doubt that we are rooted in his love for us."

"Cancer doesn't feel like love."

"No, it doesn't, because cancer is a product of sin. It's evil and part of the fallen bodies we live in. It's the destruction of the cells of our bodies. Satan comes to kill, steal, and destroy, but Jesus says He has come so that we might have life, and have it to the full."

"How do you do that when...life feels so fragile?"

Garrett dropped another dead spur to the ground. "You root deep in God's love. You know, without a doubt, that you are His, and no one can take you from Him."

"I don't even know what that looks like."

Another spur fell. "Did you know, Hudson, that the word *Yahweh* is the Jewish name for God? When Moses asked God what his name was, he said, what translates to Yh Wh. The Hebrew alphabet added the rest to give it intonation. But if you stop and say that, it sounds exactly like breathing. Yh. Wh. Out. In. The scriptures say that in Him we live and move and have our being. He is the very air in our lungs. You literally cannot breathe without saying His name. God is life. God loves you, He made you, and He keeps you breathing, even when people we love have cancer. And it's on this truth that you root your life."

He swallowed and looked at the house, and it seemed for a moment that his hand shook.

Then he sighed and turned back to the vine. "Without our rootstock, the vine dies. We die. Because life is fragile. But the rootstock of this vine"—he leaned down and put his hand around it, shook it a little—"is hearty and strong."

He handed Hud the clippers. Hud stared at them. "What are you doing?"

"Teaching you how to grow a strong vine."

Hudson stepped up to the vine, and Garrett leaned near him. "This main extension from the rootstock is called a cordon, and from the cordon, there are tiny growths, called spurs. From that grow our one-year-old canes. We're going to cut off most of the buds from this growth and leave only a couple. We don't count this little bud at the apex of the one-year-old growth, but count up a couple buds and cut there." He counted the buds that grew from the apex and then pointed to a space above it. "Cut it here."

"Just cut it?" Hud put the clippers around the branch.

"Go ahead."

Hud snipped it, and the rest of the cane fell. "It's so violent. And wasteful. I mean, what about those other buds? Won't they grow grapes?"

"Yes, but they'll be small and won't produce much fruit. It's a good metaphor for life. Less is more." He winked. "On to the next one."

He pointed to a spur with two canes. "In this case, you have two canes—we want to choose the healthier of the two."

"How do you know which one is healthier?"

"The one whose buds are closer to the cordon, or the main vine."

Hud cut the smaller cane. Then he found the two buds and cut the cane above them.

"That's it." Garrett picked up the longer clipper, the one he held on his belt, and lopped off a nub. "That's an old arm that never produced fruit."

"Gardening is a brutal business."

"Gardening, like football, is life, son." He patted Hudson on the shoulder. "Keep going." He tromped away.

"Where are you going?"

"To get another pair of clippers."

"Are you sure I'm ready?"

"Yep."

Hudson turned to the vine, found the next cane, counted, snipped.

Please, let him not be killing the vineyard.

But when Garrett returned, his clippers in hand, he inspected Hud's work and offered him a thumbs-up. Then he went to the next row and started pruning.

Hud thought he heard humming.

He finished the row, then picked up all the discarded canes. Dropped them in a wheelbarrow at the end of the row. He then went behind Garrett and picked up his discarded canes.

The sun had found its way between the trees, casting an ethereal glow upon the field as Garrett dropped his clippers and the lopper into the wheelbarrow. "I'll bet those jalapeño poppers are about done."

"That's all for today?"

"It's a lot of field. Take it one day at a time. By spring it'll be done. But I appreciate the help."

"Funny that the guys aren't out here."

"Yep." Garrett pushed the wheelbarrow toward the barn.

Hudson caught up to him. "I got that, sir."

Garrett looked at him, then set down the wheelbarrow. "Okay. I consent."

Hudson picked up the wheelbarrow as Garrett turned and headed to the house.

Consent to what?

"Don't forget to lock the barn when you come in."

Huh.

He emptied the canes, then left the wheelbarrow in the barn and headed inside.

Fraser stood at the open sliding door. "Get in here."

What? He picked up his pace, and Fraser shut the door behind him.

"What's going on?"

"There's a car driving up. Unknown."

"Are we worried?"

"We're always worried, Hud," Fraser said. "We're guarding the princess of Lauchtenland."

Right.

Okay. Because suddenly the house had turned into a black ops site, the television off, the family in the den, and Fraser and Pippa with their guns drawn.

He joined the family in the den. "So, this happens often?"

"Let's just say we don't order a lot of pizza delivery," Creed said. He and Imani had turned their video game volume off, but still directed their player around the screen.

Iris was watching the game on her phone. Seriously?

The doorbell rang, and their dog started to bark.

Jenny gathered the golden retriever up in her arms. "Shh."

"Are they going to shoot someone?"

"Probably not," Imani said. "Aw, I'm dead." She threw down her controller, looked at Creed.

"Sorry," he said, grinning.

She threw a pillow at him.

"Hudson! Get in here!"

Everyone stilled, and Hudson walked to the door, then the entryway.

A man stood in the entry, something familiar about him.

"Gripe Carlson. We met in Germany. At the Thunder dinner."

"Gripe. Wow. Uh..." Hud looked at Fraser, who gave him a look. "How did you find me?"

179

"Waylen. Who got your address from, ah, let's see, maybe your coach? I don't know. Anyway, I know what you said, or what Waylen said, but I thought maybe we could have a face-to-face, just talk it out. Could sure you use you on the team."

The rest of the family had come out to stand in the hallway. Oh, this was awkward. "Uh, Gripe, I—"

"Listen. Smells great in here—I'm actually on my way to Minneapolis. There's a dinner tomorrow night. Something casual with some of the team members and coaching staff in the area. Come to it. Let's talk there, okay?"

And what was he going to say? "Sure."

Gripe held out his hand again, and Hud shook it.

"Can't wait," Gripe said. He lifted a hand to the rest of them. "Enjoy the game."

The game? Oh. That's when he noticed Iris's maroon-and-gold sweatshirt.

Fraser closed the door after him. Turned to Hud, his expression tight. "So, who else knows where you and Iris are hiding?"

SHE COULD VERY EASILY LOVE THIS MAN.

The sense of it had crept over Iris the last few days, watching Hud join her family. Watching him laugh with her brothers, work with her father in the vineyard, play board games, shout at the television, and even help with the dishes.

Even earlier today, when they'd been in the heated garage, in the workout space Fraser had set up for himself and maybe Pippa.

She'd been doing a kettlebell routine, some lifts, swings, then simple bridges and squats when Hud came out.

He'd said nothing, just dropped onto the mat beside her and started doing pushups, plugged into his earbuds, she plugged into hers.

It'd felt easy and right and…oh, he *fit* into her life.

And she didn't know what to do with the swell of emotions. Or the fact that Fraser's words so many days ago wouldn't leave her alone. *It's just fear behind all that pride. It'll make you forfeit the grace that could be yours.*

She'd wanted to stiff-arm the words, the idea of her being afraid, but, well, the more Hud stuck around, the more her emotions started to churn.

Yes, she could love this man. And then where would that get her?

Especially when he'd asked her to attend the dinner with Gripe and the others from the USFL team. Never mind that the coach's appearance had completely freaked out her brothers.

The only reason she'd agreed to Fraser's lockdown was because the world had turned icy and cold. And tonight, she'd practically had to sneak out of the house, although Hudson had assured Fraser that he'd make sure she got home alive.

Like she might be thirteen years old.

"Fraser is driving me crazy," she said now as she got into Hud's rental car. She wore Uggs and a long wool coat over her black dress—the same one she'd worn to the dinner in Germany.

Hudson just looked over at her. He'd shaved, freshly showered, and smelled amazing.

So amazing that, "Are you sure you want me to go with you tonight?"

He'd already cleaned the ice off his windshield and now turned up the defrost. His breath hung in the air. "What? Yes, of course."

"Why? Are you seriously thinking of joining the USFL?" She didn't want to add anything to her voice that might betray an opinion.

Because if he did, gone was their conflict of interest. But he'd be in America, so maybe also gone was a chance at a future. But if he stayed in the ELF…

And maybe she was just getting ahead of herself, over her head once again. Although, he'd sneaked away more than a few times to kiss her. Once in the pantry, once in the den, and once when he'd gone outside to grab firewood, taking her with him.

Jonas had come out looking for them, so that had been embarrassing.

"No. I don't know. Maybe."

The sun hung low on the horizon, a golden simmer that cast fire upon the white fields. The drive into the city would take over an hour, but it was their first real getaway, something Hud had nearly forfeited when Fraser objected.

But he had contacted Coach Clay, who'd confirmed he'd gotten Iris's address from Yannick, her boss, and no he hadn't passed it along to anyone else. Iris had called Yannick and asked, and no, he too hadn't told anyone else.

So maybe it was a fluke.

Besides, if the goal was to eliminate officials, she was still listed on the injured list for the game next week. Yannick had suggested not replacing her and playing with a six-man lineup for the exhibition game. But they'd need the whole crew for the Lauchtenland game—a game she fully intended to officiate.

"I'm hearing rumors that the Vikings might not renew my contract and maybe I need to have some options," he said. "At first, I thought no. But when Gripe showed up, I thought...hear him out. Maybe. I dunno."

She glanced at him, the glow of the dash illuminating his handsome face, that distinct jawline. "What if one of the options was to...retire?"

He drew in a breath. Swallowed. "I've never thought beyond football. It's all I am, really."

"No, it's not. And maybe it's time to figure out what else there is."

He said nothing, his mouth a tight line. Then, quietly, "It just feels like a big leap into nothing. Without football, I'm not sure where I'd land."

She wanted to reach out, touch his hand, say something corny like, *Right here. You'll land right here.* But frankly...well, what if she wasn't enough?

The thought swept through her, and suddenly, tears burned her eyes.

What?

She looked out the window, took a breath.

"Iris? What was that sigh for?"

"I don't know. I just had this crazy memory. I was ten, and my mom was sick—going through chemo. She'd lost her hair, and I was really scared of her. I didn't like being around her, actually. It terrified me."

"Because you thought she would die?"

"Maybe."

"I get that." He looked at her. "I felt the same way when my mom was sick."

"Usually, she stayed in her bed upstairs, but this one day she wanted to come downstairs, and she asked me to help her. Just to steady her as she went downstairs. But I wasn't strong enough, because when she got to the last step, she tripped. And I couldn't catch her."

She pressed her fingers under her eyes. "She wasn't really hurt. But it scared me, and I ran out and got my dad, and he came in and picked her up. Brought her to the sofa and then..." Her hand pressed her mouth. "And then he just held her and started to cry. I'd never seen my dad cry, but he was just sitting there, holding on to her and crying, and she held him back, and I just stood there watching, horrified."

"And scared."

"Terrified. I even came over and tried to comfort my dad, but he just put out his hand, shooed me away, and I thought...I did this. I made my dad cry."

"You know that's not true, right? He was scared."

"Yeah. Now I do. Then, I thought...well, I needed to be stronger. And not weak. And if I do it right—"

"Then you won't be rejected."

Oh. "I was about to say then no one will get hurt, but...yeah, maybe." She looked away. They were entering the suburbs, houses with Christmas lights strung along their roofs, driveways shoveled. Neat and orderly. "I just...I don't want to get in the way of your future, Hud. So, if you want to play for the USFL, then... you should do it."

He went strangely quiet. Drew in a breath.

They drove the rest of the way in silence. He pulled up to the valet station at the Four Seasons in Minneapolis, and she put on her heels as he got out.

The valet opened her door, but Hud had come around to extend his hand. He met her eyes with a smile, but something seemed haunted in it.

"Hud? Is everything okay?"

He nodded, put his hand over hers as they went inside.

They walked to the concierge desk through the expansive lobby with the tall mirrored walls, golden light fixtures, leather sofas, orange accent chairs, the massive decorated Christmas tree rising from the center.

"Carlson event?" Hud asked, and the concierge directed them to the Mara Restaurant. The private area had been cordoned off with a thick orange velvet rope. A fire flickered in the massive copper fireplace, and a faux fir tree twinkled with white lights.

Mostly men in suits milled around the half dozen tables.

A man waved, and Hud slipped his hand into hers and headed toward him. "That's Gripe Carlson, coach for the Seattle Kraken." He then reached out his free hand and shook Coach Carlson's hand.

"This is Iris Marshall," he said to Carlson. "My girlfriend."

Iris froze. Wait—what?

But Hud seemed to slide right by that, continuing to hold her hand.

Okay. Yes. Maybe they were, maybe...

Just breathe.

"Glad to meet you, Iris," Carlson said. He didn't shake her hand, instead gestured to a waiter. "Would you like a drink?"

"Water."

The waiter came over with a glass of water infused with lime and she took it. Hud grabbed a frothy beer.

"Hud, you might recognize a couple guys here," Gripe said, and pointed to a couple men standing not far away. "I think you played with them at the University of Montana."

Hud waved to a man who looked over at him and grinned. Dark-skinned, big, he had a lineman look about him. "That's Duke Emory," he said to Iris. "Played center. And next to him, the big Irish-looking guy is Aiden McCowell, safety."

"They're our newest sign-ons," Coach Carlson said.

"Excuse me, Coach," Hud said and pulled her away. He walked over to the guys, hand outstretched. They greeted him with shoulder slaps and man-hugs. He introduced Iris to the men.

"You look so familiar," said Duke. "Have we met?"

"Iris was an NCAA official for a while," Hud said before she could wave him off. But maybe these men wouldn't know about the kerfuffle with Pike. Old news, really.

They'd all moved on in the four years since.

"You still officiating?" asked Aiden. Nice-looking man, blondish-red hair, cut close, green eyes.

"Not for the NCAA," she said.

"Hey, Hud." Coach Carlson came over. "Let me introduce you to our coaching staff." He gestured Hud over to a group of men.

"I'll be right back," Hud said. "You okay here?"

She nodded. She could talk football with the best of them.

"So, you're going to play for the USFL?" she asked Aiden. "Why?"

"I was tired of playing practice squad for the Browns," Aiden said. "I won't get as much money, but frankly, I just like playing."

"You look so familiar," Duke said.

"I might have officiated at one of your games. You played with Hudson, right?"

"Yes."

"I was on a crew who officiated in the Big Sky conference, and we worked your games."

"Wait—I remember you. You officiated in the game against the Bengels."

"Idaho State, the one where Hud got hurt?" Aiden said. He looked at Iris. "Yeah. You were the female official."

She stared at him. "Hud got hurt?"

"Yeah, concussion. You don't remember this?"

"It was college ball. A lot of players get hurt."

"He was carted off the field."

She stilled. "Wait." Like a fist, the memory punched her. "Targeting hit. That was Hud?" Shoot, he'd told her this story. Why hadn't she connected the dots? "I remember that. I called the hit. Ejected the player." But her stomach knotted.

Duke's mouth turned into a dark, solemn line. "You should have ejected him two plays earlier when he targeted one of our other players. But you missed it."

"What?"

"It's on the tape. The Idaho safety targeted the wideout just two plays before, dislocated his shoulder. He came off the field, and Hud went in for him."

A beat. Another. Everything hollowed out of her. She swallowed. "I...I missed a penalty?" And yes, that sounded just...lame.

"It's on the tape. Hud used it in his lawsuit against the NCAA and the player who targeted him. They settled out of court, and he's not allowed to talk about it, but yeah, that was definitely you on the field. If you hadn't missed the illegal hit..." He raised a shoulder.

Hud might be playing in the NFL.

She pressed a hand to her stomach, her gorge rising. "I cost him a year of his life."

"You cost him his entire life," Duke said, his eyes hard on her. Oh. No—

"Duke, c'mon. That's a little rough. She wasn't the one who targeted him—"

"The officials are there to keep us safe from hits—and players—like that," Duke said.

She set her glass down, her hands shaking. "He's right," she said softly. "I need...I need some air."

Aiden stepped back as she headed for the doors to the patio. But when she hit them, they were locked.

She turned, breathing hard.

And that's when, across the room, a voice rose, and then—

A man went down, scattering across tables, breaking glass, dishware shattering on the floor.

She stilled, her body ice as Hud stepped over the man, grabbed him up by the jacket.

A nearby man hooked his arm around Hud's raised fist.

Her mouth opened as Darren Pike scrambled to his feet, breathing hard. "You're going to figure out that she's not worth it. She'll betray you too, buddy. Cost you everything." He shook off Hud's hand, ran his hands down his suit.

Run. The thought pulsed, coalesced, and suddenly she was pushing through the groups of men, headed for the exit.

"Iris!"

But she ignored Hud and headed for the lobby.

He reached her just before she pushed through the circular doors.

"Let me go, Hud!" She shook away from his grip and stepped into the doors.

He stepped inside, then took one step and trapped them in the space.

"What are you doing?"

"What are *you* doing?" he practically shouted.

She stared at him, and all she could see was— "Did you know?"

He blinked at her. "That Darren Pike was going to be here? No. He's a coach—"

"No! That I was the official who—who caused your concussion. It was my miss that—it cost you everything, Hud, just like he said. *Everything.* Did you know?"

She wanted to let her legs give way, to crumple right there when he nodded.

Nodded.

"How long?"

"Since the beginning."

"Before Paris?"

"Yes."

"Before Prague."

"The whole time."

The. Whole. Time. Her breath shook. "How can you—"

"Iris. Take a breath. It's okay—"

"What is okay about me screwing up so badly that you—that you can't play football? I destroyed your life!"

"You didn't destroy my life."

She narrowed her eyes, her voice low. "Don't lie to me. I know what I did. And yet, here you are. What are you *doing*?"

"I thought you'd figured that out," he said, his voice also soft. "I'm in love with you, Iris. No—amend that. I love you, Iris."

She just blinked at him, her breaths rolling over each other.

Oh no. No. This was all her fault. She'd clung to him, needed him, and now...now she had cost him his future again. "You do know that probably the USFL won't want you now."

"Mm-hmm. But Darren Pike will probably think twice about calling you a name."

"I don't want to know."

"No, you don't."

Another couple had walked up, stared at the blocked doors. Hud gave them a look, and they pushed through the doors at the side.

He turned back to her. "Okay, so yes. For a long time, I was really angry with you. But so what you didn't catch the targeting call? You're not perfect. You don't have to always get it right—"

"Yes, I do. I'm an official. It's my job to get it right."

He reached out to touch her, but she stepped away.

"Iris," he said softly. "I'm not your dad, who is going to push you away when I'm hurt or scared."

Her eyes filled. "Just, take me home."

He just looked at her.

She folded her arms and looked away. Clenched her jaw to keep from crying.

Finally, he sighed. "Okay."

They drove home in silence, her hands folded on her lap. And it was crazy, she knew it, because the man didn't deserve it.

Didn't deserve *her* and her treatment of him. But she couldn't get past the terrible truth.

Loving her might cost him everything.

Hud picked up some McDonald's burgers for them on the way home, but she'd lost her appetite. When they got home, she went to her room, changed, and then came downstairs to make a sandwich. Instead, she stood in the bath of light from the fridge, trying to figure out why it bothered her so much.

He'd known. He'd known about it and never told her.

"Iris? You're home early." Fraser had come out of the office.

"Yep." She closed the fridge. Turned to him. Considered him. "Have you ever royally screwed up? Cost someone something that you have a hard time forgiving yourself for?"

He raised an eyebrow. "Of course. I wish I'd done a better job of protecting Dr. Hansen in Nigeria, for one."

"Does he blame you?"

"No. But I blame myself."

"And what do you do with that?"

"I guess I just try and not let it happen again. And realize I'm not perfect." He opened the fridge and pulled out a container of orange juice. "I suppose I also think that at the end of the day, it's going to happen the way God has planned, and I need to trust that He has my back. Dad told me once that God's design is for us to need help. We're not supposed to be infallible or invincible." He poured himself a glass of juice. "By the way, Coco got into Werner Vogel's phone." He put the juice back. "Apparently, he had confirmed the hit with the Orphans. He's your assassin."

"And he's dead," said Iris. "So it's over? I can go back to my life?"

"If that's what you want," Fraser said. "Probably."

"Good. Yes. That's exactly what I want." She picked up his glass of juice and took a drink.

But he was looking over her head, toward the dining room.

She turned.

Hud was standing there in a T-shirt and sweat pants.

Then he turned and headed back down the hall.

"Everything okay between you two?"

"Yep," she said. "Everything is exactly what it should be."

Then she walked to the sofa, lay down, and pulled the afghan over her head.

Because then no one, not even herself, could see her cry.

TEN

"So he walked out, just like that?"

The words, in accented Slovenian courtesy of Jonas's girlfriend Sibba, lifted from the kitchen, down the hall to her father's office where Iris was packing her bag. Not a big bag—she hadn't left Europe with much. But she had her stripes and footwear and gear, and she'd manage until she got back to Milan.

With a stopover in Amsterdam. Where she'd put this whole thing behind her and get back to her life.

Her excellent, interesting, tailored life that she'd worked so hard for.

One that didn't include Hudson Bly, thank you so much.

But yeah, he'd just walked out of her life, sometime early this morning, because when she'd gotten up, the sun pressing through the blinds of the office, breaking through the cloud cover, his rental car had been gone.

She'd walked into the kitchen, made coffee, and then, out of curiosity, walked down the hall to the guest room.

His door was open, the bed stripped, the sheets in a tumble on the floor, the blankets folded on a nearby chair.

She'd stood there blinking a long moment. Then pulled out

her phone and searched for flights. Booked herself on a one p.m. flight to Amsterdam, with a layover in LaGuardia.

Then she'd texted Yannick and told him she'd be on crew for the game.

To which he'd responded almost immediately, given it was afternoon in Prague, with a question mark and an emoji of a doctor.

She sent him back a gif of Batman offering a thumbs-up and went to pack. Her ribs felt fine-ish. Nothing some pain killers wouldn't solve. And she'd be extra careful.

Now, she toted her backpack to the kitchen and set it by the island.

Sibba sat drinking a cup of tea. Next to her sat Pippa, an eye on a tablet. Fraser had figured out how to cast the images from the security screens to a tablet he'd purchased, which made watching the screens that much more accessible.

Iris couldn't get past the notion that they'd all been freaked out by Gripe's ability to track them down. She'd heard conversations of sending Imani back to Lauchtenland sooner rather than later.

At least they'd figured out the plot to assassinate the royals, or at least Prince John—something Gunner Ferguson, head of security in Lauchtenland, had been conferring with Pippa on for the last few days. Apparently, they'd increased security to the stadium and installed bulletproof glass in the royals' box.

So, everybody needed to calm down and get back to their lives, which was exactly what Hud had been doing, probably.

"Where are you going?" The question came from her mother as she pulled fresh-baked apple muffins from the oven and dumped them onto a cooling rack. She used her hot pads to turn them over, the aroma of cinnamon and nutmeg nearly causing Iris to reach for one.

"I have a flight to Amsterdam that leaves in four hours," she said.

Silence around the kitchen, from Sibba, to Pippa, to her mother.

"Oh," her mother said. "I thought..." She turned back to the oven.

"Mom. I have a game. And a life..." Iris glanced at Pippa, who just lifted a shoulder. And Sibba made a face. The woman wore a pair of boyfriend jeans and an oversized sweatshirt, her long raven hair pulled back in a singular braid. She was smart, European, and exotic, and Iris could admit feeling a little off her mooring with the woman. But when Sibba had said she not only followed the ELF but knew a few of the teams, and then switched over to Italian, Iris decided Jonas had chosen well.

Jonas seemed downright undone by the woman and the fact that she had decided to stay in America. A couple days ago, she'd overheard Jonas talking with Fraser about her EOD skills and whether Fraser's super-elite protection team could use a bomb expert.

She just wanted to get back to her boring life, thank you.

One that, for a little while, she'd thought might include one very large wide receiver.

Perhaps she'd been hit harder than she thought, because she'd gotten way too used to seeing Hudson Bly sitting in the kitchen, eating her mother's cookies, or even helping her dad in the vineyard over the last week.

I'm not your dad, who is going to push you away when I'm hurt or scared.

No, apparently he was the breed that left in the middle of the night.

At least she waited until after breakfast. "Mom—"

"Let me at least make you an omelet." Her mother turned then, a smile back on her face. "Of course you need to leave, honey." She came up to her, pulled her into an embrace. "I just like having you around, is all."

Iris folded her arms around her mother's frame. She seemed

thinner, a little more fragile. And maybe she was imagining it, but in the light, her mother's skin seemed almost...*yellow*?

Jenny returned to the refrigerator and pulled out eggs, cheese, bacon. "Will you see Hudson in Amsterdam?"

She poured herself a cup of coffee from the station, then slid onto a stool. "I don't know what he's up to."

"Oh." Her mother set the eggs on the counter. "He went to Montana to visit his mom. He got a call from his brother last night, late, who said that he should come home."

She stilled. Her mother was cracking eggs into a bowl. "What?"

"He left early. I was on the sofa, and we chatted for a bit. He said to tell you goodbye—he didn't want to wake you. I sent cookies with him."

Of course she did. She sighed, though.

Her mother looked up. Blinked at her. Frowned. "Is there trouble between you two?"

"There's no *you two*, Mom. We're not a thing."

"Looked like a thing to me," Pippa said. "The way you laughed at his jokes."

"And the fierce Dutch Blitz competition going on the night I arrived," Sibba said. "I saw the way he looked at you when he let you win."

Her mouth opened. "He did not let me win."

Sibba folded her arms. "He totally let you win. He just stopped playing for a bit there, let you take over the game."

She sipped her coffee. "I was just so lightning fast he didn't know what to do."

Sibba held up her hands in surrender. "Just saying that he wore this silly smile, and when you won, he did too."

"I just liked knowing I could beat him at something. He's always so...capable."

"I felt the same way about Fraser when I met him," Pippa said. "Like we were competing or something. And then it sorta felt nice to let him, you know, step in sometimes. Maybe I didn't have to always be in control of everything."

"Yeah, well, that's my job. To be in control."

"Sounds tiring," said Sibba.

Iris frowned at her.

"Just saying that I get it—I have to be completely in control for my job. So being able to just sort of let go around Jonas is a gift. He's always two or three steps ahead of me anyway." She took a sip of her tea. "There's so much unknown with my job, having the certainty that I can trust him is...well, letting him love me has changed my life."

Oh. Next to her, Pippa nodded. "I'm always looking for trouble. It's nice to know that it's not all up to me."

Iris grabbed a muffin, now cool. "I'm all songs and roses for you guys and your happy endings, but it's not like that between Hud and me. I'm an official—he's a player. We can't be together without jeopardizing our jobs."

"What about this job with the USFL?" Her mom turned the bacon that now sizzled on the stove.

"Oh, I think that's pretty much...uh, not going to happen. Not after he punched Darren Pike at dinner last night." She broke open the muffin, the smell breaking out, soothing the churn in her stomach.

Her mother turned. "Really?" Then she smiled. "Oh, I knew I liked Hud."

"Mom."

"I should have given him more cookies."

Iris rolled her eyes.

Her mother scooped the bacon out of the pan and set it on a paper towel. Then she picked up the egg bowl. Looked at Iris. "You've spent your entire life memorizing rules, living your life by a plan. But your life, your rules, and your self-reliance are a prison, Iris."

"My life isn't a prison, Mom."

"It is if it keeps you from freedom. From living."

"I live."

Her mother turned and poured eggs into the hot pan.

"I have a great house and a life I like."

"Yes, you do," her mother said, turning. "But you choose the comfort of the known instead of the freedom of trusting God."

"I trust God."

"How? What in your life requires you to trust God?"

"I...listen, I went totally off-grid when I thought someone was after me."

"With Hudson."

"Yeah, with Hudson and...and..."

Silence.

"It was the best week of my life." She drew in a breath. "Okay, fine, yes, I thought maybe there was something between Hud and me, but..." Her eyes had started to burn. Maybe the smoke from the cast iron pan.

"But loving Hudson would mean letting go of that tough exterior, letting him in and receiving grace," said Pippa.

Iris looked at her.

"We feel ya," Sibba said. "But the best thing you can do in your life is swap captivity—your fear—for love. Let God be in charge of your heart, and He will surprise you."

And for a second, she was in the tasting room, Hudson's arms braced around her, hers in the scruff of his shirt, his whisper against her ear.

Because you're beautiful and strong and smart, and you make me see myself as more than I am. And I'd like a go at helping you see that too.

She closed her eyes. Saw Hudson's expression last night as he overheard her talking to Fraser. *I can go back to my life?*

No wonder he'd left. He wasn't the one doing the pushing away.

She opened her eyes. "I'm an idiot."

Sibba grinned at her. "Don't worry. If he wants you, he won't give up."

"I don't know. That's the second time I've let him walk away. But maybe I'll see him in Amsterdam. I can talk to him then—"

"You're going back to Europe?" The voice came from Shae, walking down the stairs, wearing yoga pants and a long-sleeve pullover, her blonde hair back in a low, messy bun. She held her new cell phone, the one she'd purchased when she dropped off Ned at the airport.

"I just figured out how to get email on this thing, and I have about two thousand messages," she said. "But one is from the advertising firm who hired me to take pictures of that Lauchtenland stadium."

"You took pictures of Titus Stadium?" Pippa said.

"Yeah, I told you that last week when we were looking at the blueprints. The firm wants me to take pictures of the Vienna Vikings for social media purposes, but I don't have my camera. The Petrov Bratva took it when they kidnapped me."

She said it with such nonchalance it shouldn't have silenced the room like it did, but it seemed that everyone always forgot that Shae had recently been kidnapped.

Or maybe not everyone. "You were kidnapped by the Russian mob?" Sibba said.

"Did Jonas not mention that?" Pippa said.

"Just that you were in Russia, but...wait. The Petrovs were the people who deployed a dirty bomb in my country a month ago. And who stole the caesium-137—"

"That Ned's SEAL team is trying to recover," Shae said.

Fraser had come out of the den and now stopped in the hallway. "I think that's classified."

From the stove, the omelet sizzled. Her mother added cheese, glancing at Fraser.

"Oh." Shae took a breath. "Yeah, you're right. Sorry."

Fraser walked over and grabbed the empty coffee pot.

"It's hard to keep anything classified in this family, Fraser," Iris said.

"What happened to the caesium?" Sibba said. "I thought they brought it to some secure location in Europe."

Silence. Fraser had filled the pot and now emptied it into the maker.

"Seriously?" Sibba said.

"Okay, let's just say that maybe there was a snafu with that plan." He added the coffee grounds, then set it to perk.

"So now it's on the loose?"

"Ned texted and said that they were in Germany. Ramstein Air Base," Shae said.

"So, they recovered the caesium?" Sibba said.

But Pippa was staring at Shae. "Were your pictures still on your camera?"

"Sure. I mean, I'd uploaded them, but they were on the SD card." She put down her phone and slid onto a stool. "I could use the money. They want to pay my way over to Amsterdam to hang out with the team."

Her mother flipped the omelet, then reached for a plate.

"Use your phone," said Sibba. "It's for social media, right?"

Shae nodded. "I could text Ned, ask him to meet me there."

"Pictures of Lauchtenland's Titus Stadium," Pippa said to Shae.

"Yes. Outside, inside, the land around it, the town. Hundreds."

"I'd feel better if Ned were there," Fraser said. "Just in case Iris gets into trouble."

"Hey! I can take care of myself!"

He raised an eyebrow. "And here we go again."

"Seriously, Fraser—"

And that's when, at the stove, her mother collapsed.

Just like that, she dropped to the floor, the pan still sizzling with eggs, fresh coffee brewing, the plate crashing to the floor, shattering.

"Mom!" Fraser yelled.

"Mom?" Iris said, sliding off the stool, following Fraser.

She lay on the floor, the shards of pottery around her, her eyes closed. Fraser pressed his fingers to her carotid artery. "Get Dad," he said.

Iris looked up, but Shae was already heading to the back door to shout out to their father, working in the vineyard.

Fraser picked his mother up, brought her over to the sofa. Set her down. "She's breathing."

But otherwise, her mother was limp, and suddenly, in the span of ten seconds...

Old. Frail.

Broken.

Iris couldn't breathe.

Her dad charged into the house, his boots covered in snow and mud. "Jenny?" He crouched next to her, pulled off his glove, touched his hand to her face. "Honey?"

Iris grabbed Fraser's hand as their mother blinked, slowly came to.

"Oh. I...what—"

"You fainted, Mom," Iris said, and didn't mean the accusation in her voice. Fraser squeezed her hand.

Jenny looked at her husband, then at Fraser, Iris. "I don't know what...I'm fine. Just fine."

"Like hell you are," her father said.

Fraser raised an eyebrow.

"Go warm up the car, son," her father said.

Fraser headed for the door.

Then her father leaned down and simply picked up their mother in his arms, afghan and all.

"Garrett—"

"That's enough, Jenny. Enough trying to be tough. You're going to the ER."

She sighed, then suddenly seemed to fold into her husband, as if tired. "Yes," she said softly. "It's time."

It's time?

Iris stood, frozen.

"Would someone please turn off the eggs?" her mother said as their father carried her out the door.

Maybe Hudson shouldn't have run. But Iris's words had sat in his brain all night—*Everything is exactly as it should be.*

Which was her going back to her life. Alone.

And he'd never felt so kicked in the gut as he had then.

Which was why, thirty-six hours later, he found himself perusing the late-afternoon lunch menu at the Gray Pony Bar and Grill outside Mercy Falls, waiting for his brother Harry, and maybe his parents, to walk through the doors.

The place oozed Western, with the barrel tables, the stage up front, and in the next room, a mechanical bull, a couple pool tables, darts. The sign outside boasted the best barbecue in western Montana, with live music every night.

Sure, he could have gone home, but frankly, he wasn't sure where that was right now. His parents lived in a fifth wheel and parked it close to his father's current gigs, so this seemed as good a place as any for him to check in.

"Can I get you anything besides water?" The cute waitress, with her amber-blonde hair, wearing a black Gray Pony T-shirt, low jeans and boots, the name Audrey on her name tag, set the water down on the table.

"Maybe some of those potato skins with the jalapeños and bacon?"

"You'll love them. Anyone joining you?" She reached for the silverware rolls to remove them, but he put his hand out.

"Yes, hopefully." He'd called Harry on his way through North Dakota yesterday, before he'd stopped in Billings last night for some shut-eye. Harry had said he'd reach out to their parents.

And no, Hud didn't know how long he'd be in town. Maybe

twenty-four hours, because his coach had texted him, wondering if he'd be at practice in Amsterdam in roughly forty hours.

Probably. Because what else did he have?

Onstage, a cowboy-slash-musician was warming up, testing the mic, playing a couple riffs on his electric acoustic guitar, singing a sad chorus of some ballad. Good-looking guy, he wore jeans and boots, stood almost six foot, with brown hair, pale blue eyes. He wore a half beard and seemed exactly the part of a swoony country singer.

Hud had been here once before, a few years back after his parents moved closer to Mercy Falls. His dad worked for a couple ranches in the area during branding and roundup, and hired on to ride fence during the winter or run feed out to the cattle in remote places. It was easier to live locally.

The door opened, and the late-afternoon sun blurred the image entering. Hudson held up his hand to the light and made out the outline of his older brother Harry. Not quite as tall as Hud, darker hair, Harry could still hold his own on the field—or the pitch, as his preferred sport had always been rugby.

"Bro!" Harry said as he approached the table. Hudson stood up, met his outstretched hand, pulled him in a for a quick hug, a back slap. "Seriously, what are you doing on this side of the pond?"

"Long story," Hud said as he sat back down. He signaled Audrey, who brought over water and set it in front of Harry.

"Hey, Harry," she said.

"Audrey." He glanced at the stage. "Who do we have playing tonight?"

"Oaken Fox. He's one of Dad's newest artists, up from Nashville. He's got an album dropping soon, so he's working on a tour. Dad wants to get some sound from him onto socials, so he's playing here this week. Anything besides water?"

"Let me look at the menu. Specials?"

"Sloppy Jacks. And Gray Pony fries are a family basket for three bucks."

"That's what I want, but I'll wait to order until my folks get here." He set the menu on the table as Audrey walked away.

"So, Dad's coming?"

"Yep." Harry leaned back. He wore jeans, boots, and a flannel pullover with the words *PEAK Rescue* on the chest. "Dad was pretty excited."

"Sure he was."

"Hud, you need to stop seeing Dad's reaction to your injury as some sort of rejection. He just didn't want you getting hurt. Or more hurt."

"I'm fine."

Harry gave a tight-lipped nod. "I know. But we're all just waiting for the day when you're not."

Hud shook his head and looked away. But a sigh escaped. He looked back at Harry. "I'm not sure the Vikings have a place on the roster for me next year. And I might have just blown my shot at a team here in the US, and the NFL is such a long shot, so..." He lifted a shoulder. "Maybe I should start working the rust off my cattle-roping abilities."

Harry laughed. "As if."

"What? I was a great cowboy."

"You were eight." Harry leaned back. "But, Hud, you can do anything you put your mind to—clearly football has taught you that. No one comes back from a TBI and plays pro ball again."

Audrey came back with the water and potatoes.

"Audrey, this is my brother Hudson. He's a football player in Europe."

"You play soccer?"

"American football."

"In Europe?"

He ran his thumb down his sweaty glass. "Yup."

"Cool. I'll get you more napkins." She walked away as, on stage, the musician set up his stool.

"Audrey is the daughter of local music producer and country music star Ben King."

"Really." Hud reached for a potato skin, the smell taking hold of his entire body. He hadn't eaten since scrambled eggs this morning in a diner near his hotel in Billings. "I've heard of him."

"He's had a number of hits. He's married to my chopper pilot over at PEAK Rescue, Kacey."

"How's the PEAK gig going?" He nudged the potato plate toward Harry.

"Good," Harry said. "I think I finally found my footing."

Hud considered him.

Harry met his eyes. "So, is this about the girl?"

Hud frowned at him. "What girl?"

"The woman on Insta a couple weeks ago. You two were looking pretty friendly."

"You saw my picture on Instagram?"

"Derby, one of my teammates, saw it. She follows the Vikings after Dad was bragging you up at the office a while back."

Hud stilled. "What?"

"Yeah. Dad works for Remington Ranch—Ty, the owner's son, works at PEAK. Dad happened to be dropping off a truck for Ty, came in, and we chatted. I'm not sure how, but pretty soon he was pulling up your stats and talking about the championship game and how you were going to play against an NFL team and—"

"So that's how it happened."

Harry frowned.

"His wife, Brette, came over to interview me. Said you had told her about me and the game. And I met Ty."

"Good guy. He's a chopper pilot too, but he only works part time now. Goes to seminary, wants to be a preacher. He has quite a testimony—was lost for a long time but got it all sorted after a tornado that hit Minnesota a few years ago. Oh, there's Dad." He raised a hand—the place had filled up a bit.

Hud forced away the strange ache that always tightened his chest when he saw his father. Time and work had bent him, and he looked older than his sixty-two years. He always reminded Hud a little of an older Harrison Ford. A bit gnarled by time, a swagger to his gait, a handshake that could break bones, but a rare smile that said he was listening.

Now he flashed that closed-mouth smile at Hud, even while taking the hand of Hud's mother, Evie. She spotted Hud and grinned, let go of her husband, and rushed around the tables to throw herself into Hud's arms as he got up.

He picked her up, painfully aware of how thin she'd gotten, then put her down. She wore her dark hair short, too much gray streaked in it, a pair of jeans, boots, and a canvas jacket.

"Hudson. What a surprise!"

Yeah, for him too. Because when he'd gotten in his car yesterday morning, he hadn't known exactly where to run. Just away from the brutal truth: Iris didn't want him.

Not, at least, like he wanted her.

He shook his father's hand, swallowing through the thickening of his throat. Oh, how his old man had aged, the lines around his mouth deeper, his body more bowed.

They sat down and his dad picked up his menu. But his mother took his hand. "So, tell me everything. What's going on?"

"I was interrogating him about a girl he seems to not want to talk about," Harry said.

"A girl?"

"It's nothing, Mom. We work together."

His mother raised an eyebrow. "Does she play football?"

He laughed. "No, she officiates football."

Her mouth made a round O.

"And you're not dating?"

He glanced at Harry. "No. We're just...not even friends, I think. But I've been at her home in Minnesota for the past week and thought maybe, before I go back to Europe, I should stop by."

"Montana?" His father put down the menu. "That's a long way for dinner."

He drew in a breath, then nodded.

"I used to drive a lot when your mother was sick. Just trying to sort it all out." He shot a half smile to his wife. "Or maybe I was just running."

She put her hand over his. "But you always came back."

"Yes, well, you were my solid ground, even if everything else was crumbling."

She squeezed his hand. "Because the solid ground wasn't me but Jesus, Beau."

Hud didn't know how the conversation had gone there, so serious, so fast.

But maybe that was the problem. He looked at Harry, whose mouth was a closed line. Harry raised an eyebrow.

"Hudson, is everything okay?" his mother asked.

Audrey picked right then to come up, deliver water to the table. "Are you ready to order?"

"Give us a minute," Hudson said. She nodded, walked away, and he turned to his mother. "I don't know. Maybe not."

From the front, the musician had taken the stage, introducing himself, then starting off with a song.

"I think maybe football might be over for me." He blew out a breath, the reframing of the truth somehow strengthening. "I've been feeling it ever since the championship. Like maybe it was time. But I was sort of freaked out too, so I...I did something stupid."

His father sat back, folded his arms.

"I started working for the CIA."

He raised an eyebrow.

"I know. But I wasn't sure what else was out there for me, so I...anyway, there was this girl—woman. Her name is Iris Marshall, and she is, yes, an official for the ELF, but also this amazing woman who is...more than I thought. And for a while there, I started thinking that maybe she was the next chapter in my life. But..." He leaned back, his hand behind his neck. "But I'm not sure she has room for me, so...anyway, I guess I don't know what's next."

Silence as the song lifted into the room.

Then his dad leaned forward. Took a breath. "Son, when your ma was sick, my entire world crumbled. I could hardly take my next breath, and because of that, I let everything fall apart. And you saw that."

Hudson stared at his dad. Nodded.

"And I know you were afraid."

Hud lifted a shoulder. "I'm not afraid, Dad. I mean—"

"I know you're tough and capable, Hud. But you've been dodging fear your whole life. It's why you run toward the hard things. Football. And maybe this CIA thing—"

"That's over."

"Good. But I know it's so you can have everything figured out before you get there. So you'll have the next step before the ground underneath your feet crumbles. But the fact is, and I learned this from your mom"—he put a hand on her arm—"you need to trust God for the now. Just right here, the earth beneath your feet. And then know that He'll be in the next step when you get there."

A beat. "Dad, when did you get all this faith? You've never—"

"Slowly. One day at a time, walking away from the captivity of fear, living in freedom." He smiled. "You get a lot of time to think when you're herding cattle."

He looked at Hud, then Harry. "We worry most about the things we trust God the least with. If you want God to move in your life, you need to stop trying to control everything. The root of control is fear. And God's perfect love for us casts out fear. Right, Evie?"

She patted his cheek and met his kiss. "I think you're starting to get it."

"Only took sixty-two years." He gave a chuckle.

Hud just stared at him. Where was the stoic, bitter man who'd never shown up at his football games?

Maybe Hud's expression said that, because his dad leaned

forward. And in a move that had Hud frozen, he touched Hud's arm. "I'd spent my whole life fighting God, and one day I just asked... why? Why am I fighting the God who gave me my wife, my sons, this life? What, exactly, am I afraid of? That God will put us through hard things? Maybe, but I can face them with fear, or with trust. And that's made all the difference." He let go, leaned back. "Audrey, I'll have the bison burger, double fries, and a chocolate milkshake."

Twenty-eight hours later, as Hud's plane touched down at Schiphol Airport in Amsterdam, the conversation at dinner and the evening spent on the foldout in his parents' fifth wheel still churned in his head.

Hudson put his seat up, rubbing the sleep out of his eyes, put up the shade, and watched the plane descend, the ocean beneath them, Amsterdam coming awake on the shoreline. He wasn't a fan of flying over the ocean, all that endless blue. Give him terra firma.

Trust God for the now. Just right here, the earth beneath your feet.

He *had* been hoping that Iris was his next step. But maybe she'd just been the step God had used to open his eyes.

Maybe he'd been running his entire life, looking for the next solid thing. The thing that would fill his lungs, give him peace.

You literally cannot breathe without saying His name. God is life. Yh. Wh.

He put a hand to his chest.

The root of control is fear. And God's perfect love for us casts out fear.

The landing gear went down, and he popped his ears as the cabin pressure shifted.

He was done living in fear. Done running. Done expecting life to crumble his feet.

Done trying to find answers in tomorrow instead of trusting God for today.

They landed, and Hud pulled his duffel bag out of the first-class overhead bin, slung it over his shoulder, then followed the rest of the passengers out of the plane to passport control.

After waiting in line, he stepped up to the booth and handed his passport to the security agent. Stood unsmiling as the man looked at him, then his information, then ran it and looked at him again.

Something in his eyes...

Two guards stepped up to him, both armed, although they kept their voices low. "Hudson Bly?"

He stilled, glanced at them and then the people around him. A few were looking at him, some of their expressions alarmed. What? Should he be alarmed?

"Yes?"

"Come with us, please."

He paused. "Why?"

"Please, sir. Now."

Okay, yes, he was starting to get alarmed. He took the passport from the agent, then followed the officers—one in front of him, one behind him—to a nearby booth.

They came in, shut the door.

"Put your duffel bag on the table and turn around, hands behind your back."

"What?"

"There's an Interpol alert out for you. You're under arrest on suspicion of the murder of Werner Vogel."

He turned around. Put his hands behind his back as the officer snapped on cuffs.

And tried not to feel the world turning to sand under his feet.

Eleven

Amsterdam just might be the last place Iris wanted to be. "This isn't even a real game." She dropped her backpack onto the bed of the hotel where the rest of her crew was staying as Shae walked over to the curtains and pulled them.

Against the twilight, the city had begun to glitter, the lights bright over Dam Square and the royal palace, all lit up and golden on the west side of the square. At the other end of the plaza rose the green Mint Tower, and beyond that, the flower market and the canals.

"What kind of game is it?"

"It's a fake game."

"What, they'll be wearing flags?" Shae set her weekender bag on her queen bed.

"No. But the Admirals aren't even an ELF team. They were in the World League of Football years ago, but that went down, and they've been trying to build a team since then. This game is sort of a tryout of the rebooted team, an audition to play in the ELF. They want to see how many fans show up and how well they play. But it's liable to be a sloppy game."

"And you're worried about getting hit?"

Iris frowned at her. "No, I'm worried about my *mom*."

Shae held up a hand. "Of course you are. But your dad—and the ER—said that it was just low blood sugar."

Iris unzipped her bag. "I know. I'm just worried it's something more serious."

Shae came over to her. Turned her by her shoulders. "Your dad would tell you if it was. And you can't stop anything by worrying."

Iris just looked at her. "I don't get you. You're held prisoner on a gulag ship in the Bering Sea and you're all 'don't worry, be happy'?" She sang the last words.

Shae laughed. "No. But what happened, happened. And I lived. And Ned lived. And...I guess I'm so glad to be free that I'm just refusing to let the nightmares win. It's one thing to be set free, another thing to walk in that freedom every day. If I let the past win, then am I really free? I'm ordering room service. Want anything?"

She let go of Iris and headed to the desk. "So, are you going to talk to Hudson?"

Iris had carried her toiletry bag into the bathroom. Now, she stuck her head out. "Um—"

"Because you're both here, and I was thinking...you know." She looked up. "The waffles look good."

Iris just stared at her. Took a breath. *If he wants you, he won't give up.* Sibba's words, and she hated how much she wanted them to be true.

A knock came at their door, and Shae walked over, looked through the peephole, then grabbed the door handle and flung it open. "Ned!"

He stepped into the room and swept her up. Iris exited to the bathroom, closed the door, and stared at the mirror.

Okay, maybe she should at least tell him she was in town. *Let God be in charge of your heart, and He will surprise you.*

She blew out a breath, then picked up her phone. Opened her chat app.

Stared at it.

You choose the comfort of the known instead of the freedom of trusting God.

She closed her eyes.

Her phone rumbled in her grip. Yannick.

Are you here yet? Meeting in the lobby in ten.

She washed her face, pulled back her hair, and walked out of the bathroom.

Ned was seated on the desk chair, Shae on the bed, her legs crossed. He looked up as Iris walked out, and got up. "Hey, sis."

"Glad to see you're in one piece." She hugged him. "Everything go okay?"

He nodded. "Mission goal achieved."

"You found the caesium-137?"

He looked at Shae.

"Sorry. But Jonas was there, and so was Sibba, so..."

He held up a hand. "Yes. Okay. Yes, we did. At least, the material that went missing...um..."

"I don't need to know anything," Iris said, picking up her room key. "I don't want you to have to shoot me."

Ned laughed, but maybe she wasn't kidding as she left the room and headed down the hall.

Zach was in the lift when it opened, wearing a pair of jeans and a sweater. "Hey!"

"Hey," she said, and gave him a hug.

"How are the ribs?"

"Better. Still wearing a brace."

"Good. I'd like to see you on the injured reserve though."

"Not if we want to officiate the Lauchtenland game."

He pointed at her.

They walked out into the lobby of the Hotel Amsterdam, with its sleek black-and-white tile flooring, marble columns, and expansive windows that overlooked the square. Yannick stood from a nearby grouping of tables and motioned her and Zach over. Roque, Milos, Arne, and Jakub all stood and greeted her.

Water, a couple beers, a glass of wine, and a charcuterie tray with hard cheeses, dried fruit, and meat sat in the center of the table.

"I like this version of a pregame meeting," Iris said.

"The field is used by the Ajax FC, so they had to turn over the pitch for the game," said Yannick. "Since they haven't had a professional American football team since 2007, they expect a big turnout for tomorrow's game."

"I hate not walking the field before the game," Iris said as she sat down. A waitress came over, and she ordered water and picked up a piece of cheese.

"We can get in early," Yannick said, putting down his beer. "But we're making some adjustments in the officiating." He turned to Iris. "I'm moving Zach to ump position, Iris."

She stilled. Looked at Zach. He looked away. "You knew this?"

"It's my call, Iris. And maybe just for this game, until your ribs heal. But I never want to see you get hit like that again, and umpire is the most dangerous position on the field."

"I can handle it."

Yannick leaned back, folded his arms. "Would you rather be benched?"

She held up her hand. "Okay, yes. Fine. Where am I?"

"Back judge."

"Oh. Right." But maybe there, she could keep an eye on Hudson. The story of his injury—and her mistake—hadn't walked out of her brain.

Yannick pulled out his phone and set it on the table, bringing up a picture of the field. He walked them through the field, the sun positions, then went through the starting lineup of the Amsterdam Admirals. He'd sent her film a couple days ago, so she'd watched most of it already, but he pointed out a couple cornerbacks and a safety who were rookies.

"The Admirals have a lot at stake, so they're liable to play a little off the hook," he said. "And a few of these players have come over from rugby."

"Oy," said Arne. "Then there'll be blood on the field."

"Let's keep our players safe," said Yannick. "And call a clean game."

They'd finished off their food and beverages, and Iris got up to leave with the others, but Yannick called her back. Pulled out a chair.

"Am I in trouble?"

Yannick wore a pair of jeans, a turtleneck, and a sports coat—very European. He ran a hand over his face. Cleared his throat. "There's been a complaint lodged against you. Someone from the US who says that you might be involved in a relationship that is a conflict of interest."

She looked at him. "You mean Hudson Bly."

He shrugged. "What you do after the season is your business, but...yes."

"Fear not, we're, well, barely friends. And the person who lodged the complaint was probably my old boyfriend, Darren Pike, who is a jerk, and everyone knows it."

Yannick drew in a breath. Then nodded. "Well, Hudson might not be playing in the game anyway."

"Why not?"

"He was arrested this morning when he arrived in Amsterdam. Didn't make practice."

She stilled. "Arrested?"

"Something about the death of Werner Vogel. Not sure—I overheard his coach talking about it today in the pregame meeting."

"He wasn't...I mean..."

Yannick looked up at her. Cocked his head. "You know something about Vogel's death?"

"I thought they ruled it a suicide."

"Don't know. But as of right now, Bly isn't on the starting roster. Just keep your head clear and the calls clean and there shouldn't be a problem." He got up. "See you in the morning."

She sat there, staring at her glass, her heart a fist against her wounded ribs.

Never mind costing him his career—getting involved with her could have cost Hud his *freedom*.

She got up and headed to the elevator, hit the button.

Again.

"C'mon!"

The doors opened and she got on, and it took eternity for it to reach her floor.

She didn't bother to knock before she burst into her room— hopefully Shae and Ned weren't in a clinch.

Nope. They sat at the desk, sharing a pizza, laughing.

She stopped, a warmth shooting through her at the expression on Ned's usually stoic face. Oh, he was handsome when he smiled. And for a second, her mother was in her head.

But the best thing you can do in your life is swap captivity— your fear—for love.

Love.

What in your life requires you to trust God?

Hud. Hud required her to trust God. Let Him in. Let God be in charge of her heart. Let love lead.

Love? Oh no, she *loved* Hudson Bly. Loved his humor, the way he kept showing up. If she were honest, she'd probably fallen in love with him that long night in the cave when he'd kept her alive.

When they'd kept each other alive.

She braced her hand on the wall.

"Hey, sis, what's up? You okay?"

"No. No, I'm not."

Ned got up, wiped his mouth with a napkin and headed toward her. "What's going on?"

"Hudson was arrested." She sank onto the bed.

Silence, and Ned looked at Shae, then knelt before Iris. "What do you mean?"

"This morning. When he arrived in Amsterdam. Interpol

arrested him for Werner Vogel's murder."

Ned took a breath, then got up and pulled out his phone.

"What's going on?"

Ned had dialed, and now put the phone to his ear. Held up a "wait" hand. Then, "Hey, Fraser. I think we're going to need a jailbreak."

His career was probably over.

Hud sat on the metal bench in the holding cell of the National Central Bureau, a shiny glass building four blocks from the Oude Kerk, which had rung its bells early this morning as light cascaded into the room like the heavens peeling back the darkness.

It had started as the longest night of his life as he'd stared at the ceiling of the pristine cell—probably cleaner than a few hotels he'd slept in over the years—just breathing.

Yh. Wh.

And listening to the voice of Garrett Marshall, weirdly showing up in his head. *You root deep in God's love. You know, without a doubt, that you are His, and no one can take you from Him.*

He didn't know why, because it didn't make sense, but the more he lay there, his hands folded over his chest, listening to himself breathe...

The more the knot in his chest loosed.

The more the breath, the thickness of, well, God, maybe, swept through him.

The more his mind stopped circling.

He finally closed his eyes and slept.

On the stainless steel, rock-hard bench.

Like a baby.

Call it jet lag, maybe. But when the bells began to ring, and

Hud opened his eyes and sat up, something had changed.

Then the cell-block doors opened, and an officer walked toward him. "You're free," he said.

Yeah, he was.

But also, yay, because he followed the man out to the lobby, where he received his belongings—his duffel bag, jacket, watch, and championship ring—and then the door buzzed open.

Huh.

He walked through into the white, pristine lobby.

Nearly fell over when he spotted Ned Marshall standing there, looking freshly shaved, wearing a black parka, jeans, boots.

Ned held out his hand. "Sorry it took so long."

Hudson met it. "Um. Did you...what...I don't understand."

"I made a call. Fraser made a call. I think maybe the president got involved."

"The president?"

"Of the United States? President White? Yeah. Or maybe not him exactly, but his people."

His people. Got Hudson out of an international murder charge? Although he hadn't actually been charged. "I told them everything that happened."

"Perfect. Let's go." Ned jangled keys in his hand and led Hud outside to a skinny Toyota Rav 4.

He stopped then, on the sidewalk. Around them, amidst the tall, narrow, historic buildings, bicyclists rode the cobblestone streets, a few motorcyclists drove by, the smell of street food—waffles, maybe?—hung in the air. And over it all, a gorgeous, blue-skied day, void of clouds or blemish or any hint of trouble.

Yh. Wh. He took another breath. He hadn't a clue what Ned meant, but he was okay with whatever went down.

"Iris would have met you, but she had to be at the arena."

He looked at Ned. "Iris is here?"

"She's officiating the game."

He swallowed. "Okay." Wow, he wanted to see her, but— "Wait. Did she send you?"

"Of course she did, my dude. My sister is crazy about you."

Crazy. About *him*? "What?"

"Yeah. You should have seen her last night—I think she would have dressed in black and attempted a breakout if the Caleb Group hadn't gotten involved. Get in. Hungry?"

"Famished." But his thoughts were stuck on *crazy about you*.

"Perfect. We'll pick up some food on the way to the arena."

Hud got in, his knees nearly to his chest. Ned drove out into traffic. "I can't believe they arrested you."

"Yeah, well, apparently my fingerprints were all over his flat."

"Except on the gun."

"Yep. Still, I thought I was in big trouble—they had put together a file connecting Iris and me and then Vogel and had come up with a pretty reasonable story."

"Except, no prints on the gun."

"Yep. I'd be a pretty sloppy murderer if I left prints everywhere but wore gloves to kill the guy."

They stopped at a FEBO and grabbed a burger out of vending machine, and a drink, and sat in the car and ate. Hud practically inhaled his food, which he'd probably lose in the game with one hard hit, but at least now his stomach wasn't rubbing against his spine.

They gathered up their refuse and dumped it into a trash bin, then Ned pulled out again toward Johan Cruijff Arena, located south of the city. He'd pulled up directions on his GPS.

"You okay to play today?"

Hud tried not to comment on the driving and held onto his seatbelt. "If they let me. Not sure." He sighed. "This might be my last game."

Ned looked at him. "Really?"

"I'm a walking time bomb, and it's time I stopped running and faced that. I can't play forever, and maybe I shouldn't be playing now. The USFL probably doesn't have a place for me, and even if the Minnesota Vikings or another NFL team takes a chance on me, I'm probably riding the bench, hanging out on the practice team until they cut me loose. I'm thinking I'll wait and see what God brings onto my horizon."

"Like what?"

He lifted a shoulder. "Once upon a time, I wanted to be a cowboy."

Ned laughed.

"What?"

"Nothing. You'd be a great cowboy." Ned glanced at him. "You sure?"

"I'm not sure about anything except where I'm supposed to be right now."

"And that is..."

"Right here." He looked at Ned. Smiled.

Ned frowned but turned his eyes back to the road.

The arena rose glorious and bold against the blue sky, the top closed despite the day, a hint of chill in the air. "The Ajax futbol team plays here. It holds fifty-five thousand. If we get ten, I'll be shocked. Amsterdam has spent the last eighteen years rebuilding their program. Today is supposed to be a sort of introductory game."

"Seems like the lot is pretty full," Ned said as they drove in. Hudson showed his ELF pass, and the parking attendant directed them to a players section.

Ned parked next to a giant bus, probably chartered for the team.

"Shae came in with Iris. She's got a pass to take pictures at the game, and she got one for me too, so we'll be on the Vikings' sidelines."

Hud grabbed his gear, then headed into the locker room area while Ned went to find Shae.

"Hud!" Toby lifted a hand from where he was lacing up his shoes. "You got sprung!"

Perfect. "Yep."

"Make any friends?" Felix said. He pulled his jersey over his pads.

"Funny." Hud walked over to a locker and set his bag down.

"Bly!" Coach Max had stepped out of the office. "In here."

Hudson headed over to the office where the coaching staff sat. He stepped inside, closed the door. "Listen, I got it all cleared up."

And then his gaze fell on—"Waylen?"

His agent sat back. He'd ditched the cowboy hat, but still wore the boots as well as a suit, his brown hair cut short. "Hudson."

Coach Clay sat at the end of the table. "Apparently you made a bit of fuss over in America."

Right. "Listen. That was personal business between me and Darren Pike. He's...well, he had it coming."

"Yes, he did," Waylen said. "And Coach Gripe didn't know that until that moment. He did some homework and discovered that Pike had a history of sexual assault. Apparently, he paid off or at least bargained away all his offenses. Carlson doesn't want him on his staff. But he does want you."

He shot a look at Coach Clay. "So, we're done here?"

"Sit down, Hud," Coach Clay said. Hudson lowered himself into a chair. "We're on the fence here with you. Felix is young, moldable, and frankly, not as expensive. And Max says that your head's been giving you some trouble."

"No, sir, I—"

Coach Clay held up his hand. "We see the way you've been working with Toby and Felix. They have a lot to learn from you. But you'd get less playing time."

"You have coaching in your blood," Coach Max said. "And patience. You're a natural, Hud."

"I don't understand. So, you are letting me go?"

"That's why Waylen's here. You have options."

"Coach Gripe is interested in you signing on as a wide-receiver coach."

Hud stared at him. "What?"

"Or you stay here and take on a mentoring role."

"I'd still be playing?"

Coach Max nodded. "Maybe not as much, but..."

"I want to play out my contract. Both games." He looked at Waylen.

"That can be arranged, right, Coach?" Waylen looked at Coach Clay.

Coach Clay nodded. "Suit up, Bly."

The sun had hit the middle of the sky before he came out of the locker room. He ran a lap, stretched, warmed up with the team, and kept his eyes on the sidelines.

Jack's warm-up throw nearly hit him in the head when Iris came out, dressed in her stripes, carrying her gear. She set her water bottle and bag on a bench, then started to stretch.

"Hudson! Go long!"

He glanced at Jack, who was dropping back, waving him toward the end zone.

Hudson took off, running hard, looked over his shoulder, and found the ball.

It sailed into his hands, a beautiful catch. He tucked it, then ran it in.

A few fans clapped. He turned and Felix was there. "Nice catch."

"Laces."

"Right." Felix ran back to the line of scrimmage. "My turn!"

Hudson ran over to the sidelines, where the trainers were bringing out water coolers, filling bottles to drop them into their metal baskets. Others had medical gear out. He took off his helmet and grabbed some water, the hamburger turning to a rock in his gut.

He glanced at the officials. Iris wasn't there, but he spotted Shae taking a shot of the team and walked over. She wore a jacket, jeans, and Uggs, her blonde hair back in a wool headband. "Hey."

"Hey," she said, then stepped back and grabbed a snap. "It's for social media."

"Where's Iris?"

"I'm over here." He looked up. She had a foot up on a nearby bench, was lacing her shoe. "Don't look at me."

He faced away, at the field. "Now I feel like I'm talking to myself."

Shae moved away, making it worse.

"Just stand there and listen." Iris took a breath. "I was wrong. My life isn't exactly how it's supposed to be. Not without you in it. Because you're...I don't know. You're kind and dependable and super hot and, fine, an international superhero, and I...I'm..."

"Crazy about me?"

A pause. "You're making this hard."

"Try holding on to you for six hours in a cave."

"Such a whiner. I got you out of the clink, didn't I?"

He glanced over his shoulder.

She held her hand up. "Are you trying to get me kicked off the officiating crew?"

"Calm down. I'm not going to tackle you or anything. I'm just looking." He smiled, and she put her hands on her hips.

"I look like a zebra."

"A pretty hot zebra."

"Hud."

"Listen, Iris." He lowered his voice. "This might be my last game. And I don't know what's going to happen after this, but I'd really love it if maybe we could have dinner together after the game. Maybe try and live happily ever after?"

He got a smile out of her.

"Fine. But between now and then, we're not friends, okay?"

"Not even barely friends?"

"Keep it up, pretty boy, and you'll get ejected from the game." She walked past him. Lowered her voice. "Try and stay out of trouble."

"Not on your life," he said.

She shook her head and ran out onto the field.

The sun was shining, the stadium was surprisingly full.

And Hud knew it was going to be the best game of his life.

TWELVE

The Admirals had come to play football.

Maybe after sixteen years trying to resurrect their club, they wanted some blood, but whatever it was, "It's like the Wild West out here," Iris said as she picked up another defensive pass interference flag and ran over to confer with Yannick.

"I can't decide which penalty to call—the defensive holding or the pass interference."

"Both."

"They'll be backed up all the way to their end zone."

"Get ready for another punt." She ran to the backfield, past Hudson, who glanced at her. She spotted him watching her out of the corner of her eye but didn't slow.

Maybe try and live happily ever after.

Oh, she had to stop thinking about that. Or the way he ran passing routes, or even took to the air, almost flying, grabbing one-handed passes.

The Vikings would be out of their minds to not renew his contract.

Especially when he pulled in a whopper over-the-shoulder pass in the far corner of the end zone, got both feet down, and dragged them over the white line. A small puff of black smoke confirmed her touchdown call.

Tight end Tobias West ran in the second TD, and by the start of the second quarter, they were up fourteen, zip.

But it wasn't without injury. One of the guards suffered a high ankle sprain, the new RB, Berker Rennich, dislocated his shoulder, and Hud had taken at least two hard tackles, his bell rung so hard he took his time getting off the field.

"No flag on that one?" Jakub said as he ran by her. "Unnecessary roughness?"

"Borderline," she said, but yes, she'd seen it.

Shoot. Had she hesitated? She refused to look back, took her position.

The second quarter started with the sun in her eyes, so she fought hard to keep her eye on the wideouts, to watch the play develop. Felix caught a ball on the line, and she ruled it in. The Admirals threw a challenge flag, but the replay, caught on Yannick's tablet, kept her rule.

The Vikings pushed down to the twenty, and then on fourth down, Coach Clay decided to rile the crowd—which she could admit seemed larger than usual—and go for it. He called time out when his attempt to entice the line offsides didn't work.

She ran into the bench along with Arne and grabbed her water bottle.

"Watch for the fake," Arne said.

Yep. The Vikings loved the fake punt, what with their punter a former QB for some German team.

She took the field, spotted Hud off the line, and sure enough, the center snapped it back, not to the punter but to Toby, who scrambled out of the pocket and zinged it to Hud, running hard for the end zone.

No defender, and he had a clear grab pulling it in, tucking it—

The cornerback came out of nowhere, even as she was calling the touchdown, and like a bull, came in full speed at Hud.

He hit him broadside, jerked him up, and then slammed him so hard she thought her own bones broke with the impact.

Then she just stood there, stunned.

Arne threw out his flag. "Unnecessary roughness!"

She glanced at him, back at Hud, who rolled to his back, breathing hard as his teammates came up to congratulate him, to help him up.

Hud glanced at her, something of question in his eyes, but she turned away and ran to Yannick.

He glanced at her. "Did you not see it?"

Yes, she'd seen it. But had let it sit in her brain, tossing it around, second guessing herself.

She simply didn't trust her own instincts.

"Stay on your game. We don't need any mistakes, Marshall."

She nodded, took her position even as Hudson left the field. He was getting water and having a chat with the trainer as he eased himself onto the bench.

Maybe they wouldn't be having dinner.

The Vikings booted in their extra point. She signaled that it was good, then lined up on the Vikings' line for the kick.

It sailed into the end zone, touchback, and the Admirals took the field.

The game turned gnarly as the Admirals tore their way through the line, grubbing for every yard, and turtled their way up the field, eating up most of the second quarter.

They settled for a field goal as the teams headed into the locker room at the half.

Hud seemed to be limping a little.

She tried not to look and followed her crew into their office. She dropped her water bottle off in the basket outside the door for the trainer to fill, then went inside.

Yannick had taken off his white hat, threw it on the table. Hands on his hips, breathing hard.

She slid into her chair.

"Marshall. Please tell me that you have gone blind in the last two hours. Because I cannot figure out why you haven't called one offensive pass interference or even an unnecessary roughness call on your favorite player."

"My favorite—"

"Hudson Bly." He leaned onto the table, sweat running down his angular face. "Are you trying to get him killed?"

"What? No—"

"You do realize that the Admirals have painted a target on his back. And he's fighting back. While you seem to be picking daisies out there in the backfield."

"I'm not...sir. I just...it's all borderline."

Yannick's mouth tightened to a grim, angry line. Blew out a breath. "Don't let your feelings for him keep you from doing your job."

She opened her mouth.

He held up a hand.

"And you, Zach. Two offside calls you missed."

Zach opened his mouth.

"It's sloppy. And embarrassing. And more people are going to get hurt if you don't do your job. So." He leaned down, his gaze on her. "Do your job."

"Yes, sir," Iris said and got up.

She walked out of the room into the hallway. Their water bottles were gone, the entire basket in the hands of the trainer. She spotted a woman in a pair of black pants, a Vikings jersey, a towel over her shoulder, black hair spilling out of her cap, dark tattoo up her neck. She filled water bottles from a nearby cooler.

"Will you bring those to the field when they're full?"

"Yes."

The Vikings were just coming back on the field when she arrived. She spotted Shae, taking shots on her phone, and not far away, Ned, wearing a field pass around his neck. She walked up to him.

"You angry at Hud for some reason?" he said.

"No. Just..."

"Breathe, Iris. Just breathe and do your job. Stop overthinking it. It's not training, it's game time. You know what you're doing. Go *do* it."

She glanced at him. He smiled.

Felt a little like respect.

She ran out onto the field.

Hudson didn't play the entire third quarter, but it gave Felix plenty of time to drop three beautiful passes. The Admirals got the ball and got it down to the twenty after a surprise fifteen-yard run.

Three points as the ball sailed through the uprights, and Iris was on the line for the kickoff.

The new guy, Berker, was back in the game as receiver. He nabbed the ball and took off, spinning and dodging, and suddenly he'd crossed the fifty. She'd started to backpedal as the field ran toward her, defenders trying to grab him.

Suddenly, Berker cut toward her side of the field, running hard. She sped up, heading for the sidelines, but Berker did too, along with the pack.

Oh no, oh—

Berker leaped for the sideline, and she was right there in his way—

Then, just like that, she wasn't. Someone just picked her up, danced her out of the way as the pack crashed at her feet. If she hadn't been moved, she'd have been at the bottom of said pack.

Her rescuer put her down, and she turned.

"Hud?"

He winked and turned away.

Oh. Wow. She jogged back onto the field.

"You okay?" Zach had run up. "That was terrifying to watch. Good thing Bly grabbed you out of the way."

Yeah, good thing. Her entire body shook.

"Your ribs holding up?"

"I might need some ice, but I'll be okay." She grimaced as she ran back out onto the field, but something felt...

Right.

Freeing.

She didn't know why, but the idea of Hud simply having her back swooshed a thick emotion inside her she couldn't place.

Power, maybe?

Yeah, that was it.

She felt invincible.

The Vikings easily scored, Toby and Felix doing the heavy lifting in three plays, and then the Admirals had the ball.

Three and out. Four minutes left to play. Vikings' ball.

She ignored the crazy thrill that buzzed through her when Hudson took the field. As if this was where they belonged. On the field together, her watching his back.

Him watching hers.

Sort of.

He went long for a pass, and she pulled her flag when the defender practically grabbed his helmet. "Defensive pass interference."

Hud glanced at her but didn't react as he headed to huddle.

But she felt it. The joy of doing what she was born to do. And doing it well.

So maybe she should stop trying too hard to impress, to protect herself.

Stop being so tough.

Hudson completed his next pass, went out for two plays, and when the Vikings got it down to the thirty with three minutes left, he came back in.

Apparently, the Vikings were hoping for a shot at the end zone, another quick in and out by the Admirals, and then a nice long possession to end the game.

And there it was. Ernst dropped back, faked to Toby, who ran a dogleg into the flats, then aired it out to Hud.

She ran down the field, focused on the play. He didn't push off, didn't even look at the defender, his eye on the ball as he crossed over the goal line. Gorgeous throw, right to the numbers—

Hud grabbed it, pulled it in, his feet came down, one, then the other, turned to take one more step—

The defender didn't even slow. Just put his helmet down and slammed into Hud, who'd tucked to secure the ball.

The crash was a bomb erupting in the end zone. Hud left his feet, jolted so hard his helmet loosed, jerked halfway off. The ball upended out of his hands, and he fell back, unprotected, undefended.

He slammed into the ground, his head bouncing on the turf.

The other player lay crumpled ten feet away.

She threw her flag but didn't bother with the call on her way to assess Hud.

Oh no. His helmet was mostly off now, his eyes rolled back into his head. And then he started to seize. His body drew up, his arms shaking.

"Hud! Hud!"

"Back! Get back!" The voice of a trainer, coming in now to pull off his helmet. They doused him with smelling salts, and in a second, the seizing stopped. He jerked his eyes open, groaned.

"Get back!" This from another trainer who'd run out with a backboard.

"I'm fine!" Hud pushed one of them away. But when he sat up, he had to put his hand back to stop himself from crumbling.

She backed up as the team crowded around him.

"What's the call, ref?" shouted someone.

Oh, right. She stepped back, raised her arms. "Touchdown!"

The crowd erupted, some of them booing, others ecstatic.

She turned and found Yannick, who waved her in. She ran up to join Yannick, Coach Clay, and the Admiral's Coach. "What's your rule on this, back judge?"

"He had two feet down and was making a football move. Watch it on the screen if you want, but I'm right."

Coach Clay was nodding, and then Arne joined the huddle.

"She's right," he said, and then spoke in German to the Admirals coach, who turned away, cursing.

"The ruling on the field is confirmed," Yannick said to Coach Clay.

"Wait," Iris said. "That was a targeting play—number forty-two is ejected from the game."

Yannick looked at her, but she wasn't budging.

"Okay." Yannick headed over to the other bench. Forty-two had already gotten up, had thrown his helmet down, was yelling his protest at the TD. Wait until he heard the ejection call.

Hudson was up under his own power, but leaned a little on a trainer as he headed to the bench.

She couldn't look at him.

"Back judge!"

She stilled, turned. Hudson had stopped the procession, his helmet in his gloved grip. Then he smiled. "Good call."

And she didn't care. "Good catch!"

He winked, then headed into the tunnel to the locker room.

As Yannick blew his whistle, she found her position.

Yeah, they just might have a shot at this happily ever after.

"You really got your bell rung out there, Bly." The trainer, an older man named Bastian, shot a penlight across his eyes. "You looked like you had a seizure out there on the field, but your pupils seem to be equal and reacting." He clicked off the light.

"This isn't my first rodeo."

"That's what has me concerned." He held a clipboard and was marking off the steps in the concussion protocol.

The first two—loss of consciousness and seizure—had been marked in red.

So, not a good sign.

Hudson sat on the padded table, his pads off, just his undershirt on along with his padded pants and socks, sweat still trailing down his back despite the cool air of the locker room. "I'm fine."

"I also don't like the way your neck snapped back." He picked up a neck collar. "Let's see what the X-rays say."

In the next room, the X-ray machine was processing the shots taken of his neck and spine.

Bonus of using the Ajax training center.

"Does your head hurt?"

Hud looked at him. "I just took a head shot by a man running thirty miles per hour. It was like getting hit by a truck. What do you think?"

Another red mark.

Oops.

"Any nausea?"

When he'd seen Berker headed toward Iris earlier? Um, yes. "No."

"Vomiting."

His tackle of her had kept him from seeing a collision that would have induced vomiting. But, "Nope."

Black checkmark.

"Blurred vision?"

Only when he thought about a life without Iris. He shook his head.

Balance problems. Always.

But not anymore. Time to figure out how to live his life in the now, not always two steps in the future. "Nope."

"Sensitivity to noise."

"Just the sound of your voice, Doc." He smiled.

Bastian did not. He gave him a look, then stepped away to the computer located on a nearby table. "X-ray looks clear. But my guess is that you have a sprain."

"Probably, but I don't need a neck collar."

He came back to Hud, put his hands on his neck, probed. "What venue are we at today?"

"Ajax Arena, Amsterdam."

"What half is it now?"

"Fourth quarter, just over two minutes left."

Two minutes, and then he'd see Iris, and then...then he was going to follow up that wink—what an idiot—with something a little more specific.

"Who scored last?"

"Me. I scored." He made a fist and pumped his arm.

"That's right he did."

Hud looked up to see— "Ned. How'd you get in here?"

Ned had Shae's hand, and they stopped at the door to the room. "I saw the look on Iris's face, and she's worried. I thought I'd come in and check."

"He needs an MRI," Bastian said. "His concussion protocol is inconclusive, but after that hit and that seizure, I'm pulling you from the game."

Hudson held up his hand. "Listen. I've had seizures before. And I realize the seriousness of them. I'm sticking around to the end of the game, and then I'll go in for an MRI if I need to. But I'm fine, really."

Actually, not really, because his entire body ached, and he'd probably pulled a muscle in his neck, because it did hurt, but mostly his head throbbed, so yes, he'd probably turned even more of his gray matter to mush.

Which meant, probably, his on-field days were over.

He slid off the table and grabbed a towel. Wiped it over his head and hung it over his shoulder. "I need a drink."

"Bottles are in the hallway."

He and Ned and Shae headed out into the hallway that connected the training room to the locker room. The officials' office was just down the hall. And beyond that, on either end of the tunnel, were the doorways—one to the field, the other to the parking lot.

No water bottles, however.

A trainer came in from the field. She wore a hat, kept her head down.

"Hey," said Hud. "Do you know where the water bottles are?"

She looked up at him. And then, weirdly, looked at Shae. Slowed.

"Vikka?" Shae said softly. "Wait—*Vikka?*"

The woman swallowed, then took off in a sprint.

"Who's Vikka?" said Hud, even as Ned turned, sprinted after her. "What's going on?"

Ned tackled her two steps before the door, grabbing her, spinning her around, winding her arm behind her. She swore at him, kicking, throwing back her head.

Shae and Hud had run after him, and now Ned turned the woman.

Rail thin, she had dark eyes, and her hat had fallen off, shaking out dark black hair. Tattoos ran up her neck from her shirt collar.

"Vikka. What are you doing here?" Shae ran up to her, glanced at Ned, but he shook his head.

"Who is this, Shae?"

"She was on the gulag ship with Shae," Ned said. Shook her. "Weren't you?"

Vikka's jaw tightened.

"I thought you died."

"Nyet. But I was recaptured. Along with Zurab." Her eyes bored into Shae. "Only you got away."

"What about...what about Judah?"

Vikka lifted a shoulder. "Dead."

Shae's shaky hand covered her mouth.

"But what are you doing here?" Ned said. He turned to her. "What's going on?"

Vikka's eyes widened, and she looked from Ned to Shae, then Hudson. "I had no choice."

No choice. And with those words, a hard ball formed in his gut.

"They have Zurab. And I...I'm sorry, Twenty-Three."

"Sorry?"

Hud looked at her. She nudged a memory inside him, but he couldn't place it.

Wait. Earlier— "You filled the water bottles."

Vikka's jaw tightened.

"The water. Oh my gosh—the *water*."

Ned looked at him. "What about the water?"

"Abe Bartmann was poisoned. I watched him on camera. He fell right after—oh no." Two-minute warning.

Iris would come off the field and...

He looked at Vikka. "It's in the water bottles."

He didn't wait for her confirmation, just turned and took off down the tunnel. The far doors were propped open, and he ran out onto the field.

Two minutes, four seconds left on the clock, according to the massive scoreboard, and the Admirals still had the ball.

A run play, and as Hudson searched for the officials' bench, the player was called down.

The clock stopped at Yannick's call of the two-minute warning, and the players broke for the sidelines.

Hud spotted Iris on the field, running up to Arne. Together they began walking off the field toward their bench.

He was still fifty yards away. She was jogging, thirty yards, twenty...

He took off, bumpering past players, dodging trainers.

"Bly!" someone shouted, but he ignored it.

She'd reached the bench. Was listening to something Arne said, now laughing.

Reaching for the bottle.

He cleared the last of the players and nearly took out a linesman with the down markers. "Iris!"

She didn't hear him as she flipped open the top on her bottle. Smiled and nodded again at Arne. Twenty yards away.

"Iris!"

Ten.

She jerked, hearing her name, looked even as she lifted the bottle to her lips.

Her eyes widened as she spotted him, even as he vaulted her bench, his body flying toward her.

He didn't mean to take her out. Just wanted to swat the bottle away. But she put up her arm—a defensive move—and he had no choice.

He wrapped his arms around her, pulled her close, and then turned.

Bam! They slammed into the turf, skidding, his body half under hers as the wind knocked out of him.

They skidded to a stop, and he just lay there, gasping, his mouth opening like a fish, no air.

She'd grunted with the landing, then lay there too a long second.

He fought for breath.

She pushed herself up, looked at him. "Hud?"

There—a long, wheezy gasp, and suddenly his lungs ballooned. He let out the breath, gulped in another.

"Hud, are you okay—what's going on?" She'd dropped the water bottle, and now Arne and a couple other officials came over to them.

Zach had run up, breathing hard. "What, you guys playing your own game here on the sidelines?"

Hud swallowed, found another breath, then sat up, breathing hard. "She—the..." He took another breath. "The water is poisoned."

She blinked at him. Arne looked at his water, then threw his bottle away. Yannick too held a bottle but now closed it.

"What are you talking about?"

"You said that Abe was poisoned, right?" He directed the question at Yannick.

Yannick nodded. "That was what the coroner said—but it wasn't confirmed until a couple days ago. Thallium."

Iris's mouth opened, then she turned to Hud. "How did you—"

"It's a long story. But don't drink the water." He got up, pulled her up to himself. Meant to let her go, but she held on to his shirt.

"You...are...over-the-top, Hudson Bly."

"I promised your brothers I would keep you safe," he said, smiling.

"For how long?"

"Does until death do us part sound okay?"

She raised an eyebrow.

"Aw, just kiss the man already," Zach said.

"Hud?" She put her hand on his chest. "Wait. What about... the future?"

"God has the future in His hands. Right here, right now, my future is you."

She smiled. "I really feel we're heading toward a penalty."

"Absolutely." He lowered his head.

"I'm thinking a neutral zone infraction."

"Yep."

"Illegal hands to the face," she said softly, her eyes shiny.

"I was thinking offensive holding."

"I might have to throw you out of the game." She wove her hands around his neck. "So make it worth it."

"It's always worth it."

She glanced up. "We're on the jumbotron."

"Perfect." He waved, then slid his arms around her. As the crowd cheered, he lowered his mouth to hers and finally, beautifully, kissed her.

Now that was a viral post he could like and share.

And for her part, she kissed him back, maybe not as much

ardor as in the tasting room or even that one time in the pantry at her house, but she still managed to leave a message.

The rest of the officials had left them to stand in the corner of the field, outside the end zone. He lifted his head and saw Toby watching him, raising a fist in triumph.

Oh brother. But his head no longer hurt, and he'd never felt freer in his life.

"I gotta go," Iris said.

"I know. I'll be right here, on the sidelines."

"Two more minutes," she said, backing up.

"Two minutes to the rest of our lives."

She rolled her eyes and ran out onto the field.

He walked up to the team, a few slapping him on the shoulder, the back.

"Well, that's one way to end your career," Coach Max said.

"Yep," Hud said. He looked at Max and grinned. "Best play of my life."

"YOU STILL HAVE ALL YOUR TEETH, RIGHT?"

Iris made a face at her mom through the zoom screen. "Yes."

"I didn't hit her that hard, Mrs. M." Hud sat on the floor, his back to the sofa of his hotel suite, Iris's phone up on the ottoman, casting a video of her family—well, her father, mother, Pippa, and Fraser.

She glanced at Hudson. "I can take a tackle, Mom."

The memory of his takedown, the feel of his body cradling hers even as they fell...somehow it imprinted on her as a metaphor.

The way it should be between them. Her, trusting his arms around her. Trusting *God's* arms around her. And her, letting go.

The night swept into the large windows that overlooked Amsterdam, glittering and bright. The castle shone with lights, and in the center of the square, a Ferris wheel spun, celebrating the upcoming holiday season.

"So where is this Vikka now?" Fraser asked.

"I turned her over to the Dutch police," said Ned, standing behind the sofa. He held a can of Fanta, the other hand holding a piece of pizza. Shae sat beside Iris on the sofa.

"I can't believe you recognized her," Garrett said.

"She's very hard to mistake," Shae said. "And we have history. I feel sorry for her, really. She was pretty messed up, despite her tough exterior. Lukka had done a number on her, and now her brother is still somewhere in Siberia, so she's frantic."

"What I can't figure out is why the Petrov Bratva wanted to poison Iris." This from Pippa.

"It wasn't just Iris," said Ned. "They tested the water in all the bottles. Trace elements, although Iris's had the most. The crew was treated—everyone is fine. Hud stopped them before they ingested enough to kill them."

Iris took his hand, squeezed.

"And then he kissed her, right on the jumbotron," said Shae.

Iris looked at her. She grinned.

"Really," said her mother. "Does that mean you'll be home for Thanksgiving?"

A pause, and Iris glanced at Hud.

"Yes," he said.

"What about your upcoming Lauchtenland game?"

"It's not for a month—two weeks before Christmas. And we'll be back for it," Iris said.

"I'm not playing," Hud added. He didn't even sound upset. "I'll be on injured reserve for the game, so on the sidelines, but mostly I'll be around to coach up Felix and the other wideouts. At least until my contract ends at the end of the year."

"And then?" Fraser said.

Hudson took a breath. "Then, we'll see what the next step is. I know God has something good...I just need to wait for it."

In the screen, her dad nodded. "Well done, Hud."

"How are you feeling, Mom?" Iris asked. Her mom seemed just as fragile as when Iris had left, although she'd been cleared of any immediate issues.

Like cancer.

"We're having some tests done tomorrow. We'll let you know if there's anything to worry about." Her father smiled, but worry haunted his eyes.

"Ned, are you and Shae headed to Minnesota or back to San Diego?"

Ned had put down his pizza, then put his hand on Shae's shoulder. "Would you be too upset if we...eloped?"

Silence. Iris looked at Ned, who looked down at Shae. She was nodding.

"Where?" her father said.

"It's a secret. But we'll tell you when we come home for Thanksgiving." Ned winked.

"What about your uncle, Shae? Won't he—"

"He'll be fine," she said.

"Congratulations," Fraser said, and Pippa echoed it.

"I'll need a lot of pictures," said her mom.

"Pictures!" said Pippa. "That's it! Shae—you said that when you were kidnapped, the guy who took you—"

"Arkady Petrov."

"Right. You said you thought they wanted the pictures on your camera."

"Yes."

"Of Titus Stadium."

"Yes." Shae looked at Iris. "And Vikka was sent by them to poison Iris—"

"And her crew," Fraser said.

"So that means, what? That the Petrovs were planning to kill Prince John? Why?" Ned said. "Why would the Russians want to kill the prince?"

A beat.

"It doesn't matter now," Ned said. "We stopped them, and you said your team has extra security, right?"

"Yes," Pippa said.

"And so does the ELF."

"So, it's over?" Shae said. "We foiled their plan? I feel like I should have a mustache to twirl."

Her joke didn't hit. Pippa looked at Fraser. He made a face. "I don't know."

"I think it's time for Imani and me to head back to Lauchtenland."

Fraser blinked at her, frowned, and then gave her a look that said maybe right now wasn't the time to have this conversation.

"You let us know when you're coming home," her father said, leaning forward to pick up the phone. Now it was just his face in the screen. "Iris. I love you. Hud? Take care of my girl."

"Dad."

"Iris—"

"Thank you."

He smiled.

"Yes, sir," Hud said, and they hung up.

Iris turned to Shae. "Eloping?"

Hud shook Ned's hand. "Okay, so Iris and I are going to get out of here and let you figure that out." He got up. "C'mon."

"Where are we going?"

He pulled her toward the door. Handed over her jacket. She slipped on boots, a hat, and he did the same.

Oh, he was cute in his puffy black parka, his hat that turned his blue eyes rich. The man was unbearably handsome.

And he was hers.

He took her hand again and led her downstairs, through the lobby, then outside to the square, where music bounced off the cobblestones into the star-strewn night. Street vendors hawked caramel stroopwafels and french frites with mayonnaise, ginger cake and poffertjes—pancakes with powdered sugar.

Musicians busked in the corners of the square, their violin or guitar cases open for money.

Hud made a direct line for the Ferris wheel. He bought a ticket at the counter, then added them to the line.

"What are we doing?"

"We are...taking a moment." He put his arm around her, pulled her close.

"A moment?"

"Yep." He climbed into the hanging basket, and she settled in beside him.

The Ferris wheel began to move.

He pulled her close, against him.

"I thought it would be good to just...leave the earth for one moment. Get away from bullets and bombings and assassination attempts and..."

"Trouble."

The Ferris wheel brought them higher, the lights of the city glittering all around them. The canals caught the colors, reflected them back, and overhead, the moon watched.

"Oh, I know better than that, Iris Marshall." He turned to her, touched his big hand to her cheek.

"Encroachment," she said softly.

"You bet it is." Then, as the basket swung up into the star-strewn endless sky, he definitely encroached.

WHAT HAPPENS NEXT

He wasn't ready.

Garrett stood at the window of the waiting room, watching the snow peel from the sky, trying not to let the snarl of emotions in his chest escape out into the room.

"I wonder if the storm will disrupt Thanksgiving. I hope the kids can get in."

Jenny sat in a chair behind him, having shed her jacket, although she still wore her wool beanie hat, a thick sweater. Lately, she constantly shivered.

"I think it'll be okay. They'll get here. Iris called and said she and Hud were in New York, switching planes."

"Did you see the pictures from Shae and Ned's wedding? Such great shots. We should have eloped."

He glanced at her. She gave him a smile. Her skin seemed so sallow, and she'd dropped weight. "Your parents would have murdered me."

"I don't know. Think of the money we could have saved."

"Don't tell me for a second that you're not dreaming of Iris's wedding." He was trying. Really. But weddings and thanksgiving dinner were the absolute *last* thing he wanted to talk about.

"Oh, I hope she and Hud get there."

And soon. But he didn't say that, just turned to look again out the window, fighting to hold it all together.

A beat, then Jenny's hand slipped into his and she stepped up behind him, curling her other hand around his arm, setting her chin on his shoulder. "Breathe."

He slipped his hand over hers. Fought to clear his thickening throat. "Yep."

"It's going to be okay. No matter what the doctor says." She moved around him, turning him to make him stand in front of her. "I trust God's plan. No matter what it is. We both know that this is not the end."

His eyes burned, and he pulled her to himself before she could see him tear up. The last thing she needed was him crumbling. But inside, he already felt shattered.

That's what happened when you found your beloved wife collapsed on the kitchen floor, her panicked children around her. Didn't matter that Fraser had fought wars, that Jonas chased storms, that Iris stood up to burly football players, even that Creed had seen way more than he should, way too young. When he'd run into the kitchen and seen Jenny, pale and broken, they'd all become small children in his eyes, watching their beloved mother fade into eternity.

"I beat it once, I can beat it again," she said, pulling back.

Oh shoot, too soon because moisture rimmed his eyelids. She put her hands to his face and used her thumbs to wipe it away. Smiled.

He nodded, unable to speak. But she seemed more frail every day.

Twenty years ago, she'd been strong, robust, and ready to fight.

Today... He pulled her close, wrapped his arms around her, and simply held her. Thirty-five years.

No, he couldn't say goodbye. Not yet.

"Jenny, Doctor Brian will see you now." A nurse stood by the door to the office of Jenny's oncologist. How Garret never wanted to see the University of Minnesota Cancer Center ever again. Still, he found a smile and followed Jenny in.

Dr. Brian Holland met them at the door, and Garrett met his hand. "Good to see you, Garrett."

Garrett nodded.

"Jenny, Garrett, have a seat." He motioned to the orange chairs and only then did Garrett notice the remodel, the teal walls, the new carpet, the pictures of Brian's children, now grown, on the desk. Outside, the heavens dropped soft snow, as if trying to gentle the blow.

Jenny sat. Garrett stood behind her, his hands on her shoulders. She gripped his hand.

Brian leaned against the front edge of his desk. Folded his arms. "It's not what you think."

Garrett gave him a hard look, his chest tight.

"You already know the initial tests showed the cancer isn't back. Thank you for the extra tests, Jenny. The MRI, the Pet-scan, the blood tests. It's all confirmed—you're still in remission."

Garrett just blinked at him, not sure if he heard him right, trying to let the words settle.

Remission.

Except. "Then why the look, Doc?"

Doc Brian leaned up and went around to his desk, logged into his computer. The remodeled office included a flat screen, and now he picked up a remote and turned it on. An x-ray showed on the screen. His remote control included a laser and he flashed it over a darkened area on the screen. "This is your liver, Jenny."

"We should be worried that it's so black, right?" Garrett said, now letting go of Jenny and walking nearer the screen.

"Yes. It's diseased, and our tests showed that it's failing."

Garrett steadied his hand on his desk.

"It was the chemo, wasn't it?" This from Jenny, and Garrett

glanced at her. She had sat up, her arms around herself. "It was one of the side effects."

"Yes," Dr. Brian said. "It's been a slow decline, but now we're here."

Garrett walked over, sat in the other orange chair, and reached for her hand. Maybe more for himself than her. "So, now what, Doc?"

He flicked off the monitor. "There's good news. The liver can be transplanted by a *live* donor. It's intensive surgery, with a four-month recovery time, but you have four children—"

"Five," Jenny said.

Dr. Brian took a breath. "Four, for the purposes of the transplant. But there is a high possibility that one of those four is a match."

"You'd take out part of their liver, and put it into Jenny?" Garrett said.

"Yes."

"And then what? Is it like losing a kidney?"

"No, their liver can grow back. And Jenny's would too—the healthy liver."

"And she'd be better? Healthy again?"

"She'd have to take anti-rejection meds for the rest of her life, but yes, if she takes care of herself."

He wanted to weep with the terrible rush of light through his body.

"Oh, I don't know."

He stilled, looking at Jenny, but her attention was fixed to the doctor. She pulled her sweater around herself. "How risky is it? I don't like the idea of putting my children's lives in danger."

"Jenny! Our children would do anything for you!" Never in a thousand years did he believe she'd even consider not—

"This is too much."

He just stared at her. She met his gaze, and everything inside it chilled him,

"I don't think we should tell them."

He just blinked at her.

"I mean..." She looked at Garrett. "They have lives..."

"Jenny!"

"Ned could lose his career! And Fraser—he's been through so much, and Jonas wants to go back overseas, and Iris *lives* overseas..."

He turned away from her, beseeching the doctor for a little backup. "I can't believe I'm hearing this."

"Can I get on a donor list?"

Dr. Brian raised an eyebrow. "Yes. But your former cancer diagnosis will be a hiccup."

"Let's do that."

"I can't even..." Garrett got up, walked to the window, braced his hands on the window ledge. "I can not—"

"It's my life. My choice."

"It's *our* life!"

Oh, he didn't mean to explode. Not here, not in front of Doc Brian, who just sat at his desk, hands folded, looking nonchalant.

Clearly this wasn't the first marriage argument waged in his office.

But it was one of the first in years between he and Jenny. Usually, they always...saw...eye to...

"Jenny, what's going on?" He'd lowered his voice, turned it soft. Walked over to her and knelt in front of her. Tears rimmed her eyes. "Tell me what's happening here."

She gave him a sad look, then directed his gaze at Doc Brian. "Is it possible that the surgery won't work?

"Yes, of course, but—"

She held up her hand. Looked at Garrett. "That's why. Imagine how one of our children would feel if they gave up part of their liver and I still died. The sense of failure, and helplessness and frustration and..." She touched his face. "I love you Garrett, and I love our children. But I need some time. I just..." She sighed. "Please put me on the list, Doc."

Garrett knew that look. He'd get nowhere if he pushed today. But, "This conversation is not over, Jenny."

She pulled her sweater even tighter. Looked out the window.

And even he knew.

There was a storm coming. And he wasn't sure any of them would survive.

THANK YOU FOR READING IRIS.

I hope you loved Iris and Hud's love story, and are excited for Creed, the big finale to the Minnesota Marshalls series.

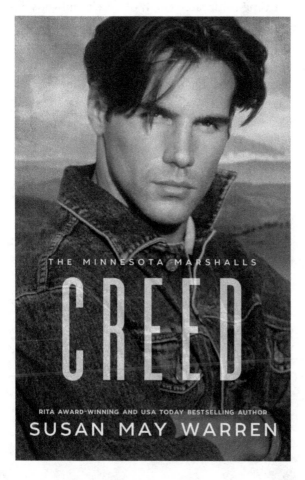

He's a criminal—who must become a prince to save the princess he loves. But will she have to become a criminal to save him?

In the heart-pounding conclusion to the epic Minnesota Marshalls series, Princess Imani finds herself once again in peril as she becomes the target of a deadly plot. She needs Creed – only problem is, he's facing charges in Lauchtenland. But he's not going to let that stop him from protecting her...even if he has to become a fugitive. But who is trying to kill her? Together, they race against time to unravel a web of deceit and conspiracy that seems to entrap the entire family. As their journey takes them from the palace to the high mountains, and finally back to Minnesota, Imani and Creed must discover the truth before tragedy destroys everything—and everyone—they love.

Read the thrilling finale of the Minnesota Marshalls series, where the fate of a family and destiny of a kingdom hang in the balance.

Turn the page for a sneak peek...

CREED

THE MINNESOTA MARSHALLS || BOOK FIVE

CHAPTER 1

They'd called him a hero so many times, Creed had actually started to believe it.

Even now, as he stood at the top of the stairs, again, the dream so familiar he wanted to shout—*stop!*

But no, in this dream, his legs worked, his body juiced with adrenaline as he watched beautiful Princess Imani of Lauchtenland on the dance floor.

In the arms of Prince Xavier Neville of Keswick.

The jerk.

But Creed's focus wasn't on the couple waltzing around the crowded dance floor but on a man in the wings, dark hair, dressed in black, a gun leveled at Imani.

Fredrick Ferguson, former protection officer from Her Majesty's Security Detail turned traitor.

Turned *murderer*.

And it seemed only Creed saw him.

"Stop!" He started down the stairs—

And that's when the dream turned on him. Again, he tripped, started falling.

Again, he grabbed for the rail, and found only air.

Again, he plunged forward.

Again, his legs had vanished. Both of them, whittling away to nothing right before his eyes.

And again, he tumbled headfirst, the pain blinding as he careened down the massive staircase.

His shout lifted, jerked him out of the nightmare.

Breathe. He blinked awake. Sweat coated his body, his good leg tangled in the sheets, the other still in a brace. His breaths fell over each other, even as he blinked, orienting himself.

"That one was louder," said a voice, soft, from the doorway.

He glanced over.

Jonas. He stood, arms folded, his hair mussed, still in his pajama bottoms, wearing a Vortex tee-shirt. He'd grown a beard since returning to Minnesota from Slovenia, like a man trying to figure out his life.

"Sorry."

"I was awake, little bro." He walked into the room. "Same dream?" He reached for the pain meds on Creed's beside table.

"Yes. And no meds. I'm trying to stay clean."

"You're clearly hurting."

Creed had grunted while sitting up. He leaned his head back on the headboard. "It's not terrible."

Jonas made a noise and set the container back on the table. "Define terrible."

"Shards of glass shooting up my leg, a constant hammer on my bone, and sharp, stomach-churning flares of agony when I move the wrong way."

"Fun."

"It's a blast. Especially in the morning when my thigh muscles contract, flushing out all the toxins gathered during the night." Even now, he drew in a long breath, waiting for his muscles to release.

Finally, he exhaled and swung his legs over the edge of the bed, easing the injured one down to the floor. "At least I can walk. Sorta." He reached for the crutches.

"You'll get there," Jonas said. "You're getting stronger every day. Tell me about the dream."

Creed stood up, balanced, then walked to the window. Outside, the sun layered red along the horizon, dark clouds cluttering the sky. Crystalline, white snow covered their dormant vineyard, little puffs of snow whisking from the tops of the sleeping vines by a bully wind.

"Looks like a storm is headed this way."

"Mmmhmm."

Jonas wore his curious-scientist tell-me-everything expression.

"It was just a dream."

"I know." His brother's gaze didn't waver. Because, of course, he knew the story.

"Fine. It might be a premonition." His mouth tightened. "Probably not."

"Tell me."

Creed sighed. "I'm at some fancy event. Wearing a suit. Fraser is there too."

Jonas raised an eyebrow.

"Imani is dancing with a guy. That prince she's been writing to."

"She's been writing to a prince?"

"Yes—no. Sort of. He's a friend of her stepfather's, and she met him during her gap year world tour. Apparently, he's some distant cousin of Prince John."

"Aren't all the royals around the world distant cousins?"

"I don't know. Maybe. But Imani is adopted, so it doesn't matter. But her stepdad did write to her and asked her to go to some Christmas ball with the prince, so—"

"That's what the fight was about."

"You heard that?"

"The entire house heard that, Creed. For cryin' out loud—

fish or cut bait, man. You can't tell Imani who she can correspond with if you're not going to ask her out."

Creed just stared at him, his chest rising and falling. "It's complicated."

"What's complicated? You like her—she likes you—"

"She's a princess!" He shook his head and crutched over to his dresser. Pulled out a fresh tee-shirt.

Silence.

Creed pulled it on, one handed. Glanced at Jonas. "It can't work."

"Fine. Tell me about the dream."

Creed pushed past him to the bathroom down the hall. "It's stupid."

Jonas clearly didn't get the hint and followed him. Stood outside the door as Creed brushed his teeth. "Why is it stupid?"

Creed stared at himself. He hadn't shaved in a week, dark whiskers grazing his chin. He looked wrecked, tired, in pain. And frankly, he didn't love the view.

He'd never been a victim, thank you.

So he opened the door, gave Jonas a look. "Someone is about to shoot Imani, and instead of saving her life, I fall down the stairs."

Jonas just blinked at him.

"My legs vanish."

His eyebrow raised.

"It's just a stupid dream!" He pressed past Jonas and headed toward the stairs.

He gripped the stairs, then, he hopped on the railing.

"What on earth are you doing?"

"I saw it on YouTube. It's parkour, and I figure if I can't go down the stairs the regular way, I'll slide."

"Great idea. Break your head as well as your leg."

Yeah, well, Jonas had two working legs.

Creed slid half-way, balancing, then stopped himself at the bottom and lowered himself down, holding in a grunt. The tantalizing smell of cooking bacon, eggs, and flapjacks, not to mention the sound of laughter from the Marshall family brood, urged him into the kitchen-slash-great room.

He spotted Fraser sitting at the long kitchen island, eating eggs over easy, bacon, and some flapjacks. He nursed a cup of coffee. His oldest brother, a former SEAL, still wore a cast on his hand, but he worked his fingers against the granite countertop. But that was Fraser—always moving.

Now he looked up and lifted his cup to Creed. Invalids in arms, maybe.

His mother turned from the big six-burner stove. She looked better today, wearing an apron over her jeans, her blond hair back.

Creed still couldn't purge from his mind the image of her collapsing a week or so ago right here in this kitchen.

"Morning, son," she said, and slid him a plate with scrambled eggs.

"Thanks, Ma." He reached for a couple flapjacks from the big plate in the center.

Jonas had followed him downstairs. "Can I get one of those?"

His mother winked at him. "Runny eggs for you?"

Jonas nodded and sat next to Iris. She wore her blond hair back, and an over-sized Vienna Vikings sweatshirt—probably on loan from football boyfriend Hudson Bly. The big wide-receiver sat next to her, also finishing off eggs. He dwarfed the Marshall boys, which was saying something, but Creed liked the Aussie. Hud might be the one man who could stand up to Iris.

The only sibling missing was Ned, but he was off on his honeymoon, so no one really expected him for Thanksgiving.

Weird that Imani and Pippa weren't eating breakfast, too.

"Is Pippa watching the perimeter?" Creed asked as he slid onto a stool.

"Nope," Fraser said, sort of snippy, even.

Creed frowned at him. "Did I do something?"

"You tell me," Fraser said, now holding his coffee.

"Apparently, you read Imani's mail?" He cocked his head at Creed.

Creed glanced at Jonas.

"Told you," he said, accepting a plate of eggs from his mother. He grabbed toast from a platter.

Swell. "Yes. Her *email*. She was sitting on the sofa, right there next to me. It wasn't like I unlocked her computer and went snooping. I mean, we practically lived on the sofa for the last two months. She read a lot of my mail, too."

"Even reading over someone's shoulder is a violation of privacy," Iris said. "Is that what you were fighting about last night? Hud and I could hear you from the kitchen when we got in."

"Yeah, I know. Listen, she was upset, and so I read it. Whatever." He didn't know his sister well, but clearly his memory of her bossiness wasn't wrong. "And yeah, we got into a fight. What would you do if the father of the girl you liked suggested she date someone else?" He pushed his plate away, suddenly not hungry. "So what if he's the future king of Lauchtenland. Doesn't mean he gets to pick her husband. The days of arranged marriages are over."

"Not for royals," Fraser said. "Pippa said this guy is a lesser prince, but still in a royal line. And according to her, the email was just a suggestion from her father that Imani attend some charity ball with him. Not marry him."

Creed picked at his eggs. "I know."

"Pippa said that there is some unrest in the country over a possible American in the royal line of succession, so maybe this was a gesture from her father."

"Stepfather."

"The future king of Lauchtenland," Fraser said.

And he didn't know why Fraser's words just sat in his chest like a shard of glass. Maybe because Fraser had been there to witness how hard he'd fallen for her.

It wasn't every day that he helped a princess escape a

murderer. Or took her home to Minnesota to hide in his parents' home-slash-winery while his brother and her bodyguard, Pippa Butler, stood guard.

Wasn't every day that he got shot trying to protect her.

And it was probably only Fraser who really knew how Imani had found her way inside his heart. Made him fall for her laughter, her smile. Made him feel like they belonged together. A couple of refugee kids.

Probably because Fraser had fallen for Pippa.

But Fraser wasn't Creed. And that, maybe, burned him the most. He leveled a look at Fraser. "So this was the king's attempt to keep up appearances that his princess stepdaughter not marry an American kid from the streets."

Silence, and even his mother turned.

After a second, "You're a Marshall, Creed. Full stop. Your past is not you. Not anymore."

He hated the sudden thickness in his throat. "Whatever."

"And I don't think for a second that's what Imani cares about." She gave him a smile.

Fine.

She turned down the heat on the stove. "Besides, you don't know the whole story. Don't take offense at something that wasn't meant to harm you."

He picked up the syrup. Swallowed. "Problem is, it wasn't her first email from this guy. Xavier. In fact, they'd been emailing for months." He swamped his pancakes in the syrup. Set it back on the counter. "Apparently, we're not exclusive."

"Are you two even *dating*?" Iris said. She picked up her coffee cup. "Because, like you pointed out, it sort of looked like you've been sitting on the sofa playing video games."

He stared at his sister. "I was shot in the leg! I have pins holding my freakin' bones together. What do you suggest I do, go outside and play a little one-on-one with her?"

Iris raised an eyebrow. "Just calling it how I see it."

"For your information, we were...dating. I think. And, we

kissed, not that it's any of your business, but it's not like it's secret. Fraser and Pippa caught us and nearly came unglued. Try 'dating,'" and he finger-quoted the word, "with your spec ops brother and her overzealous bodyguard watching your every move."

Fraser rolled his eyes.

"Believe me, no one wants to get back on his feet faster than me."

"Of course you do, Creed." This from his mother. "You've always been the guy who goes after what he wants. Ever since you joined our family, you were the fighter. Remember how you kept those kids alive in the school after the tornado?"

"I was just one of many, Mom. The teacher was there—"

"But you were the captain. You led the team, you found water. You kept their spirits up as we searched. And even your track scholarship—"

"Please don't talk about track," he said, reaching for the orange juice. "I'll be lucky if I walk again."

"Oh, I've met you. You'll walk again," Fraser said. "Run, even."

He didn't know why those words seeded inside him, filled his throat. "Yeah, well, not anytime soon. And I understand Imani getting sick of waiting for the guy who saved her in Europe to get off the sofa. *I'm* ready to get off the sofa."

"Please," Fraser said. "I drive you to physical therapy every other day. I watch you sweat and fight and try not to howl. So that's not why Imani left."

He stared at Fraser. "Wait. *What?*"

"Imani and Pippa left about four hours ago," Iris said quietly.

A punch to the solar plexus. Taking out his breath would have had lesser effect. "No, that can't be..." He slid off the chair and headed up the stairs. His stupid brace made it hard to take the steps at any impassioned pace. Still, he made it to the top, then crutched his way down the hall to her room—Iris's old room.

Empty. The morning sun shining across the stripped and remade beds, the sheets in a tumble on the floor.

Gone.

The floor creaked behind him. Fraser had followed him up. Now he folded his arms, drew in a breath.

"You just let them go?" Creed said, wanting to push him back. Or punch something. Or—run.

Just run.

Wow, he missed running. The freedom, the power of pushing his body. The sense of not being helpless, but in control.

Not falling down stairs.

Fraser held up his hands. "Listen. Pippa says that Lauchtenland wants her back. She's been putting it off now for weeks. Especially now that the assassin is in custody—"

"We don't know that!" Creed shook his head, pushed past him to his room, formerly Jonas's, and picked up his cell phone. He depressed her number, holding his phone to his ear even as Fraser came to stand in the doorway. "She could be in danger right now."

"Dude. Pippa is with her—"

"Pippa nearly let an assassin find her—pick up, Imani!"

But his call went to voice mail. He pressed end, and dialed again. "They found our house. They can find them."

"And since then, we've had no attacks, nothing to make us think she's in danger," Fraser said quietly. "It seems, based on Gunner Ferguson's investigation, she's out of danger."

"What does he know?" Still not picking up. He hung up.

Fraser was giving him a look. "Right. He's only the captain of the guard in Lauchtenland. What could he possibly know—"

"He didn't believe her—*us*—when we told him she was being stalked. If it was up to him, she'd be dead already." He tossed the phone on the bed, went to the closet. Pulled out his duffel bag.

"Bro. What are you doing?"

"Going after her."

"On crutches?"

Oh, if he could have gotten to him, Creed would have. Just launched himself over the bed, taken his way-too-smug brother down. Probably would have managed a couple good hits before Fraser shut him down.

But yeah, he was *on crutches*. And, yes, sometimes pain meds. He couldn't even drive, so that was super-duper convenient and totally helped him make good on his impassioned statement.

He stared at the bag. "I can't believe she just...left. Just...*left*?" And he wasn't going to do something stupid and cry, but his chest tightened, and he crutched over to the window, stared out at the snow and ice and the barren, frigid world, the oncoming storm.

Gritted his jaw.

So, clearly he'd been right.

He meant nothing to Imani at all, if she could just leave him without a word.

He closed his eyes and refused to let the past take a run at him.

"Sorry," Fraser said softly.

Creed drew in a breath. "Good thing I never told her I loved her."

Silence.

Another beat, then. "Yeah, good thing."

Creed swallowed past the terrible burn blocking his throat.

"Pippa said she'd check in every twelve hours. I promise, I'll keep you updated. But maybe this is a good thing."

Creed turned then, narrowed his eyes at him.

Fraser was looking at his hand, still in a cast. He wiggled his fingers.

"Maybe you double down on your PT. Get yourself back in fighting shape." He looked up at Creed.

It wasn't until this moment that Creed realized that when Imani left him...Pippa had also left Fraser. So maybe the words weren't just for him.

"Are you...are you going after Pippa?"

Fraser's mouth tightened around the edges. "Not sure, exactly, how I fit in her world, either."

Creed had nothing.

Finally, Fraser lifted a shoulder and walked away.

Creed followed him downstairs. Heated up his plate of food. In the adjoining room, a football game played. Iris was already on the sofa, criticizing the refs.

"This will be a loud day," Hudson said, grinning.

Anything to drown out the terrible shouting inside that said somehow, he'd blown it. Caused someone to abandon him again.

And he hadn't a clue how to win back the heart of a princess of Lauchtenland.

Or if he should even try.

Want More Like This?

Meet the Montana Marshalls, a family with Big Dreams, and Big Trouble, under the Big Sky, and cousins to the Minnesota Marshalls!

A cowboy protector. A woman in hiding. Forced proximity might turn friends to sweethearts if a stalker doesn't find them first...

Montana rancher Knox Marshall's danger years are behind him. A former bull-rider, he now runs the Marshall family ranch, raising champion bucking bulls for the National Professional Bullrider's Expo (NBR-X). Wealth and success are his, and he's not looking for trouble.

But trouble is looking for county music star Kelsey Jones. Onstage, the beautiful rising star of the Yankee Belles becomes the person she longs to be - vivacious and confident - burying the brokenness she carries from a violent assault. But her attacker just might be on the loose...

Knox and Kelsey's paths collide when an explosion at an NBR-X event traps them in the rubble, igniting Knox's obsession to find the bomber and protect Kelsey...no matter the cost.

Thank you for Reading

Thank you again for reading *Iris*. I hope you enjoyed the story.

If you did enjoy *Iris*, would you be willing to do me a favor? Head over to the **product page** and leave a review. It doesn't have to be long—just a few words to help other readers know what they're getting. (But no spoilers! We don't want to wreck the fun!)

I'd love to hear from you—not only about this story, but about any characters or stories you'd like to read in the future. Write to me at: susan@susanmaywarren.com. And if you'd like to see what's ahead, stop by www.susanmaywarren.com .

And don't forget to sign up to my newsletter at www.susanmaywarren.com.

Susie May

About Susan May Warren

With nearly 2 million books sold, critically acclaimed novelist Susan May Warren is the Christy, RITA, and Carol award-winning author of over ninety novels with Tyndale, Barbour, Steeple Hill, and Summerside Press. Known for her compelling plots and unforgettable characters, Susan has written contemporary and historical romances, romantic-suspense, thrillers, rom-com, and Christmas novellas.

With books translated into eight languages, many of her novels have been ECPA and CBA bestsellers, were chosen as Top Picks by *Romantic Times*, and have won the RWA's Inspirational Reader's Choice contest and the American Christian Fiction Writers Book of the Year award. She's a three-time RITA finalist and an eight-time Christy finalist.

Publishers Weekly has written of her books, "Warren lays bare her characters' human frailties, including fear, grief, and resentment, as openly as she details their virtues of love, devotion, and resiliency. She has crafted an engaging tale of romance, rivalry, and the power of forgiveness." *Library Journal* adds, "Warren's characters are well-developed and she knows how to create a first rate contemporary romance..."

Susan is also a nationally acclaimed writing coach, teaching at conferences around the nation, and winner of the 2009 American Christian Fiction Writers Mentor of the Year award. She loves to help people launch their writing careers. She is the founder of www.MyBookTherapy.com and www.learnhow-towriteanovel.com, a writing website that helps authors get published and stay published. She is also the author of the popular writing method *The Story Equation*.

Find excerpts, reviews, and a printable list of her novels at www.susanmaywarren.com and connect with her on social media.

f facebook.com/susanmaywarrenfiction

O instagram.com/susanmaywarren

y twitter.com/susanmaywarren

BB bookbub.com/authors/susan-may-warren

g goodreads.com/susanmaywarren

a amazon.com/Susan-May-Warren

The Marshall Family Saga

THE MINNESOTA MARSHALLS

Fraser

Jonas

Ned

Iris

Creed

THE EPIC STORY OF RJ AND YORK

Out of the Night

I Will Find You

No Matter the Cost

THE MONTANA MARSHALLS

Knox

Tate

Ford

Wyatt

Ruby Jane

A complete list of Susan's novels can be found at
susanmaywarren.com/novels/bibliography/.